THE SACRED ARROWS

The Pawnees broke and ran, but not all fell back. One old Pawnee jumped down from his horse and sat on the ground singing his death chant.

"I will go and count coup on this ancient one," Bull said, holding his lance high, the medicine bundle tied near the point. Slapping his pony, he charged toward the lone man. But the Pawnee ignored the frothing horse and its frenzied rider. As the old one dodged Bull's lance again and again, the Pawnees screamed their admiration.

"How can this be?" Younger Wolf cried. "The sacred Arrows should blind the enemy!"

Stone Wolf, too, grew uneasy.

Then the unthinkable occurred. The old Pawnee reached up and tore the lance from Bull's hands. Bull steadied his horse and tried to retrieve the lance, but the Pawnee lunged forward and the lance's sharp point opened a gash in the side of Bull's pony. As Bull kicked his wounded pony to safety, the Pawnee discovered the medicine bundle and held it high overhead.

"The Arrows are lost," Younger Wolf said. "The Pawnees have broken our power."

"No!" Stone Wolf shouted. "We must recover our heart! Come, brothers, carry the fight to our enemy! Strike hard and save the day!"

THE
MEDICINE TRAIL
STONE WOLF'S VISION

G. CLIFTON WISLER

ZEBRA BOOKS
KENSINGTON PUBLISHING CORP.

ZEBRA BOOKS

are published by

Kensington Publishing Corp.
475 Park Avenue South
New York, NY 10016

First printing: November, 1991

Printed in the United States of America

Prologue

Long before the white man came to the plains and the mountains, when Bull Buffalo shook Mother Earth with his numbers and Horse was still a distant dream, the People were there. *Tsis tsis tas,* they called themselves. Others knew them as Sandhill Men. Later the strange speakers, the white-skinned men of prophecy, used their word for dog, *chien.* By the time words were put on treaty papers, and snows no longer remembered were given numbers, the ten bands had become the Cheyenne. They were a fierce people, a nation of warriors without equals. But as the death song says, "Nothing lasts long. Only the earth and the mountains."

Heammawihio, Man Above, gave the People a hard road to walk, but he granted Sweet Medicine vision to see the dangers that lay ahead. Sweet Medicine, in turn, shared his dreams with others. He saw the coming of Horse and spoke of the freedom it would bring. Sweet Medicine also had a darker dream—the sickness and death brought by the white man.

"You must avoid these strange ones," the prophet warned.

Sweet Medicine feared his words lacked the power to prevent disaster, so he climbed *Noahvose*, the heart of the world, and brought the People *Mahuts*, the four sacred Arrows. Two had the power to blind enemies, and were turned toward men. The others brought success to the hunt, and were shown to Bull Buffalo. So long as *Mahuts* remained safe, and the ceremonies were kept, the People would remain strong.

One

It was early, and a dampness hung in the air. The sweet scent of spring flooded Stone Wolf's nostrils, awakening in him memories of boyhood adventures — of long rides and hard fights. Most of all he recalled the days passed in the lodge of his grandfather, Cloud Dancer, the Arrow-keeper.

"Your medicine was always strong, *Nam shim'*," Stone Wolf whispered. "As were the People. Now there's much uncertainty."

In those good, remembered times, Cloud Dancer would have offered counsel, sought a dream. Now the old man had climbed Hanging Road, and only the wind was left to whine an answer. As for *Mahuts,* the sacred Arrows, they now rested in the care of Stone Wolf, who too often wondered if their power could protect a people with so many enemies.

"Perhaps the others were right," he said, gazing through the haze toward the distant camp. "I'm too young to keep *Mahuts.*"

But who else was there? Iron Wolf, who might have

followed his father's path, was long dead. Of the sons left behind, Stone Wolf was eldest.

"It's for my brother to do," Younger Wolf had insisted when older men had challenged Stone Wolf's right to keep the Arrows. "He knows the ceremonies and the healing cures. He bears many battle scars, though he's still young. He walks the sacred path, doesn't he? Who else can be trusted to put the welfare of the People above all else?"

"Ayyyy!" the men had howled. And those who still disputed Stone Wolf's merits had left to ride with another band.

Sometimes, reflecting on the burdens of an Arrow-keeper, Stone Wolf wished another would step forward and lift the burden. Obligation had aged the Wolf. Others might have passed their twenty-fifth spring in the young men's lodge, sharing stories and raiding horses. But a man of the People had to see to the welfare of the defenseless—the very old and the young.

It was necessary. Cloud Dancer had added his voice to the warnings left long ago by Sweet Medicine.

"I see many enemies tormenting our people," Cloud Dancer had said. "I see clouds of blue soldiers coming to rub our names from the children's memory. But the greatest danger to the People, and to *Mahuts,* comes if the Arrows are abused."

"Nam shim'?" Stone Wolf had exclaimed. "You know me. I will not dishonor your trust. I will keep them well."

"You will come to face a terrible challenge, here," Cloud Dancer had warned, placing his wrinkled hand on Stone Wolf's chest. "You'll know grief and loss.

8

You'll hunger to kill. An Arrow-keeper must always hold the well-being of the People foremost in his heart, though. You must put yourself above worldly matters."

"I don't understand," Stone Wolf had cried.

"You will, *Nisha*," Cloud Dancer had assured him. But the future remained obscure. Stone Wolf's dreams didn't reveal everything, and he worried his devotion to *Mahuts* would not be enough to fend off the terrible prophecies of Sweet Medicine and Cloud Dancer.

"Now is no time for heavy thoughts," Younger Wolf had argued when the two had risen that morning. "You have a son waiting to be born. Everywhere the earth is being remade. Come. We'll hunt."

Stone Wolf had accepted the invitation with a glad heart. Walking the hills with his brother, seeking meat for the camp, he could set his other concerns aside for a time. True, they never entirely left him, but then the hunt had barely begun.

Off to his left Stone Wolf watched as Younger Wolf stepped lightly through the trees, silently weaving a path up the hillside. Just ahead lay a good spring where deer liked to drink. The hillside was full of tracks, and the wind tickling Stone Wolf's chin would not betray his scent to the prey.

Brother deer, we ask the life of your children to make the People strong, Stone Wolf prayed silently as he spotted the first creature. *Give my bow the true aim that death may come quickly and without pain.*

Younger Wolf was likewise making his prayers, for Cloud Dancer had taught his grandsons the old ways. The brothers then drew arrows and prepared to kill.

9

Younger Wolf, who had always led such hunts, shot first. Stone Wolf loosed his arrow a moment later. Both found their marks, and two deer fell.

Others might have slain a third, or even a fourth. Not the brothers. Already they had enough meat for their own needs, and plenty besides to offer the hungry. To take more was to disturb the harmony of the sacred hoop that was life.

"Your aim is good as ever," Younger Wolf observed as he began skinning his kill. "I feared your Crow wife's sharp tongue would unsettle you."

"Star Eyes is with child," Stone Wolf reminded his brother. "It's wise to consider that when judging her words. Birthing doesn't come easy to her."

"Nor does anything else," Younger Wolf grumbled. "Except talking. I've never known a woman with such a fondness for hard words!"

"That's her Crow upbringing," Stone Wolf said, laughing as he slid his knife from its scabbard. "She hasn't learned our ways yet, Brother."

"No," Younger Wolf muttered.

They spoke no more of Star Eyes. Instead they devoted their efforts to the butchering. Soon they were riding through the camp, offering meat to families without hunters, or to the old and sick with no one to fend for them. Stone Wolf presented the hides to Red Willow Woman, who had come to take care of his small son and daughter.

"You've had a good hunt," the old woman noted. "These will make good shirts."

Star Eyes peered at her husband from the far side of the campfire. Mornings found her pale and weak, and she barely acknowledged Stone Wolf's return.

"Soon?" he called to her.

Star Eyes grunted a reply, and Red Willow Woman sighed.

Stone Wolf received a warmer greeting from his small son and daughter. Dawn Dancer raced over and hugged her father's leg. Arrow Dancer followed, his three-year-old legs striving to keep pace with his sister.

"How is my son?" Stone Wolf asked as he lifted the boy onto one shoulder.

"Hungry, *Ne' hyo*," the little one whispered. "You brought fresh meat?"

"He's always hungry," Dawn Dancer complained. "Until he eats. He only chews a little and leaves the rest."

"He's small," Stone Wolf said, setting Arrow Dancer on the earth and sitting beside his daughter. The girl climbed onto one knee and let her five-year-old back rest against her father.

"You pamper them," Star Eyes complained.

Yes, Stone Wolf confessed to himself. *As their mother should.*

Red Willow Woman seemed to read his thoughts, for she scolded Star Eyes for keeping so late to her bed.

"I bore eight children," the Oglala declared, "but I never let my husband ride to the hunt without an encouraging word."

"I wasn't raised to be a dog's slave," Star Eyes insisted. "Hunt? It must have been a small animal! You've brought only some ribs and a shoulder!"

"It was a big deer, *Nah' koa*," Dawn Dancer argued, pointing to the hides.

"Coyotes must have eaten the rest," Star Eyes said,

frowning. "Or else Stone Wolf has given all the best pieces away!"

"A man of the People has responsibilities," Stone Wolf said, staring hard at his wife. "Others have needs, too."

"And your family must survive on what remains," Star Eyes grumbled. "See what I have come to? A poor sick woman kept captive in a camp of fools!"

"No one's captive here," Stone Wolf said, glaring. "Once, when we were both young, I offered you the chance to leave, go back to the Crows. You stayed."

"I've regretted that often," Star Eyes said, grinning slightly as she observed the sting of her words. "But you dog people killed my father, my brothers! Who would care for me?"

"You've not been mistreated," Stone Wolf told her.

"No?" she cried. "I am the daughter of a great man. In my father's camp I was honored above all women. Among the Crows, who are known as a great and powerful tribe! My father's fathers were great men, and the songs of their brave deeds filled many winter lodges. I was destined to give life to chiefs, and I expected kind words and beautiful things. What have you brought me, Stone Wolf, for all my grief? Promises. Empty words."

"Is that all?" Stone Wolf asked, drawing the children closer. "How have you suffered? Red Willow Woman keeps our camp. She cooks and tends the children. She makes our clothes."

"Sometimes I think she enjoys your favor, Husband, more than I!"

"Sometimes she deserves it!" Stone Wolf barked.

12

"But you're my wife, and I've never turned to another."

"No, but your heart is rarely with me. You give yourself to the Arrows, to the curing of the sick and the feeding of the poor. With so much meat you might have traded for fine moccasins. You could buy me a good blanket and glass beads when the white traders return."

"Would that make you happy? A blanket and some beads?"

"At least then the other women would know me as a person of wealth and importance."

"Is their opinion important?"

"Yes," Star Eyes declared. "You don't know how it is for me. They whisper behind my back. 'There goes the Crow woman!' They find fault with everything I do. If I walk the river path alone, they say I value myself too highly. If I speak to someone, they accuse me of loose morals!"

"You speak too freely with men," Red Willow Woman said as she placed one of the hides on a stretching rack. "You neglect your proper work."

"Who are you to speak to me that way!" Star Eyes shouted. "Old woman, you're fortunate we take you to our lodge. Your sons leave you to starve, and you dare scold me!"

"My sons . . ." Red Willow Woman began.

"Enough!" Stone Wolf demanded, rising to his feet. "I won't have the harmony of my camp disrupted."

Red Willow Woman dropped her eyes and went on with her work. Star Eyes grunted and gazed skyward.

"Do they argue much?" Stone Wolf whispered to the children.

"Not much, *Né, hyo,*" Dawn Dancer replied. "Always."

Stone Wolf grinned, and the little ones giggled. It was not, however, the end of the discussion.

That evening Star Eyes led him to the river path. There, away from the stern gaze of Red Willow Woman and the chattering children, they sat beneath a tall cottonwood and watched the stars dance overhead.

"The night brings peace to the land," Stone Wolf observed.

"To some," Star Eyes said, sighing as she took his hand. "Not to me."

"Is your life really so cruel? I spare you the hardest work."

"Work," she muttered. "That's all your women know. Or understand. Have you seen the way the others look at me? When I was heavy with child, who came to tend me in the women's lodge? No sister. No cousin. Strangers!"

"Red Willow Woman is no stranger," Stone Wolf argued.

"Worse. She dislikes me. I've heard her speaking with the children—my children! She poisons them against me."

"Do you want me to send Red Willow Woman away?" Stone Wolf asked.

Star Eyes paled.

"Who would do her work?" she asked.

"Ah, that would be a problem," Stone Wolf confessed. "When we sent her away before, you soon wearied of the tasks. I could take another wife."

"No!" Star Eyes shouted. "Perhaps you could find

a Crow woman to help, someone I could look upon like a sister."

"I know of no one," Stone Wolf lamented. "Maybe when we raid horses."

Star Eyes frowned heavily. For a moment she closed her eyes. Then, growing harder, she turned with angry eyes and declared, "You must speak to the other men."

"Of what?" he asked.

"Of me," she explained. "You took a chief's daughter to your lodge, and she deserves the respect of the other women. You don't notice their rude manners, the way they block my path and whisper behind my back. When the traders come, I am kept from their blankets until all the best goods are taken. Small children throw mud at me when I walk to collect wood. I worry our child will be harmed."

"Why do they behave this way?" Stone Wolf asked. "What do they say?"

"They call me 'that Crow woman'! I'm the wife of the Arrow-keeper! Don't I share my husband's standing?"

"They don't understand your ways," Stone Wolf explained. "Among our people a woman tends her camp, cooks, and sees to the raising of the children. A woman doesn't walk alone through the camp to visit the white traders."

"They say I'm unfaithful."

Are you? Stone Wolf wondered. He wanted to voice his concern, but the words wouldn't form. He feared the answer.

"I was born to my people," Star Eyes said somberly. "Many times I've wondered if fate might have been

15

kinder to those who were slain. Here I am, a stranger among your people, unloved and misunderstood. Hated by many."

"Loved by some," Stone Wolf said, taking her head in his hands. "Maybe it was wrong to keep you with me, but your eyes captured my heart. Younger Wolf says I should have made you learn our ways, but the hardness would have rubbed the shine from your eyes. I'll speak to the men. They'll talk to their wives and sisters, and your path may be smoother. I pray so. You must try to adopt our customs. Red Willow Woman can teach you so much if you will heed her advice."

"I promise to try, Husband."

"We're both young, Star Eyes. There's so much left to learn. If we're patient, our path will not disappoint us. Soon I'll climb the hills and make prayers. You will bring our child into the light. That should be a cheering notion."

"Yes," Star Eyes agreed. She rested her head on his bare shoulder, and Stone Wolf hoped the past troubles would fade into memory. They didn't.

Two

Star Eyes soon took to the women's lodge to prepare for the birth of her child. The thought of a third child brought a glow to Stone Wolf's lodge. Dawn Dancer argued for a sister.

"*Ne' hyo,* Red Willow Woman is old," the girl noted. "She won't always cook and tend camp for us. There's too much work for a single woman, and I'll need a sister's help."

Arrow Dancer frowned at the thought and objected in his small voice that men were needed to hunt and fight.

"Please bring us a girl, *Ne' hyo,*" Dawn Dancer pleaded as she nestled under her father's arm.

"A brother," Arrow Dancer stubbornly insisted.

"Man Above will decide it," Stone Wolf told the children. "Put the welfare of your mother first in your thoughts. Son or daughter, I only hope the child will enjoy strength and wisdom."

He hoped, too, that a sucking infant would lead Star Eyes back to her family. Motherhood was a

17

strong instinct, and the needs of a helpless one struck deep into one's heart.

"Don't expect too much of her," Red Willow Woman counseled. "She speaks only of white traders and remembers her Crow days."

"I wish she had relatives here to speak to her," Stone Wolf replied. "I don't understand Crow women."

"It's not Crows," Red Willow Woman argued. "There are many among the People raised by those other people. I don't see others neglect their work, ignore their children."

"We've spoken these words already. Soon I must seek a dream, and I don't want my thinking clouded with dark notions."

"No, and I have work waiting me. The child will be a boy. Bring him a good name from the hills."

"A boy?" Stone Wolf asked. "What makes you believe that?"

"I felt it move," Red Willow Woman boasted. "Women know such things. It's good you should have another son. Our family isn't blessed with numbers, and your brother has no children."

That was all too true. But Younger Wolf wasn't an old man yet, and Stone Wolf would have other little ones.

Two days hence Stone Wolf left the camp with his brother to make the birth prayers and seek a name for the little one. Such occasions were serious times, and the brothers took care to observe the ceremonies carefully. A fire was kindled on high ground, and Stone Wolf performed the pipe ritual, invoking the aid of the spirits in the upcoming trial. He smoked, and Younger Wolf smoked. The sky overhead cleared, and a thousand stars sparkled in the ebony vastness.

"Man Above, bring me a dream," Stone Wolf pleaded as he stood before the fire, bare as a newborn. Younger Wolf brought a knife, and Stone Wolf drew the blade across his chest, his thighs, his forearms. Bright red blood trickled across his body, and a warm glow spread through Stone Wolf's insides. He danced, singing old warrior chants and praying for a dream.

All night and most of the morning Stone Wolf danced and bled. He took no food, and only a little water. Gradually a fever began to take possession of his senses, and by nightfall, Stone Wolf had lost consciousness. Younger Wolf covered him with a buffalo hide and stoked the fire before walking off to leave his brother in the hands of the spirits.

The dream came quickly. Before, when awaiting Dawn Dancer and Arrow Dancer, Stone Wolf had fasted and danced and bled three nights. Now the vision came with great urgency.

It began, as others had, with a great white cloud. Sometimes Bull Buffalo would step from the cloud, leading his brothers in a great charge across the earth. More often Wolf would howl a greeting. Such was not the case this time. Instead faces emerged from the mists.

Cloud Dancer was there. Iron Wolf, the father who had died when Stone Wolf was a boy of nine summers, stood beside the old Arrow-keeper. Others, dead cousins and friends, appeared as well. Their stern faces forewarned of danger.

From out of that spectral throng emerged one unlike the others. He wore skins marked in ancient symbols, and his wrinkled face and odd manner brought forth half-remembered stories from Stone Wolf's boyhood.

It was the strange one — Sweet Medicine.

"Yes, it's I," Sweet Medicine whispered in a melodic voice. "I who brought *Mahuts* to the People, who gave laws and customs to keep them safe in these times of great peril. Hear me, Arrow-keeper!"

Sweet Medicine's eyes became fireballs, and the cloud glowed yellow-bright like the sun itself.

"Long ago I warned the People of the pale ones," Sweet Medicine lamented. "But what are words? Whispers on the wind. Useless to those with no ears to listen. Now the danger has come, and my counsel cannot save the People from their fate."

A great moaning ensued. Sweet Medicine sighed and turned away. Slowly, silently, he disappeared in the fiery cloud and was gone.

The dream continued. Stone Wolf heard other voices, other warnings. But they were nothing compared to the despair etched in Sweet Medicine's brow. Finally Stone Wolf felt himself floating above the earth, carried along as a speck of dust. The rich land beside Muddy River became covered with wagon lodges. White men erected villages where the People had always camped. *Noahvose* itself was violated.

Bull Buffalo became a ghost. Wolf vanished. Eagle flew no longer. Only Stone Wolf remained, a man alone on a high cliff, listening to the mourning wails of the wind and feeling the terrible cold that loss and isolation brought.

"Man Above, what can I do?" Stone Wolf called.

"See," a haunting voice answered. "Remember," it added. "Warn the others."

"Can I stop these terrible things?" he cried. "Man Above, tell me how!"

Stone Wolf screamed his plea over and over. He was shouting it still when Younger Wolf shook him from the dream.

"*Nah nih,* what have you seen?" Younger Wolf asked. "Brother, what is it?"

"The future," Stone Wolf answered, shuddering at the realization. "The death of all the world we know."

"How?"

"The white men will bring it," Stone Wolf explained. "We should have heeded Sweet Medicine's warnings. We must avoid the pale people."

"How is that possible now," Younger Wolf asked. "They're everywhere. Every season more come. How can we fight our enemies without the guns they trade us? Our women are accustomed to the shiny beads and fine cloth the traders bring."

Younger Wolf's words rang true. Stone Wolf wanted to argue otherwise, but there was no turning away from truth. How would Stone Wolf guide others from the traders when he couldn't persuade his own wife to avoid them?

Younger Wolf built up the fire. Meanwhile, Stone Wolf treated his sacrificial wounds and tried to share the apocalyptic vision.

"Surely *Mahuts* will shield us from these things," Younger Wolf suggested.

"I pray so," Stone Wolf replied. "A world without Bull Buffalo means starving winters."

"Did a name come to you?"

"A name?"

"For the child," Younger Wolf reminded his brother. "You came to seek the name, didn't you?"

"Yes, but I saw much more. Cloud Dancer would have thought of a proud name, but I . . ."

"A child doesn't need a proud name," Younger Wolf argued. "He'll win a brave heart name for himself when it's time. What will we call him now?"

"You're certain it will be a boy?"

"Red Willow Woman said so. She knows such things."

"Then we will name him for his mother's people. Crow Boy."

"His mother has too much to remind her of the Crows already. There are those, too, who will trouble a boy so named."

"A hard road makes a man strong."

"But it too often kills a young one," Younger Wolf argued. "I'll tell them in the camp. Then I'll return with a horse so you may ride homeward. The walk won't ease your fever."

"No, but I know cures for fevers." *And none for this terrifying future Man Above has shown me!*

Red Willow Woman was right about the child. It was indeed a boy.

"More like a worm," Younger Wolf pronounced when he held the wrinkled brown bundle the first time.

"In time he'll carry the stringless bow," Stone Wolf declared. "He, too, will join the Fox Warriors like his father and uncle."

"It's hard to imagine," Younger Wolf insisted.

"We all begin small, Brother. Even Younger Wolf once squirmed and crawled. Crow Boy won't disappoint us."

Younger Wolf returned the infant to its father and smiled. The little one had already burrowed its way into Stone Wolf's heart.

Crow Boy enjoyed no like success with his mother. Star Eyes distanced herself from the child immediately.

"He cries too often," she complained.

"He's little and knows no better," Stone Wolf argued. "He's probably hungry."

That meant little to Star Eyes. No sooner had she regained her feet than she refused to nurse.

"He bites," Star Eyes complained.

"Bites?" Red Willow Woman cried. "He has no teeth!"

There was no persuading Star Eyes, though, and Red Willow Woman took charge of the child. Little Wren, the young wife of Prancing Elk, eagerly agreed to nurse the little one. Her own son was born early and breathed but a few times before drifting off in a dream.

"His crying doesn't trouble me," the Wren told Stone Wolf. "It's the sound of life, after all."

Red Willow Woman regarded Star Eyes with new contempt, and the other women renewed their hostility.

"See how they insult me!" Star Eyes complained to Stone Wolf.

"They expect better behavior of you," he responded. "I hoped for more myself."

23

"Who are you to speak ill of me!" she answered. "I thought I married a great man, but you are no chief! Arrow-keeper! That's an empty title. You give away our possessions as if they are nothing. A shrewd trader would fill our lodge with fine things!"

"A wise woman would see the wealth around her," Stone Wolf scolded. "Three children. A loving husband. What want haven't I satisfied?"

"You speak of wealth, but you list only burdens."

"Maybe you should leave my lodge then," Stone Wolf said sternly. "There are Crow camps nearby. I'll give you good horses. It's an easy ride."

"So now you would dishonor me!" she exclaimed.

"You do that yourself," Stone Wolf said bitterly.

"Do I? You listen to the others too much."

"I have eyes. I see you neglect our children!"

"I won't be chased from my home."

"Leave or stay," Stone Wolf grumbled. "Choose. But if you intend to remain my wife, bring no more trouble to our lodge. Be a mother to my children."

"I gave them birth," she said angrily. "How easily a man finds fault. He doesn't know a woman's pain!"

Stone Wolf frowned heavily. He shook his anger off and offered a comforting hand. She avoided it, stalking off angrily.

"Why doesn't our mother share our love?" Dawn Dancer asked afterward.

"I don't know," Stone Wolf confessed. "She was taken away from her family when still a girl. Perhaps that's reason enough."

"You lost your father, too," Red Willow Woman pointed out.

"Yes, and I wanted children young so I might see

24

hem grow tall. I might have given her time to learn our ways first."

"She'll never learn," Red Willow Woman muttered. "Many would eagerly step into her shoes. I sometimes wonder what ill wind blew her to us. How unfair that she should enjoy such long life and Little Wren's son be born dead!"

"That's enough of such talk," Stone Wolf said, and Red Willow Woman moved to the far side of the lodge and sat silently.

"Do you think she'll go?" Younger Wolf asked when the brothers sat beside the fire together late that night.

"Maybe," Stone Wolf answered. "If she's unhappy . . ."

"She's not," Younger Wolf declared. "Not when she's down at the river. I wish she would leave. She'll only bring you sorrow."

"Joy, too," Stone Wolf said, closing his eyes and imagining the children beside him.

"Hold them close, *Nah nih*," Younger Wolf urged. "I fear you'll need their strength."

As spring flowed into summer, Stone Wolf found little time to worry about Star Eyes. An Arrow-keeper's duties never seemed to end, and when he wasn't invoking a blessing or performing a healing cure, he was lending the power of the Buffalo Arrows to hunting parties.

Dark dreams of the white men plagued his sleep,

but there was no avoiding the newcomers. Every river knew the hairy-faced hunters, and traders traveled with many bands of *Tsis tsis tas.*

"We need the lead they bring to make balls for our guns," the hunters said.

"Their cloth is good and warm," women argued.

When Stone Wolf reminded his companions of the spotted sickness that had killed so many of the People, spoke of the empty Mandan camps on Muddy River, the young men simply smiled.

"We don't remember the Mandans," they said. "Save your stories for old women."

"Show respect for the keeper of *Mahuts!*" Younger Wolf shouted.

"Old arrows don't kill buffalo," Snake Eater, a young Elk lance carrier complained. "My father spoke of how the Arrow-keepers kept us from accepting guns until the Crows grew strong and powerful. See how our cousins the Lakotas have grown! We, too, should change our ways."

"We are *Tsis tsis tas!*" Stone Wolf shouted. "If we turn from what we know, who will we be?"

"Not who," Snake Eater answered. "What! Alive. If the Arrow power is so strong, why not use it to defeat our enemies? When was the last time *Mahuts* led the warriors into a fight? Show us your worth, Stone Wolf. Bring the people a victory over the Crows."

"What would you know of such things?" Younger Wolf said, scowling. "My brother has counted coup on the enemy. You carry a lance, but how did you earn it? Your uncle made a present of it to you."

"I've killed the enemy!" Snake Eater cried.

"You shot a Ree boy with your rifle," Younger

Wolf replied. "A child of twelve summers. No more. One surely left to hold his brother's horses. When you touch the lance to the enemy's chest, then speak to Stone Wolf of fighting Crows."

"We all know of Stone Wolf's battles," Snake Eater said, laughing. "With Crow women. Perhaps there should be six Arrows. Two to blind women."

"Enough!" Badger, Snake Eater's uncle, barked.

"It's only the truth, Uncle," Snake Eater continued. "You've seen Star Eyes in the trader's camp yourself."

"It's a sad thing," Badger agreed. "But speak no more of it. And never insult *Mahuts*. You haven't seen their power. They are the heart of the People."

"Heart, yes," Snake Eater agreed. "The Foxes have heart enough. But I wonder if they've lost their stomach for fighting. When did their young men last ride against the Crows?"

"Would you organize a horse raid?" Younger Wolf asked. "When the hunting is still good? Now's the time to gather food to keep hunger from our winter camps."

"And when the hunting is finished, will the Foxes join in raiding the Crows?"

"Join?" Younger Wolf cried in disbelief. "When did the Foxes follow anyone? We lead the way. So it has always been. So we will always do."

"I will remember these words," Snake Eater declared. "As will others. If your hearts remain brave, you will come with the Elks. Or lead as you choose."

"Lead," Younger Wolf said, glaring at young Snake Eater.

"*Ayyyy!*" Snake Eater and the other Elks cried. "It will be a fight to remember!"

27

Afterward, Stone Wolf drew his brother aside.

"It's easy to talk of coups," Stone Wolf argued. "To boast of war. We remember fighting the Crows."

"Yes," Younger Wolf admitted. "And it's foolish to rush into a thing. We'll prepare ourselves. You will ask *Mahuts* to counsel us, and I will see we avoid ambush."

"Be careful, Brother. My sons need their uncle."

"They'll grow tall at my side. This fight is necessary. Snake Eater's voice is a loud one, and others share his views."

"Then the torment of my dream is already upon us," Stone Wolf lamented. "And hard days lay ahead."

Three

Snake Eater was young to lead men to war, so it was Badger that carried a pipe among the warriors, organizing the party. Even so, when it was time to consult *Mahuts,* Snake Eater was the one who appeared outside the Arrow Lodge, cradling a pipe in his leathery bronze arms.

"I come to consult *Mahuts,*" Snake Eater said when Stone Wolf emerged from the sacred lodge.

"Yes," Stone Wolf replied, frowning as he examined the lance carrier. Snake Eater wore only moccasins and breechclout. His hair bore no ornaments, and he smelled of horses. "I expected you," the Wolf added, "but not this way."

"No?" Snake Eater asked angrily. "And how should I come to you?"

"Are you blind to think it's me you seek?" Stone Wolf cried. "You would step inside this sacred place, stand before *Mahuts!* Go, speak to Badger, your uncle. Learn from him and the other Elks. Don't return until you can speak with respect, and you free yourself of dung scent."

"I've been riding among the many bands," Snake Eater explained. "Gathering men."

"It's good to have strong numbers," Stone Wolf observed. "But preparations are as important. Purify yourself in the sweat lodge. Think of the road before you. Then come before *Mahuts* in your best clothes, bringing a suitable gift that I may place before the Arrows."

"Then you will ask *Mahuts* to bless our undertaking?"

"I will help you discover what is to come."

"That's what I ask. I'll do as you say and return. Then we will speak to *Mahuts* and go to kill the Crows."

Snake Eater did, indeed, return. Badger led him to the Arrow Lodge. The Elks were dressed in fine buckskin shirts and beaded breechclouts. Their hair was oiled and decorated with elk teeth and eagle feathers. The two received a welcoming nod from Stone Wolf.

"My nephew brings a pipe to *Mahuts*," Badger explained. "He would ask a question."

"It's always good to have a guide when you first walk a new road," Stone Wolf said, motioning the visitors inside the Arrow Lodge. "There's so much for a young man to learn."

Snake Eater scowled as if to say, "You're not so much older that you should scold me!" Stone Wolf ignored the look. *Mahuts* would be offended by discord in that sacred place.

The Arrows hung in the center of the lodge as was customary. The men carefully made their way around the outer rim of the lodge, taking care not to pass between *Mahuts* and the entry. Stone Wolf then sat beside a small fire and motioned for his visitors to sit nearby. Then the Wolf performed the pipe ritual and smoked. After passing the pipe to Snake Eater, who smoked and passed the pipe on to his uncle, Stone Wolf accepted the pipe and emptied its ashes in a small pile beside the embers of the fire.

"You come to ask *Mahuts* a question," Stone Wolf noted. "Do you bring a present?"

"We bring these small gifts," Badger said, presenting a glimmering yellow stone, a polished buffalo horn, and two eagle feathers.

"These things are acceptable," Stone Wolf noted as he tied each in turn to the Arrow bundle. "White eagle's tail feathers bring power to our talk. Bull buffalo's horn adds strength. This yellow rock reminds us of the permanence of Earth, which will remain when our bones are only memory."

Stone Wolf spoke the ancient prayers, then invited Snake Eater to pose his question. The lance carrier told of Crow horse raids against the People and recounted the hard fights waged against the Crows in times past. Finally Snake Eater argued the need for an attack to punish these enemies and assure the safety of the People's summer camps.

Stone Wolf closed his eyes and drank in all he had heard. Then he opened his eyes and watched as the sacred bundle turned slowly overhead.

"Yes, you will lead your raid," Stone Wolf spoke slowly, reverently. "But there's danger for the People in this thing."

"How so?" Badger asked.

"Many Crows ride the buffalo valleys this summer," Stone Wolf explained. "Most camp nearby while our bands are scattered. Be careful not to bring them all down upon us."

"They are only Crows," Snake Eater muttered. "We're unafraid."

"Be quiet, Nephew," Badger scolded. "You haven't seen what I have. What does *Mahuts* tell us?"

"Two things," Stone Wolf said, breathing deeply. "The Crows have many good horses. We will capture these ponies in a great raid that will long be remembered. But we must kill no one. So long as we don't strike down the Crows, none of our men will be harmed. If the Crows pursue, their eyes will not find us."

"It's a war party I'm forming," Snake Eater complained. "You counted coup against the enemy once. Do you deny us the chance to earn honor in the same way?"

"Nothing was said of counting coup," Stone Wolf pointed out. "You may strike the Crows with a quirt or touch them with bow or lance. But if blood is shed, it will be nothing to the river that will follow."

"And if a Crow kills one of us?" Snake Eater asked.

"No Crow arrow will find us," Stone Wolf insisted. "I will make charms to turn them away."

"And will you then ride with us?" Badger asked. "Perhaps *Mahuts* will come?"

"I will come," Stone Wolf reluctantly agreed. "But only to make the proper prayers and recount the warning. It's for you, the leaders, to keep the young men in check."

Badger nodded, and Snake Eater rose with his uncle.

"We'll heed your counsel," Badger pledged. "Your words, as always, carry the weight of wisdom."

"They do," Stone Wolf agreed. "But only if they are followed."

After invoking the protection of the spirits and tying elk tooth charms behind the ears of the young horse raiders, Stone Wolf accompanied Younger Wolf and a handful of Fox Warriors as they rode out across the prairie. Summer had painted the land yellow-green, and the grass was thick and high. It was a good time to hunt buffalo, and Stone Wolf wished the men were seeking game instead of Crow ponies. In spite of Snake Eater's promise, a foreboding filled the Arrow-keeper's entire being.

"You've done all that's possible," Younger Wolf argued as they rode. "Everyone heard your words. Even the youngest horse-holder understands the weight of an admonition from *Mahuts!*"

"Does Snake Eater?" Stone Wolf asked.

"No one wishes to be remembered as a man who brought death to the People," Younger Wolf said as he pointed to where the lance carrier was riding up ahead. "And Badger is at his side."

But neither of them planned the raid. Scouts were sent to find the horse herd, but no effort was made to strike with stealth. Instead Snake Eater screamed like an eagle and urged a charge. Many young Elk Warriors followed, and Badger was left behind. Younger Wolf kept the Foxes back, and they struck the flank of the herd and cut out a hundred good ponies for their use. Up ahead the firing of rifles and loud cries told of a bloody confrontation.

"How can you warn a man who won't hear?" Stone Wolf cried out in frustration.

"You can only tell a man what lies ahead," Younger Wolf answered. "If he's determined to ride to his death, then he'll do it."

"He won't die," Stone Wolf muttered. "No, that's for others to do."

Younger Wolf nodded somberly, then instructed the younger Foxes to drive the captured ponies back to the camp.

"We others must rescue our brothers," Younger Wolf said, gazing at the seven who remained.

"First paint your faces," Stone Wolf advised. "Then make your prayers. It's a hard fight we'll find up ahead."

So it was. Stone Wolf watched in dismay as the raiding party split into twos and threes and tried to flee with captured ponies. Snake Eater galloped past, driving before him a midnight black mare and screaming defiantly. The Crows were forming a line of sorts on a low ridge. Once twenty had assembled, they mounted a charge. Badger and another scarred veteran made a brief stand to halt the Crows, but there were too many. The Crows swept over them like a flood, and a bare-chested young man soon emerged from dust swirls, holding Badger's lance in one hand and a bloody scalp in the other.

"We're too late," Younger Wolf declared.

"To stop the blood from flowing," Stone Wolf said as he drew out his bow. "We can occupy the Crows here or lead them to our camp."

"The young ones will warn the camp," Younger Wolf said, frowning. "We can run the Crows."

Stone Wolf nodded. It was always the hard things a man of the People was left to do. Fools like Snake Eater could boast and shout and run away. Not so Stone Wolf.

"Nothing lasts long," Younger Wolf screamed. "Only the earth and the mountains!"

The other Foxes shouted in response, then followed as Younger Wolf led them toward the enemy. The Crows were too busy celebrating Badger's death and recovering horses to notice the approaching danger. Younger Wolf struck down one, and a young man called Thunder Coat buried his lance point in the thigh of another. Stone Wolf unhorsed one young Crow by slapping him across the chest with a bow. The Crows broke and fled.

"Ayyyy!" the Foxes howled.

Younger Wolf held them back from a second charge, though.

"The danger's elsewhere," he warned.

Stone Wolf nodded grimly, and the Foxes began the long ride homeward.

The camp was a whirlwind of activity. Young horse raiders boasted of their exploits and paraded their captured animals. Snake Eater told of striking down the Crow guards.

"Two coups I counted!" the lance carrier cried.

"And who shot his rifle?" Stone Wolf demanded. "Who broke the medicine?"

"A Crow raised his rifle," Snake Eater explained.

35

"He would have killed Badger, my uncle."

"And where is Badger now?" Younger Wolf asked.

"Dead. Scalped by the Crows."

"No," Snake Eater said, glancing around in a furious effort to locate his missing relative. Badger's wife and daughter began the mourning cry, and others among the People rushed to search out their fathers or brothers. Soon other cries rose.

"How did my uncle die?" Snake Eater asked, his face growing pale.

"He stayed behind to drive off the Crows," Younger Wolf said angrily. "As a lance bearer would do."

"To protect those who followed him on the war trail," Stone Wolf added.

"It was for me to do," Snake Eater muttered.

"He took the pipe among the camps," Younger Wolf said, glaring at the young Elk. "He felt the obligation."

"I'll return to the Crows and bring back his body!" Snake Eater vowed.

"It's nothing now," Stone Wolf argued. "The danger is to the defenseless ones. The Crows will follow the horse trail and find our camp. We must move quickly."

"Before mourning the dead?" an old woman objected.

"We must wait the three days," Snake Eater insisted.

"We can mourn elsewhere," Younger Wolf suggested. "Or stay and mourn others."

A murmur of agreement met his words, and women hurried to break down the lodges. Soon the camp was packed up and moving off. They left a clear trail be-

36

hind, though, and Stone Wolf knew the Crows wouldn't be long in finding it.

They came at dusk the next day. Small warrior bands had ridden out to watch for enemies, but the Crows were clever and avoided their enemies' eyes. Only a small party attacked the camp. Most of the Crows were content to steal horses and chase the pony boys. Those who did strike the lodges came with angry eyes and a hunger for revenge. They hit hard and swiftly.

Stone Wolf was in the Arrow Lodge, preparing healing herbs, when the yelping of the camp dogs warned of danger. He paused only long enough to grab his bow before hurrying outside. Already the dust thrown up by approaching horses shrouded the dying light of day, leaving a burnt orange haze hanging on the western horizon.

"Ne' hyo!" Dawn Dancer called in alarm as her father notched an arrow.

"Go inside the lodge," Stone Wolf commanded. "Look after your brothers."

The girl bowed her head respectfully and raced back to the lodge. Red Willow Woman gripped her hand and pulled her inside.

"Nah nih, here!" Younger Wolf then called, and Stone Wolf followed his brother's voice to where the Crows were battling a group of Elks on the western fringe of the camp.

Stone Wolf paused to usher curious children to safety before taking his place in the thin line between Younger Wolf and Thunder Coat. The Foxes were the largest warrior band in the camp, and their numbers swelled as men saw their families to safety, armed themselves, and hurried to defend the camp. Crows made weak attempts to break through the warrior line, but mostly men fought with lances. One man was knocked down, and a second wounded, but little blood was shed.

Among the Crows was a tall man who had painted his face and chest red. While others fought on foot, he rode a swift horse behind them, shouting encouragement and hurling insults.

"He owns strong medicine," Thunder Coat cried. "See how he avoids the arrows."

The red-faced man seemed charmed. Each time an arrow flew in his direction, he seemed to melt into the sky. It was an unnerving thing to watch, and Stone Wolf decided it should come to an end. He drew back from the fighting, notched an arrow, and spoke a brief prayer of apology as he drove his arrow into the heart of the tall Crow's horse. The animal screamed as it went down, hurling the red-faced demon into the embers of an abandoned campfire.

The Crow cried in pain as he dragged himself free of the coals. His left leg remained bent, and he couldn't steady himself. Snake Eater rushed through the line to kill the lame Crow, but Red Face produced a knife and threw himself forward, slashing so violently that Snake Eater was caught by surprise. The lance carrier fell backward, and the Crow pounced. The knife cut deep, gashing Snake Eater's thighs and opening up his belly. Red Face then carved away his enemy's forelock and raised it skyward with a howl of celebration.

38

The Crow didn't live to enjoy his victory. The Elks, enraged by the sudden loss of their young leader, surged. The outnumbered Crows retired to safety, found their horses, and made good their escape. Red Face, horseless and lame, chanted his death song and vanished in a wave of Elk fury.

Red Face's death was scant compensation for the losses suffered by the People. Seven lodges were destroyed, and fifty good horses had been stolen. Besides Snake Eater, four others were slain. Winter Bear, one of the old man chiefs, had fallen protecting his grandson. Two small sons of Long Ear were cut down inside their lodge, and a daughter of Dove Moon was hit by an arrow.

Many, both warriors, women, and children, were wounded. One of the pony boys, Thunder Coat's brother White Horn, bore seven wounds. But he was strong. Stone Wolf attended the boy himself.

"I think these Crows don't like you much," Stone Wolf observed.

"They liked my horses," White Horn replied. "They would have left me alone, but I'm a slow runner. Others outran the lances, but not me."

"I saw no wounds on your back," Younger Wolf noted. "A man is hurt on his chest when he fights."

"*Ayyyy!*" Thunder Coat agreed. "He's a brave one."

"They took the horses," White Horn said, sighing. "Broke my bow, too."

"I'll make another," Thunder Coat promised. "He will heal?"

"His spirit's strong," Stone Wolf said, spreading ointment across the gashes. "My medicine will make him whole."

"I'll have scars," White Horn said, staring at his bloody chest and thighs.

"Ah, the women will like them," Younger Wolf said, touching the youngster lightly on the shoulder. "Soon you'll join your brother among the Foxes."

"Yes, soon," Thunder Bear agreed. "Rest now, Brother. And mend yourself."

Four

The Crows were not content with their solitary raid. The mourning cries of women spurred the men to embark on revenge forays, and the People were constantly moving their camps and striking back at marauding enemies. Autumn found Stone Wolf's band east of their traditional autumn camps, near *Noahvose*, the sacred center of the earth.

"It's here Sweet Medicine brought *Mahuts* to the People," Stone Wolf told the young ones. "My grandfather, Cloud Dancer, came here to start the long walk up Hanging Road, as did his uncle, Touches the Sky, before him."

"Is it a place of death then, *Ne' hyo?*" Dawn Dancer asked her father.

"No, it's the heart of all the world," Stone Wolf explained. "When the Arrows were stained with blood flakes, it was to Noahvose they were brought for renewal. This high place is close to the sky. It brings on dreaming. A place of death? No, it's a place of beginnings."

41

As autumn cast its amber brush to the hills and valleys, it was hard to imagine beginnings, though. Nights were growing longer and colder. Bull Buffalo's coat grew long and heavy, and the men were busy hunting. Winter coats and dried meat were made ready against the approaching need.

Stone Wolf occupied himself preparing the young men for the hunt. He painted their chests and offered charms. Mahuts advised the scouts where to seek Bull Buffalo, and Stone Wolf made the appropriate prayers. If a man or boy was hurt, the Arrow-keeper treated the wound or injury and restored the injured to vigor.

More and more the woman's part of the healing cures was taken by Red Willow Woman. The Oglala had a calming touch, and her devotion to the sick brought her praise throughout the camp.

The same tongues which held Red Willow Woman in high regard questioned the absence of Star Eyes from her husband's side.

"Where is the Arrow-keeper's woman?" they asked. "Off with the traders."

Younger Wolf was blunt.

"She should join the Crows," he suggested. "You should send her away, *Nah nih*. She brings dishonor on our family."

"She lacks the healing touch," Stone Wolf argued. "And there are the little ones to look after."

"Yes, and she should take them in hand!" Younger Wolf demanded. "Dawn Dancer is too young to bear all the burdens of the lodge. She tends her brothers and watches the cook pot when Red Willow Woman helps you in the Arrow Lodge. Soon Little Wren will

42

be finished with Crow Boy. It's time his mother provides for that child!"

Stone Wolf knew his brother was right, and he led Star Eyes to the river to talk.

"You neglect your obligations," Stone Wolf told her. "I bear the hardness in your heart for me. But your children want a mother."

"They have Red Willow Woman," Star Eyes declared.

"Perhaps the Oglala should take your place at my side," Stone Wolf said icily. "She's more wife than you."

"And more husband than you," Star Eyes replied, laughing. "What do you want of me, Stone Wolf? I've given you sons. And some measure of pleasure. If you've grown old and wrinkled and need a woman to warm your feet, ask one of the old ones to do it. I'm the daughter of a chief and expect more."

"And what of your obligations?"

"If I owed you my life once, then surely three children are payment enough."

"Don't you feel anything?"

"What should I feel? Love? When have I ever been numbered among the important things in your world? First always are the Arrows. Then the little ones. The shoeless boy or gray-haired old woman find your protection, but me? No, you allow the others to torment and humiliate me. I asked your help, but you had other duties."

"Do you wish me to leave our lodge?" Stone Wolf asked.

"Oh, that would be a fine thing! I would have three children and no one to provide meat!"

"What do you wish, Star Eyes?" Stone Wolf asked. "To return to the Crows?"

"My family is dead," she grumbled. "Who there would treat me with honor after so long a time among the enemy? I don't demand you buy me silver bracelets or glass beads. Leave me to walk my own path."

"Among the traders?"

"When they are among us, I'm useful. I translate their words and signs for others. They reward me with fine gifts."

"It's not proper work for the wife of an Arrow-keeper."

"Maybe you should give the Arrows over to someone else then," she suggested. "It's their burden that blinds you to the good things all around you."

"Blind?" Stone Wolf cried. "No, *Mahuts* opens a man's mind to all. I see well enough."

"Do you?" she asked, smiling shyly as she had when he first took her to his lodge. "I wonder."

Stone Wolf frowned heavily. Younger Wolf was right to say Star Eyes was no longer a wife. But how could a man force his children's mother from his lodge? He was an Arrow-keeper! Such disharmony would darken the Arrows and bring disaster to the People!

Stone Wolf tried to cast the gloom from his life. He found distraction in his work, and delight in the company of the little ones. Dawn Dancer repeated remembered tales beside the evening cook fire, and her father nodded proudly as she spoke. Arrow Dancer often rested on one knee, or else chased Younger

Wolf around the fire, uttering high-pitched war cries and pounding his uncle with a small bird arrow — as big a lance as a boy of three summers could manage.

Crow Boy, too, was growing, although he occupied a cradle board more often than not. At dusk he would rest in his sister's arms or roll on a sea of elk hides, reaching his chubby hands out toward the fire and examining all the world.

"He misses his mother," Red Willow Woman continued to complain.

"Mother?" Dawn Dancer cried. "What mother? He misses Little Wren."

"Star Eyes has gone to speak for the traders," Stone Wolf said, motioning his daughter close. "Sit with me, little one, and I'll tell you how my grandfather brought Horse to the People."

"Will that bring our mother to us?" the girl whispered.

Stone Wolf frowned, but Dawn Dancer stroked his cheek and offered a cheerful grin.

"It was long ago," Stone Wolf began, and the old story warmed them against a chill wind.

It wasn't long thereafter that a dark dream came to him. It began as others had, with a gray wolf howling on a distant hillside. After a time the wolf stopped and turned toward the valley, where a camp of the People spread out beside Shell River.

"Hear me, brothers," the wolf called. "Hard days are coming."

Stone Wolf shuddered at the icy tone of the wolf's words. The camp stirred in alarm as a cloud swept across the land, obscuring the slope and its prophetic beast.

"Run, brothers," the voice of the wolf urged. "Run! Your enemies are approaching!"

From beyond the clouds they came—Crows, Rees, Snakes, Pawnees—from north, south, east, and west. Run? Run where?

"Come, stand tall with me!" Younger Wolf screamed as he rallied the young Foxes. "Protect the defenseless ones!"

"Ayyyy!" the Crows howled furiously as they charged. The young Foxes shrank from the charge, leaving Younger Wolf and a few others to meet the Crows. In a swirl of gray dust the warriors were overrun, and the Crows galloped on into the camp, scattering lodge poles, splitting apart skins as they searched for captives. Drying racks cracked beneath war axes, and little ones screamed with fright as the enemy struck them down or carried them off. The women tried to protect themselves, but it was hopeless. The old ones died in a heap beside the river, rubbed out by cascades of arrows.

"Where is *Mahuts?*" the survivors called. "What has become of our protector?"

No hint of the Arrows could be seen, though, nor of Stone Wolf. The enemy bands ravaged the camp, taking what they wished and burning what was left. When they finished only ashes remained to stand beside the dead.

"This must not happen," the wolf whispered.

Stone Wolf awoke in a sweat. He sat up, shivering, and stared at the darkness around him. Star Eyes was fast asleep. Dawn Dancer and her brothers were bun-

46

dled in their buffalo hides and otter skins, warm and untroubled by their father's dream. Only Younger Wolf stirred.

"Your dreams trouble you, *Nah nih,*" he whispered.

"Yes," Stone Wolf confessed.

Stone Wolf rolled out of his bed and dressed himself. His brother did likewise, and the two of them stepped out into the predawn stillness to share the dream.

"It's a hard thing you've seen," Younger Wolf observed afterward. "What must we do to keep the People safe?"

"Seek a vision," Stone Wolf replied. "As always. I will climb *Noahvose* and starve myself until Man Above shows me the path we must walk."

"I'll go with you," Younger Wolf volunteered. "As always. There are Crows about, and . . ."

"If there are Crows nearby, you will be needed here," Stone Wolf argued.

"No!" Younger Wolf objected.

"Yes, Brother, the winter hunting isn't finished. The children will need looking after, too."

"You can't go alone, *Nah nih!*"

"I'll ask one of the young men," Stone Wolf explained. "It's time others were introduced to the sacred path."

"White Horn is young, but he remembers things, and he walks the earth with respect."

"It's a good choice," Stone Wolf agreed. "I'll ask him."

"Be wary," Younger Wolf urged. "White Horn has courage, but he's young."

"We were all young once, Brother," Stone Wolf

47

said, managing a smile. "Never too young to learn, though."

Younger Wolf agreed, and they shared recollections of other days for a time. When dawn finally exploded across the eastern horizon, Stone Wolf set off to find White Horn. The young man readily accepted Stone Wolf's invitation, and they returned to find Younger Wolf had horses and provisions ready for the journey.

"Be watchful," Younger Wolf admonished White Horn. "Learn from him, but most of all keep him safe. We are lost without his vision."

"I place his life before my own," White Horn answered, putting on the fiercest gaze any fourteen-year-old ever managed.

"Don't worry," Stone Wolf said, clasping his brother's wrists. "Man Above will watch over us both."

Younger Wolf nodded, and Stone Wolf climbed atop the buckskin stallion he preferred for short rides. Waving White Horn along, the Arrow-keeper then led the way from camp and toward the looming slopes of *Noahvose*.

Many times Stone Wolf had climbed into the hills to seek a vision. Even as a boy spirits had come to him in dreams, and his grandfather had taken note of the young man's medicine in passing *Mahuts* into his care. Now more than ever it seemed to Stone Wolf there was need of power—of medicine strong enough to fend off the perilous nightmare foretold by the gray wolf.

With White Horn trailing along behind, Stone Wolf rode ever higher. *Noahvose* seemed to call him, urge him onward.

"Here?" White Horn called as they came to a clearing marked by the charred remains of many council fires.

"Higher," Stone Wolf answered. The shoulders of the butte were somehow inadequate this time. He sought the very summit.

Once there Stone Wolf dismounted and searched a place where he might glimpse both the beginning and end of day. He located a rocky clearing and sat down. As he set his medicine pouches beside him, White Horn collected kindling for a fire.

He was a good choice, Stone Wolf thought. *He senses what needs to be done and works quietly, respecting this sacred place.*

Indeed, White Horn seemed in awe of the mountain. He built a small fire and lit the kindling while Stone Wolf readied a pipe.

"Sit," the Arrow-keeper urged, pointing to a place on the far side of the fire. "Keep a flame rising from the wood."

"At night, too?" the boy asked.

"Until I have awaken from my dream. I need the flame to invite the spirits."

"If there are enemies about, they'll see it," White Horn warned.

"Man Above knows we're here," Stone Wolf assured his young companion. "We must rely on his power."

Stone Wolf then filled the pipe and began the sacred ceremony. He tossed tobacco to earth and sky, to the cardinal directions, and spoke the old medicine prayers taught him by his grandfather, the Arrow-keeper Cloud Dancer. The Wolf then painted himself and adorned his hair with elk's teeth and shells. Later he painted his face and chest. Although the provision bags were full, Stone Wolf took no nourishment and only a little water.

"The starving will hurry the vision," he explained to White Horn. "When night comes, I will hurry it more."

All day Stone Wolf chanted and danced. He spoke ancient invocations and recounted the origin stories. Finally, when the western sky swallowed Sun, Stone Wolf rose to his feet and drew out a knife.

"No, Uncle," White Horn cried, rushing to Stone Wolf's side. The boy wasn't really a relative, just a young Fox who had agreed to undertake a serious task. But it was good to speak to an elder with respect. Stone Wolf warmed at the boy's concern, but assured him nothing was amiss.

"It's necessary I suffer," Stone Wolf explained. He stripped himself bare, then cut the flesh of his chest and arms. Bright red blood trickled down his taut bronze flanks, and the wind stirred.

"Hear me, *Heammawihio*," Stone Wolf called. "Man Above, enter my dreams. Bring me power, that I may see what is to be. Show me the way to lead the People from peril!"

Stone Wolf howled and danced furiously, allowing his blood to flow freely. As he exerted himself, the hunger and pain produced fatigue and later fever. He finally collapsed, shivering, and White Horn covered him with buffalo hides.

For a time Stone Wolf lay silently atop *Noahvose*. It was as if Man Above was cradling him in mammoth hands, gently easing his pain and healing his wounds. Then a great white cloud formed in Stone Wolf's mind, growing taller and wider until it seemed to engulf the world. From its midst roared the sacred White Buffalo Cow, mother to the world and wisest of all creatures.

"You come to me troubled, little brother," White Buffalo Cow spoke. "you fear for the People, but they are blind to many warnings. Didn't Sweet Medicine warn of the pale ones? Didn't the Mandans die of spotted sickness that you might learn from their mistake? And now the hairy faces visit your camps, dishonor your women, shed your blood, and you do nothing."

"The world has changed," Stone Wolf heard himself answer. "The white man's guns have fallen into the hands of our enemies. We, too, take them so we won't be rubbed out."

"You take more than weapons," White Buffalo Cow complained. "You set aside the old ways. You kill game you don't eat. You foul sacred waters. You ride against enemies with angry hearts, not to earn honor by counting coup. No, the People have changed. Perhaps it's better they should die."

"No," Stone Wolf pleaded. "Show me another way. Give us protection from the white man's bullets and eyes that can see the danger ahead."

"You've long walked the sacred path," White Buffalo Cow said somberly. "This must continue. You ask for protection? Listen, see, and I will give what you ask."

Indeed. White Buffalo Cow climbed the clouds and stood among her mighty sons. Bull Buffalo spread in all directions as far as the eye might see. From a great brown bull White Buffalo Cow took the hide and rounded it into a circle. The tough hide was matched with a second hide, this the gift of antelope. Horse hair was stuffed between the two and sewn into a shield which a man could strap onto his arm.

White Buffalo Cow then blessed the shield with a blood sacrifice and painted it in wild symbols. On its head was a white buffalo skull, and surrounding it were arrows and thunderbolts.

"This shield will guard against all dangers," White Buffalo Cow promised. "It bears the power granted by *Heammawihio*. So long as a man rides with a brave and pure heart, he need fear no enemy."

"I will make these shields," Stone Wolf promised. "For each one I will invite a dream."

"Then it's good," White Buffalo Cow concluded. She turned and thundered back into her cloud, and a calm spread over *Noahvose*. Stone Wolf found the deep sleep that came with peace.

Five

When Stone Wolf awoke, it was midmorning. The autumn sun showered the face of *Noahvose* with golden hues, and the world below stretched far and wide.

"Water?" White Horn asked, rising from his place beside the blazing fire.

"Yes," Stone Wolf answered. "I will eat, too."

"Then you had your dream?" the boy asked.

"Yes," Stone Wolf said, nodding solemnly. "Man Above has shown me the way to make strong medicine."

"Then it was worth the starving. And the bleeding."

"Always the best power comes from sacrifice," Stone Wolf explained. "One day soon you will hang in the New Life Lodge and gain power for yourself. It's a hard thing at first. Later, pain becomes only another river to cross."

"You grew tall in the Arrow Lodge," the young man said respectfully. "So much remains a mystery to me."

"There's time to learn."

"You will show me?"

"It's a hard road, the medicine trail," Stone Wolf warned. "There's greater glory among the warriors."

"Thunder Coat says there's no greater honor than to be known as a man of the People. Unless it is to be Arrow-keeper."

"Honor," Stone Wolf said, chewing the word. "Responsibility. I always knew I would keep *Mahuts* when Cloud Dancer gave up his burden. There was no choosing for me. I stepped onto the hard road as a boy, and now the trail is steeper. Sometimes I would give much to be a simple man."

"The People would suffer."

"Yes, my heart tells me that. And so I continue to bear the burden. No man lives forever, though. If your brother agrees, come and live with me and learn the ceremonies. Even if you are not chosen to keep *Mahuts,* you will learn the healing and gain power."

"It's all I ask, Uncle."

They spoke of many things, high on the mountainside. Stone Wolf read the eagerness in White Horn's eyes and remembered his own boyhood. Old stories flowed from his lips, and as he introduced White Horn to old mysteries, he found himself recalling the words of his grandfather, Cloud Dancer.

"The man who chooses the easy path never grows hard or tall. When the deep snows come, he lacks the needed strength to endure winter's hardships. Man Above, give me great enemies that I may grow strong! That is my morning prayer."

When dusk came, Stone Wolf sent White Horn to ready the horses. It was time to return to the camp. All that day he'd spoken nothing of the Buffalo Shield.

"You don't wish to share the dream," White Horn muttered.

"It's not the dream I will share," Stone Wolf replied. "It's the gift brought us by the vision. You will help me bring it to the People. But I will not reveal the vision, for that might steal its power."

The boy didn't understand, and his perplexed look troubled Stone Wolf. Still, it was best the boy learn slowly.

They rode into camp as the sun passed from view. A crowd soon assembled, hoping for news, but Stone Wolf shared no more with them than he had told White Horn.

To Younger Wolf, he merely said, "We have a task to accomplish, Brother. We'll start tomorrow."

After greeting the little ones and chewing tubers offered by Red Willow Woman, Stone Wolf entered the Arrow Lodge and smoked a pipe. He passed the night alone there, pondering the task ahead.

The making of the Buffalo Shield was a remembered thing. Stone Wolf first selected a strong buffalo hide. Younger Wolf offered an antelope skin, and the brothers brought both to the Arrow Lodge. Next Stone Wolf kindled a fire and invited Younger Wolf and White Horn to smoke. Then the Arrow-keeper instructed White Horn to dig a rounded hole in the earth the depth of his foot and the width of a man's arm.

"Now we make the hide strong," Stone Wolf explained as he heated stones. His companions studied him intently, wondering what purpose such unusual preparation had. But the Wolf kept his own council.

Once the stones were hot, Stone Wolf had them placed in the pit. Then the buffalo hide was pinned over the hole with the thickest, neck section near the center. Water was poured over the stones so that steam rose, thickening the hide. Stone Wolf sat beside the fire, overseeing the actions of his companions and chanting softly entreaties to the spirits. Once the hide was readied, hot water was poured over the hair side, and White Horn scraped it clean.

Time passed, and a considerable crowd gathered to watch the strange actions of the Arrow-keeper. Finally Stone Wolf satisfied himself the hide was properly prepared. He ordered it removed from the fire. While Younger Wolf and White Horn held the hide in the air, Stone Wolf selected the strongest section and pierced it with a small punch. He then used a strip of sinew to measure a circle and cut the hide to its intended size.

"Ayyyy!" Stone Wolf howled. "It's done."

Stone Wolf next spread a buffalo hide on the earth so that the shield hide wouldn't be marred or stained. With a flat stone the Wolf pounded the shield hide again and again, erasing every wrinkle and making it smooth as an iced river. Small holes were burned in the shield, and an armhole of otter skin was laced to the back. Then Stone Wolf motioned for the antelope hide.

"These hides will be joined," he announced. "The power of Bull Buffalo and Uncle Antelope will join their strength and power to protect the People."

Now the shield began to take shape. Other tribes used hide shields to fend off arrows, and as Stone

Wolf stuffed buffalo and horse hair between the skins and sewed them together, he first told of how White Buffalo Cow had given him the vision of this new protective power.

"Now, Brother, bring singers," Stone Wolf urged. "Summon a drum. The important work remains."

It took some time to assemble an appropriate group, for Stone Wolf turned some away. He wanted only brave men with many coups to their credit, and he insisted they paint themselves and dress in their best clothes. Stone Wolf admitted them to the Arrow Lodge, then stepped in himself and pinned the flap shut. He rested the shield on a bed of white sage and lit a small fire.

Stone Wolf next placed four sticks in the ground nearby, representing the cardinal directions. Once the fire had burned some time, the Arrow-keeper placed a solitary coal in the center of the stakes. He sprinkled sweet grass over the coal so that a pleasant white smoke rose skyward. Stone Wolf then let the smoke purify his hands.

"It's well," he pronounced.

Now Stone Wolf performed the pipe ceremony. He offered tobacco to earth, sky, and the cardinal directions, then invited Man Above's guidance in the work at hand. After smoking out the pipe, the Wolf emptied the ashes, refilled the pipe, and set it on the earth between the stakes and the shield.

"Now," Stone Wolf told the drummer, and he began his beat. The singers joined their voices, and the Arrow Lodge filled with brave heart songs.

Stone Wolf readied his paint and began marking the shield. He began with the center, placing the white skull of Bull Buffalo there. He worked carefully, patiently, using the mixture of paint and buffalo hoof glue that would make the image permanent. Each time the singers finished, Stone Wolf set down the brush and smoked. Only when the pipe was finished and refilled did he allow the singers to resume.

It was a long, arduous task, the painting. Stone Wolf worked with inspired precision affixing the image of the buffalo skull and surrounding it with the four sacred Arrows. He added elk teeth and small shells, long symbols of his personal medicine crafted into warrior charms. Later he would add hair from enemy scalps offered by Younger Wolf, but now he contented himself with decorating the shield with buffalo hair.

The singers concluded the song, and he listened to their murmurs of approval. Stone Wolf relit the pipe, though, and smoked again. When he finished, he nodded for the singers to resume. As they took up the ancient chants, Stone Wolf cut the flesh of his arms and allowed blood to touch the shield. In sacrificing his strength, he hoped to give the shield even greater power. Now it was finished, and when the singing was over, Stone Wolf turned the shield toward his brave companions.

"It's done, Brothers," he announced. "Here is the first Buffalo Shield of the People. See how its medicine will turn back the enemy!"

"*Ayyyy!*" the others howled.

The singers then passed into Stone Wolf's hands feathers marking brave heart deeds, and he attached them to the shield. Finally the singers rubbed white clay over their bodies, and over their clothes, bringing them power.

Stone Wolf was satisfied, and he opened the lodge covering. Outside, women had prepared food, for the singing had lasted much of the day. The singers ate inside the Arrow Lodge with Stone Wolf, and afterward they departed in reverent silence. Stone Wolf then placed the shield beside the door, and men, women, and even little children stepped in to gaze at the wondrous thing. Each touched one hand to the powerful shield, invoking its blessing.

Afterward a sweat lodge was erected across from the Arrow Lodge. The shield was placed atop the lodge, and Stone Wolf and the singers entered together, joining their voices in song. Inside they enjoyed the cleansing of the steam and sweated out their troubles. When they emerged, still singing, it marked the true conclusion of the shield ceremony.

"Brother, erect a tripod," Stone Wolf told Younger Wolf. He then explained the shield must rest beside its owner's lodge except when taken down to go to war. "No one may touch the shield without permission, and should it fall, it must be purified, or the medicine will be destroyed."

"It's a fine thing, *Nah nih,*" Younger Wolf observed when the shield was placed on its tripod. "But it's only one shield. Others will surely be needed."

"Yes," Stone Wolf agreed. "But only the bravest men can win a Buffalo Shield. Others may choose to fashion their own shields, and many will hold power. But Man Above sends few visions, and I will make only two shields until he shows me another dream."

"Only two?" Younger Wolf asked.

"Tomorrow I will make another," the Arrow-keeper

explained. "For my brave brother, Younger Wolf, who would lead the young men. He will need its protection, even as I need his strong arm at my side."

So it was that Stone Wolf resumed his labors that next day. Again a medicine shield emerged from the Arrow Lodge. This time the buffalo head was surrounded by prowling wolves, for each shield would borrow from its bearer's personal power. Warriors shouted their approval, and boys gazed in admiration and envy at the second shield.

"I, too, will win a Buffalo Shield," young men boasted.

"First grow hairs to pluck from your chin, *Naha'*," their fathers admonished. "There's time for great deeds later."

As winter gripped the land, the first light snows came. Shell River was lined with a beaded necklace of clear ice. The coughs and shivers of the young and old tormented the camp, and Younger Wolf led the young men out on a hunt.

Stone Wolf found that season of hard face moons the time of new beginnings his heart had ached for. The children were growing tall and strong under Red Willow Woman's wing, and White Horn was both a help and comfort in the Arrow Lodge. There was more need than normal for healing cures, and the boy's eager eyes and soft words brought fresh hope to the sick.

Star Eyes, too, seemed to change. The new prestige Stone Wolf enjoyed after bringing the Buffalo Shield to the People brought his wife envy and attention.

With the traders in their winter lodges on Muddy River, she passed her days beside the cook fire, playing with the children or sewing heavy robes.

"Her tongue is sharp as always," Red Willow Woman grumbled. "But she keeps to her place. Maybe you can win her to your heart yet."

It was in that time of snows and mournful winds that the Pawnees came to Shell River. Their winter camps were south of their old hunting grounds, and they stayed there most times. There was a young war chief among them hungry for revenge against the old enemy, though, and he found thirty men to follow him. They avoided Younger Wolf's hunters and struck the camp unseen. The snows were already deep, and their horses found the going difficult. Nevertheless they killed an old man named Lame Dog and took seven captives—three women and four girls.

The camp was already alive with mourning cries and calls for revenge when Younger Wolf returned.

"Lame Dog was a Fox," Younger Wolf told his brother. "His death must be punished."

"It's more important to regain the captives," Stone Wolf argued.

"We'll do both," Younger Wolf vowed. "It's time the Buffalo Shields went to war. *Nah nih,* join us."

Stone Wolf was reluctant to leave the camp, for many were in need of his healing skills. The People gazed upon the sacred Buffalo Shield, though, with high expectations. Hadn't he asked for the vision so that he might safeguard the People? Surely Man Above expected brave deeds.

The brothers assembled a small party of Foxes. Their intent was to strike rapidly at the fleeing Pawnees. The snows would slow the enemy, and even observing the three days mourning would not allow the Pawnees to flee unscathed. Eight men in all set off the fourth day, and two carried the medicine shields. White Horn's brother Thunder Coat rode at Stone Wolf's side, and the young warrior clearly hoped to win the third shield for himself.

By keeping to Shell River, the Foxes exposed themselves to the eyes of their enemy, but they made rapid time. That first morning they recovered one of the women and the four young ones.

"We walked slow, and they grew impatient," Reed Woman explained. "They left just two boys to watch us, and we sneaked off in the night."

"The others?" Younger Wolf asked.

"Where is my sister?" Red Bird anxiously asked.

"Still captive, but not yet harmed," Reed Woman answered. "They aren't far ahead. You'll catch them this day if you ride hard."

The Foxes did just that. Just before dusk they came upon the Pawnee camp. With wild cries, Younger Wolf and Red Bird led a charge that split the enemy. One band formed a line and turned their bows on the Foxes, but Stone Wolf rode before them, holding his shield to the light. The blinding medicine confused the Pawnees, and their arrows failed to find a mark. Younger Wolf and Red Bird recovered the stolen women and escorted them to safety.

The leader of the Pawnees was a tall man dressed in elk shirt and trousers, with a bright silver medal hanging from a necklace around his neck.

"Raven Eyes, he's called," Thunder Coat said as he joined Stone Wolf. "He's troubled our hunters."

"He's unafraid," Stone Wolf noted. "But he doesn't know our power."

Even so Raven Eyes had twenty men at his side, and only five Foxes remained at Stone Wolf's flanks. The Pawnee chief raised a war whoop and motioned his companions onward. They charged furiously, but again the snow slowed them. Stone Wolf notched an arrow and killed one. The other Foxes followed their Arrow-keeper's example, and three other Pawnees fell. Their companions hesitated, and Stone Wolf charged Raven Eyes. The young chief was surprised at the boldness of the outnumbered enemy and lost heart. Others turned and ran wildly toward Shell River.

One Pawnee stood his ground, though. A scarred warrior of forty summers, he carried a lance. Now he jumped off his horse and staked himself in the snow, crying out a challenge and waving his painted lance.

"He's a brave man," Stone Wolf declared. "Who will answer his taunts?"

"It's for me to do," Thunder Coat said, raising his own lance and starting toward the enemy. The Pawnee planted his lance in the snow, drew out a bow, and killed Thunder Coat's horse. The young Fox jumped clear, gained his feet, and continued on. Now the two faced each other, each holding a lance, and they struggled each in turn to gain an advantage. The Pawnee could not match Thunder Coat's moves, for his right leg remained anchored.

"Kill him!" the Foxes urged, but Thunder Coat darted to one side and instead of piercing the Pawnee's side severed the thong tying him to the earth. Freed, the Pawnee cried angrily and struck Thunder

63

Coat a fierce blow which the young man deflected with his lance. Now the Pawnee's chest was exposed, and Thunder Coat drove the point of his own lance under the ribs and pierced the older man's vitals.

The Pawnee dropped to his knees and chanted his death song as the Foxes raised their lances in tribute. Thunder Coat waited for death to cloud the brave heart's eyes before touching his lance to the corpse and counting coup. He then took the man's scalp but otherwise left his body undisturbed.

"This is a remembered thing!" Younger Wolf announced, and the others howled their agreement.

"Yes," Stone Wolf agreed. "He's won a shield."

Six

When the Foxes returned to the winter camp with the rescued captives, a great cry rose from the People.

"Ayyyy!" the men howled. "Here are the brave hearts who have brought back the stolen ones!"

"Ayyyy!" others added. "Surely the medicine shields are strong. All the young men have come back."

Stone Wolf accepted the praise directed his way, but he was quick to recommend Thunder Coat to the camp.

"He was the one to slay the Pawnee lance bearer. Yes, that was a brave one," Stone Wolf declared. "Thunder Bear holds his scalp. Soon the hair will rest on a Buffalo Shield."

"Yes," the People shouted. "He's earned the honor."

Stone Wolf didn't begin making that third shield right away, though. He knew the power in his own medicine, and he knew the path Younger Wolf rode. This young man, Thunder Coat, was a mystery, though. The Arrow-keeper intended fashioning the shields to augment a warrior's power, and how could that be done without understanding the shield carrier?

So it was Stone Wolf invited Thunder Coat into the Arrow Lodge. The two smoked and talked of many things. Later, they took a sweat. Finally Stone Wolf led the way into the hills, and Thunder Coat kept watch while the Arrow-keeper sought a vision.

The dream came easily, and Stone Wolf saw himself standing on a tall mountain, surrounded by dark clouds. Lightning painted the sky with its golden daggers, and Thunderbird shook the earth. Hawks and eagles screamed overhead. Then Thunderbird flapped its wings furiously, and a solitary rider emerged from the clouds, riding a white horse and calling to the skies for power. Red arrows decorated his bare chest, and his braids held two coup feathers.

"Yes," Thunderbird whispered. "This is my son, Thunder Coat, a brave heart."

When he awoke, Stone Wolf gazed solemnly at his young companion.

"What did you see?" Thunder Coat asked.

"A bare rider on a white horse," Stone Wolf answered. "His chest was painted with red arrows, and . . ."

"I, too, saw the dream," Thunder Coat said solemnly. "Man Above makes my burden a great one."

"It's a hard road a man of the People walks," Stone Wolf agreed. "A shield carrier must be certain he wishes such a life."

"What man ever chooses his way?" Thunder Coat asked. "Man Above directs my feet. Can I be other than myself?"

"No," Stone Wolf confessed. "I will make the shield. It will be a fine thing and bring you power. But to accept it, you must understand it takes its medicine from this vision, from your courage, and will hold it so long as you keep the old ways. Live your life in a sacred manner. Always hold first in your heart the welfare of others. No medicine can protect a man from rash and foolish actions."

"I understand, Uncle," Thunder Coat said, nodding somberly.

And so Stone Wolf repeated the shield-making process. All was as before except the white buffalo skull was surrounded by red arrows and the crooked lance symbol of the lightning bolt. The shield was a thing of awe and beauty, and the other warriors looked upon it with envy.

"*Nah nih,* you stand tall among all the warriors," White Horn told his brother. "Perhaps one day I, too, will win a shield."

"Maybe," Thunder Coat answered. "Your task is to help with the cures, though. This work's important, too."

White Horn grinned at such recognition, but his eyes remained fixed on the wondrous shield.

As winter snows melted, and spring brought new life to the land, others performed brave heart deeds and were given shields. The People grew strong, and their enemies shrank from the medicine of the Buffalo Shields.

"Your vision restored the People's greatness," Younger Wolf told his brother.

Stone Wolf began to believe it himself. Never had the hunting been better, and the Crows rode west to the Big Horn country to escape the fury of their old enemy, the *Tsis tsis tas*.

It was a time of contentment for the Arrow-keeper. Stone Wolf accompanied the young men on hunts and made the healing cures. He delighted in the growing children, and his dreams promised peace and prosperity. As the snows of his twenty-seventh winter melted, and spring smiled on Shell River, the Wolf hoped the good days would continue.

It was while making the New Life Lodge that word came of new traders traveling Shell River.

"These pale ones come with many good presents for the Arrow-keeper," Prancing Elk announced.

"What time is this to come to me with gifts?" Stone Wolf cried angrily. "This is our most sacred season, the time when all the bands gather to renew the earth! Can we never escape the torment of the pale ones?"

"This trader is different," Prancing Elk continued. "He speaks our tongue and understands our ways. He walks in silence, with respect."

"How is this possible?" Younger Wolf asked.

"Your uncle's son is with him," Prancing Elk explained. "This yellow-haired one has wintered with the Oglalas, and now Long Walker, son of Little Sky, brings him to the *Tsis tsis tas.*"

Stone Wolf frowned. He couldn't be bothered at this crucial time. Still, this trader had earned Little Sky's confidence. Why else would a man send his son with a stranger? Long Walker was still a boy of sixteen summers. Maybe Prancing Elk was right. Could this trader be different from the rest?

"Tell my cousin to make camp," Stone Wolf suggested. "We haven't yet remade the earth, and pale people aren't welcome to share this sacred time with us. I will meet later with the trader. Now I have a ceremony to conduct."

Only rarely did the ten bands of the People gather together. It was hard to find adequate game for so many, and so the bands split into smaller camps to hunt and make their way. In midsummer, though, the People gathered to perform either the sacred Arrow renewal or to make the New Life Lodge.

Other tribes knew the New Life Lodge ceremony by other names. The Lakota called it the Sun Dance, although the dancing was but a small part of the ritual. If no harm had come to *Mahuts* and the Arrows didn't require renewal, the medicine chiefs would call for three men to sponsor the New Life Lodge. The ten bands would gather, and the ceremony would begin.

From time to time sickness or peril would afflict the *Tsis tsis tas,* and men would vow to make the New Life Lodge or make a sacrifice to bring a cure. Now men stepped forward to fulfill their vows.

"I'm growing tall," White Horn announced. "It's said you hung by the pole when no older. I, too, will suffer."

"Yes," Stone Wolf admitted, "but there's much pain to endure. There was great need when I hung by the pole, but the People enjoy good times. You should wait for a time when your blood and pain is needed to bring a cure."

"Suffering brings a man power," White Horn argued. "How can I earn a shield and take my place among the warriors if I don't walk man's road?"

69

"He's a boy no longer," Thunder Coat added, gripping his brother's shoulders. "He can bleed to bring the hunt success."

Stone Wolf argued against it, but boys much younger had undergone the ritual suffering, and White Horn would not wait.

Stone Wolf oversaw the arrangements. First the warrior societies gathered on the south side of the camp circle. Two young men were chosen to lead each band. Next came the warriors, followed by their chiefs. Afterward the boys of the camp rode along on horses. It was an inspiring sight, especially when they sang their brave heart songs. They made one turn inside the camp circle and a second outside. Then they entered again, and the group broke up, each man going to his own lodge.

Once the parade was over, the people began packing up the camp. The People broke down their lodges four straight days and moved short distances. It was hard work, but before the People adopted skin lodges, it had been far more difficult. In each new place Stone Wolf prayed and smoked.

The day before the New Life Lodge was erected the Elk warriors rode out and killed a jackrabbit. Strips of rabbit fur were cut and tied to the buffalo robes worn by the lodge-makers.

Next several structures were erected. First came the gathering lodge and the Only Lodge. Then the New Life Lodge itself was raised, as were two coverings for the use of the warrior societies who had charge of the ritual.

Once the ceremonial lodges were built, Stone Wolf called all those who had previously made the New

Life Lodge to the gathering lodge. It was time to plan the ceremony. The three sponsors, who were there to learn the ceremony, kept silent.

On the day before the hanging pole was cut, Stone Wolf again assembled this group. Now they went to the Only Lodge, and each new maker carried a pipe.

The lodge-makers sought out instructors from among those who had previously sponsored the New Life Lodge. Together with these helpers they smoked a short-stemmed pipe in a special ritual. Then the advisors instructed the lodge-makers. An instructor spoke a sentence, and the lodge-maker repeated it. There were prayers and offerings, for all the powers and influences of the world were invoked. Each thing—animals, birds, hills, rivers—were prayed to and given small gifts. The prayers were spoken four times by each advisor, and the lodge-maker repeated them each time.

When these prayers and offerings were over, they smoked again. This time a long-stemmed pipe of black stone was used, and different ritual words were spoken.

The next day was spent in meditation. Few words were spoken, but few were needed. In the solitude of the Only Lodge, the lodge-makers pondered their vows and prepared for the suffering to come. Then, as the sun started its descent into the western hills, the advisors led their three charges outside. They walked eastward, following Stone Wolf and the other medicine chiefs across the plain. When they stopped, the lodge-makers were formed in a row, facing south. Stone Wolf and his companions made a second row, facing north. The advisors took up places behind this second row. Finally, a small fire was kindled at the south end of the line.

Stone Wolf, who was called Earth Maker, drew a small circle in the ground, representing Earth. After Stone Wolf had whittled three pipe sticks, Bold Eagle, the first sponsor, filled a pipe and brought it to Stone Wolf.

Next Dancing Antelope, the second sponsor, brought a coal from the fire and placed it before Stone Wolf, who moved the pipe around the earth circle before lighting it. Then the lodge-makers each took a smoke and passed the pipe along.

After they finished with the pipe, the lodge-makers moved away from the others, toward the southeast. There, sitting on their buffalo robes, they performed a second pipe ritual. When it was finished, they returned to the camp. In their absence, men from the camp had moved the Only Lodge into the center of the camp circle.

The lodge-makers entered the Only Lodge and were presented several sacred bundles to bring to the New Life Lodge. These contained medicine herbs and bone charms passed on by old ones, and their power would enhance the ceremony. Next the lodge-makers were instructed to remove all their clothes except breechclouts. They left the Only Lodge then.

Beaver Skin, the third sponsor, stood beside the New Life Lodge, holding a buffalo bull's skull. After a short ceremony, the head was taken inside the New Life Lodge and placed in the back, facing east. The lodge-makers were then brought in and made to sit on the southeast side. To the west sat Stone Wolf, flanked by the three advisors. Again

Earth Maker made a circle in the ground.

Another pipe was lit, but this time only the sponsors smoked. Then men stepped outside and summoned the warrior societies. Each society promised dancers, and they carried on wildly outside while inside the rituals continued.

Bold Eagle approached the buffalo skull. He knelt beside Red-tailed Hawk, an old man, who took the lodge-maker by the right hand and guided him in, reverently drawing a yellow line from the top of the skull, between the horns, down to the end of the nose. Next the Hawk made ritual motions over arms, leg, and head. Then Stone Wolf lit a pipe and beckoned Bold Eagle come over and smoke.

This time the pipe ceremony was an odd one, with many complicated motions. Stone Wolf also blew smoke over arms, legs, and head, as if to wash away the old with sacred smoke. Finally he emptied the ashes in the heart of the fire and cleaned the pipe. The dancers entered, and Stone Wolf turned to advise them. "You will suffer much," Earth Maker noted, "but from pain we learn respect and patience. These hard times bring power to your dreams and strengthen your heart. It's good you suffer."

Stone Wolf couldn't help studying the serious eyes of the dancers. He nodded gravely at the younger ones. White Horn was there, helped by his brother, Thunder Coat, who busied himself painting White Horn's face and readying him for the dancing. Meanwhile a drum was brought in, and the smoking continued. Long periods of silence often filled the New Life Lodge, during which the men prayed. Four drummers came in and sat beside the drum.

A great amount of drumming and singing followed. Four wolf songs were sung. Then the lodge-makers and the dancers stood and danced, blowing on eagle bone whistles which hung by a cord around their necks. The dance was restrained, with little more than the bending of knees as the bodies moved up and down to the beat of the drum.

The dance concluded, and Bold Eagle took a pipe to the drummers. The music stopped, and the dancers rested. After smoking, the drummers resumed their labors. They sang four songs before the dancers rose. And then the dancing went on until Bold Eagle again took a pipe to the drummers.

Four times the dancing started and stopped in this way. From time to time food was brought in, provided by the lodge-makers for those who had not vowed to undergo a starving. When the fourth pipe was brought back from the drummers, the day's activities were finished. The dancers lay on beds of white sage and rested. Spectators returned to their lodges.

In the final four days of dancing and ritual, the interior of the New Life Lodge was transformed. The tall cottonwood pole which dominated the center of the lodge was joined by others — box elders and chokecherries. Branches formed a small forest. A large buffalo wallow had been ceremoniously cut in the earth. Strips of hide and medicine bundles hung suspended by rawhide strips.

All this time the medicine chiefs had made prayers. The People had sung and danced while warriors performed mock combat. Now came the climax of the ceremony — the torture dance.

The call went out, and dancers stepped forward to

be prepared. First the young men's bodies were painted. Then they lay on their beds of white sage while the skin of their breasts was pinched and pierced with sharp pins. They were then made to stand on white sage while the ropes were attached to the pins.

Members of the family gave presents in honor of the dancers, and cries of encouragement were shouted by advisors and friends. Then the drumming and singing resumed, and the dancers began their suffering.

White Horn danced with great energy, blowing his eagle bone whistle as he strained to free himself from the rawhide strip. The pins stretched, opening tears in his chest, and blood ran down his bare stomach. Pain flooded his face, but he merely blew his whistle and continued.

Man Above, give him strength, Stone Wolf prayed silently.

The suffering had scarcely begun, though. The bravest men flinched as pain tormented their flesh. Eight songs had been sung when the first dancer managed to pull himself free. The dislodged pins dangled from the rawhide, and the People shouted. The dancer stared at the jagged scars left on his chest and steadied himself until his family came to carry him off.

Another dancer freed himself, and several others, exhausted, fainted. Each in turn was cut free by his advisor. White Horn continued, even though his bone whistle lost its energy. He went on straining at his rawhide, and blood painted him with red streaks. Stone Wolf frowned, and Thunder Coat drew out a knife.

"Not yet," Stone Wolf whispered, praying Man Above would lend new strength to this brave heart. No one would find fault if the boy faltered, being young, but to fail when first stepping onto man's road was a hard thing to swallow.

Thunder Coat could stand no more. He held his knife to the strap, but White Horn pulled away. Spitting out his whistle and screaming with fury, the boy flung himself backward, ripping the pins from his flesh.

Younger Wolf and Thunder Coat lifted White Horn from the earth and held him high. Even the old men chiefs howled with approval. Others, too, cheered while Thunder Coat painted the gashes on his brother's chest with healing ointment.

"It's a great thing you've done," Stone Wolf said as he drew the young man against his side. "I could be no prouder of a son."

"Now I can stand tall," the boy whispered. "And you can show me the sacred rituals."

"Yes," Stone Wolf agreed. "*Mahuts* welcomes the brave."

Seven

Stone Wolf did not ignore the presence of the white trader, but he had duties to perform. The summer hunt was led by the Buffalo Arrows, and he was occupied for some time leading the way against the great herds of humped beasts. Only when the bands separated, and the warrior societies took charge of the hunt, did Stone Wolf meet his Oglala cousin, Long Walker, and the white trader, Marcel Freneau.

"My father wintered in the lodge of old Cloud Dancer, the Arrow-keeper," Freneau explained. "I remember his stories of Iron Wolf, your father, and Long Walker's father, Little Sky. He was happy in the camp of the *Tsis tsis tas.*"

"He is the son of Corn Hair," Long Walker explained, nodding toward the amber-haired young trader.

"I know of this white man," Stone Wolf admitted. "He came to the Shell River country before I was born and was taken captive. Ah, he was a strange sight entering our camp!"

"Just a boy," Freneau said, laughing to himself.

"The men who found him stripped his clothes and took his rifle. Papa was never a big man anyway, and he must have seemed like a skinned rabbit to people unaccustomed to white men."

"Grandfather said he was lost when they found him," Stone Wolf said, studying Freneau. "You have a guide. Why do you trouble the People?"

"I didn't come to cause you trouble," Freneau insisted. "I came to trade you good blankets, powder, flints, iron kettles, and good tobacco. Buffalo and elk hides are in demand. You'll find me a fair man to treat with."

"I don't wish to treat with you," Stone Wolf replied. "White men bring bad things to the People! Sickness and death."

"Yes, I've seen such it," Freneau readily agreed. "But I am not sick. I carry no tainted goods. There's no whiskey in my canoe, and I don't steal your women. To be a strong tribe, you need the goods I will provide. Your enemies possess them already, and you can't fight them with flint-tipped arrows and war clubs."

"That's not for you to say, trader," Stone Wolf argued. "You have these things, but your father was killed by white men. His lodge was burned on Muddy River. This is true."

"Yes," Freneau confessed. "Papa was killed because he traded fairly. Others wished to cheat the Lakota and *Tsis tsis tas,* and they killed him. My brothers and I were away. Also our uncles and cousins."

"The bad men who burned Corn Hair's camp were punished by the blue coat soldiers," Long Walker added. "Corn Hair was mourned by my father. When

78

Young Corn Hair came to us, he was welcomed. No sickness tormented our children. He walks a straight road, Cousin, and you can trade with him."

"I know your heart, Long Walker," Stone Wolf said, sighing. "You think to do us good by bringing this man. But your mother is Oglala, and you perhaps don't know of Sweet Medicine's warnings. We avoid the pale people."

"Ah but do you?" Freneau asked. "Other traders travel Shell River. I've seen them camped beside your lodges, barely beyond the circle. These men abuse your friendship, cheat your men, and dishonor your women."

Stone Wolf rose in anger at these words, and Freneau dropped his chin.

"Young Corn Hair meant no insult," Long Walker said, placing his hand on his cousin's arm in a quieting manner.

"He doesn't belong here," Stone Wolf argued. "He speaks our words, but he understands nothing of what we are. His flesh is pale, lacking life. His eyes hold the sky captive, and his hair is yellow like winter grass. Bear and Bull Buffalo seem more brother to the People, and they walk on four legs."

"It's true," Freneau said, shifting his feet and pushing his thick yellow hair back from his forehead. "I come to be among the *Tsis tsis tas,* to listen and to learn."

"You come like a thief to steal what we are," Stone Wolf muttered. "White traders come. It's true. They do as you say, and we are unable to prevent it. Our ways don't permit us to kill without hatred and reason, as white men do. I remember the tales of Corn

79

Hair, and I read in your eyes you intend no harm. The harm will come, though."

"Perhaps," Freneau admitted. "It may come anyway. It's not in my heart to hurt you or your people, though. I barely remember my father. He died when I was small, and I hoped to stay here a time and understand what he found in your grandfather's lodge that brought him peace."

"This has been his wish for many summers," Long Walker added. "He is white outside, but his heart is like mine, and yours, Cousin."

"I'll go," Freneau announced. "I didn't intend harm."

"No, but it would come, as I said," Stone Wolf responded. "We must be what we are, Corn Hair. There is no other person you can be."

Freneau left as promised, but his departure didn't end the white incursion on the plains. Others traveled up Shell River, bringing whiskey and games of chance. Some of these pale traders brought with them Lakota and Pawnee wives. Others invited young women into their camps.

Sweet Grass Woman, a girl of only fourteen summers and the daughter of a Bowstring chief, was stolen by a white trader called Beaumont. His name meant beautiful mountain, or so the white men said, but after Sweet Grass Woman's father found him, there was nothing beautiful about him. His fingers and toes were cut off, and the skin of his forehead flayed most horribly. He was then blinded, stripped, and left to crawl naked across the land. A party of

Oglalas said they discovered him still alive being gnawed by wolves and set upon by birds.

"This we should do to all the whites!" some said.

Stone Wolf argued against punishing the innocent, but he spoke strongly against treating with white traders.

"But we need their good guns," the young men objected.

"They have good, strong blankets to keep us warm against winter's cold," the women said.

"They have no ears for your warnings, *Nah nih*," Younger Wolf observed.

"Is it such a bad thing, accepting these goods?" White Horn asked.

"Sweet Medicine has told us the future," Stone Wolf answered. "Our bones will be scattered by the wind, and no one will remember we walked Shell River. Even the Buffalo Shield won't prevent these things from coming to pass if we ignore the warnings and walk this false road."

Stone Wolf's words carried less and less weight with the young men. The chiefs accepted generous gifts and invited the traders to stay. Warriors staggered along Shell River, their spirits confused by whiskey. Men gambled away their lodge skins and winter robes. Some even sold their daughters to pay debts.

"Listen, brothers!" Stone Wolf called. But their ears turned elsewhere, and the traders stayed.

Of all the traders to walk Shell River, the worst was known as French Pete Dumont.

"True, his father was French," Younger Wolf told Stone Wolf, "but that's all the truth he's spoken. His mother was half Pawnee, and he stands low in the

81

sight of the other whites. He cheats a man when he trades, and he's killed men over silver. His only skill is the making of whiskey. He gives some to the young men and then, when they thirst for more, he trades it for their best possessions. I've seen boys return to camp nearly naked, having given away their shirts and leggings for Dumont's whiskey!"

Stone Wolf found all white men a source of trouble, but Dumont brought forth from him rare anger. It was this man who invited Star Eyes to his lodge, for he spoke only some Crow besides the white man tongues.

"He gives me many nice things," Star Eyes explained, displaying silver jewelry and fine beadwork. "I speak for him to the others."

"This must end," Stone Wolf declared. "Go no more among the whites. My dreams are troubled with visions of sickness. Winter comes soon, and the hard face winds bring trials to even the strongest child. The little ones need no sickness to add to their burdens!"

"They will leave soon, Husband," Star Eyes argued. "I'll stay just a little longer."

"No!" Stone Wolf insisted, and she lowered her eyes in a sign of compliance.

Stone Wolf was glad of it, for soon word spread of a new blister sickness.

"I've heard of this," Red Willow Woman said, her eyes betraying great fear. "Smallpox, the whites call it. It kills everyone. Whole bands of Pawnees have died of it."

"What can be done?" Stone Wolf cried in horror.

"Burn all the sick have touched, and keep away from the dying."

"I must help the sick," he objected.

"You will die," she warned. "Only one who has had the blister sickness is safe. And most who grow sick die."

Red Willow Woman's words held great truth. The blister sickness crept among the lodges of the *Tsis tsis tas* as a prairie fire, taking first the young and the old. Strong men became swollen with the red blisters, grew feverish, and died.

"Dumont brought the sickness to our camp," Younger Wolf declared angrily. "He had a Pawnee girl with him who was sick. He didn't worry, for he suffered with blister sickness as a boy. It won't trouble him now. There's talk of hunting Dumont and bringing him a slow death, even as he has brought the People such a fate."

"No, Red Willow Woman warns of touching Dumont or his Pawnee. We must wait and pray and hope Man Above saves us from our folly."

Of all the trials a man ever had to endure, Stone Wolf judged the blister sickness worst. It swept like a shade through the camp, striking first the small and helpless ones.

"Two Claws played with the Pawnee girl," Dawn Dancer explained when Red Bird's young son boiled over with fever.

"And you?" Stone Wolf cried. "You avoided the trader's camp?"

"As always," the girl said, resting her head against her worried father's side. "I remember the stories of Sweet Medicine and the grandfathers. And I don't like the crazy hairy faces. *Ne' hyo,* they are strange!"

"Yes, they are," Stone Wolf agreed. He almost

managed a grin, but the odor of death lingered nearby, and he could not erase it from his thinking.

The first hard face moon of winter saw thirty die. By the time eight suns had risen and fallen, another fourteen were gone. Those who recovered took charge of the sick, but their knowledge of healing cures was small. They offered warming blankets and cool water to drink, but they held no powers to restore strength or chase away fever and torment.

"I must go to them," Stone Wolf finally declared. "They are my people, and I must help them."

"I, too, will go," White Horn added.

"No, you'll grow sick yourself," Stone Wolf argued.

"As you will," the young man noted. "But afterward, when Man Above restores our strength, we will help many regain their lives."

Stone Wolf looked into the solemn eyes of the young man and wondered if he dared risk such a life. Others among the men spoke against it.

"Who will show us the way when our Arrow-keeper is gone?" they cried. "We will all of us perish!"

Stone Wolf, as always when facing difficult choices, sought a dream. This time he saw nothing, but his heart told him his place was among the sick.

"Someone who understands the ceremonies must remain," Stone Wolf told the others. "Yes, that must be. Younger Wolf will go to the high hills and keep watch over *Mahuts*. If Man Above calls me to walk Hanging Road, my brother will know how to keep the Arrows and renew the earth."

"Yes," the others agreed. "It's good."

Stone Wolf then drew his brother aside.

"Always you've walked at my side when the hard

84

face winds have gnawed at my soul and the hungry times have darkened the world," Stone Wolf recounted. "It's a hard thing I now must ask. Take the little ones away from this camp of death. Look to their needs and those of my wife. If my road takes me away, know I don't worry for my family's welfare."

"You will see many winters, *Nah nih*," Younger Wolf answered. "But I will watch the little ones until you return to us."

Stone Wolf then said his farewells, embraced his children, and walked a bit with Star Eyes. Finally he collected his healing herbs and powders.

"It's time," White Horn said.

"Yes," Stone Wolf agreed, and they walked together to where the sick lay.

Thereafter Stone Wolf danced and sang and fought the blister demons from the souls of the People. He remained fearless even when his own flesh and that of White Horn were afflicted.

"Come, you must rest," White Horn urged as the Arrow-keeper's head dripped with sweat. "Take this cool drink, Uncle."

Finally Stone Wolf's eyes clouded over, and he dropped off into the deep sleep of the near dead.

It's no hard thing, this dying, Stone Wolf decided as his shade drifted between heaven and earth. *I've known little peace among the living. Only silence walks Hanging Road.*

But the sound of a drum and tearful children called him back. He saw feverish faces and shivering shoulders.

"Who are you to walk the smooth road, Arrow-keeper?" White Buffalo Cow asked. "You who were given *Mahuts,* the sacred Arrows. You, Stone Wolf, who I gave the vision of the Buffalo Shield. Have you ever hid from danger, run from the hard fight? No! Turn and save the little ones!"

Stone Wolf awoke days later, his skin still blistered and moist, but his thinking clear once more.

"You've come back to us," White Horn, who had likewise recovered, observed. "It's good. There's great need of your skills."

"As there was before," Stone Wolf answered.

"More so," the young man insisted, stepping aside so that Stone Wolf could view the blistered face of little Dawn Dancer.

"No!" Stone Wolf shouted. "She avoided the sick camp. I sent her high into the hills!"

"The sickness went with her," White Horn explained. "Dawn Dancer avoided the traders, but not so your wife. She, too suffers."

"Star Eyes?" Stone Wolf asked. "And the boys?"

"Well now," White Horn replied. "As is your brother and Red Willow Woman. Star Eyes passed little time with them."

Stone Wolf frowned. *She went to the Frenchman knowing the danger,* he told himself. *She brought this torment to our daughter!* Many things might be forgiven. But this?

Stone Wolf had neither time nor strength to waste with anger. He devoted his energy to making medicine. Those with the greatest fever were laid in the snow, and those strong enough were taken to the sweat lodge. Stone Wolf fought hardest for the life of his daughter.

"Man Above, spare her," he pleaded each dawn as

he made the morning prayers. "She's my heart!"

But Dawn Dancer grew worse. Star Eyes, her flesh scarred by the blisters, also appeared close to death. But her fever broke, and she regained her strength.

"It's a poor bargain," White Horn declared when Star Eyes left her bed. "She brought the sickness to her daughter, but she will retain life. Dawn Dancer, who did no wrong, grows weaker."

When the fevers shook the little girl with all their fury, Stone Wolf took her hand and offered all his strength and power to fend off encroaching death.

"You can't have her!" he shouted. "Little one, brave up. Your father is here beside you."

But the torment continued. All around them children were dying or recovering. Only Dawn Dancer hung between, clasping the final strand of life tenaciously.

"Look at her, Uncle," White Horn finally said. "She has melted away into a shadow of herself, but she fights on. Your words have touched her, and she will not give way."

"Her heart's as strong as Bull Buffalo."

"But see how the blister sickness tortures her. I, who have hung from the pole, never knew such pain. Stone Wolf, you are a father to me, and Dawn Dancer has been my sister. Release her spirit. Give her up to the Great Mystery. She'll know no pain there, and her feet will find the climb up Hanging Road a smooth one after the trouble she's known in life."

"You don't know what you ask?" Stone Wolf cried. "I would cut off my arm before I would lose her!"

"You would hold her here, in this world of suffering?" the Horn asked. "It must not be."

"No, it must not," the Arrow-keeper agreed. He embraced the little figure and released his grip. Howling and tearing open his shirt, he sang the old song.

"Nothing lives long. Only the earth and the mountains!"

Dawn Dancer stirred a moment, and her lips moved. A whisper emerged, a solitary word of farewell. Then her shade passed to the other side, and her father began his mourning cries.

Eight

Cloud Dancer cut his hair and put aside his good clothes. When he made the dawn prayers, he remembered the cheerful face of his daughter and clung to her ghost.

"Let her go," Younger Wolf urged. "Don't hold her here with you."

"You don't know," the Arrow-keeper cried. "You have no daughter!"

"Wasn't the girl my blood, too?" Younger Wolf asked. "Others need your curing touch, *Nah nih!* Go to them. Bring them back to the People."

Indeed, the blister sickness continued to plague the camps of the *Tsis tsis tas*. Even those thought safe grew feverish and broke out in blisters. Arrow Dancer and Crow Boy collapsed. Younger Wolf joined his nephews.

"Man Above, spare these others," Stone Wolf prayed. "I will suffer for them," he vowed, cutting the flesh of his arms and chest. "Here, take my blood and release them."

White Horn, too, prayed.

"Man Above, I hung from the pole," the young man solemnly said. "Give me power to turn the blister sickness from the little ones."

Stone Wolf tended his brother and sons with great devotion, but the bleeding and praying and labor among the other sick brought new fevers to the Arrow-keeper.

"*Heammawihio* calls him," White Horn said as Stone Wolf fell into a deep sleep. Death was near.

Stone Wolf floated between heaven and earth three days. White Buffalo Cow urged him to return to his obligations below, but now he heard Dawn Dancer singing, calling him to accompany her on Hanging Road. The voice was sweet and inviting, and its pull was strong.

"What am I to do?" Stone Wolf screamed through his dream. "Man Above, which path must I put my feet upon?"

A calming wind seemed to stroke his face, and serenity engulfed him in a cloud. When he awoke, he found himself gazing into the knowing eyes of Red Willow Woman.

"There's work for you here," she whispered. "Rest now. Tomorrow you must see your sons."

"The blister sickness?" he cried.

"Has passed," she assured him. "Younger Wolf is well again, and the little ones have cast off their fevers in the sweat lodge."

"Star Eyes?"

"She's always well," the Oglala grumbled. "She who brought these dark times to our lodge! Already she busies herself in the camp of the new trader."

"New trader?" Stone Wolf asked.

"Young Corn Hair," Red Willow Woman explained. "White Horn brought him, hoping he might know a cure for this white man's sickness."

"Did he?"

"No, but he tended the sick as a brother, and he has earned honor here in this camp. I know you fear the whites, Nephew, but this one's heart is good. He'll bring us no harm."

Stone Wolf frowned, but he spoke no more of ordering Freneau from the camp. The young trader did, indeed, tend the sick, and White Horn judged Arrow Dancer and Crow Boy owed their lives to Young Corn Hair's efforts.

"Their fevers had broken already when I arrived," Freneau told Stone Wolf. "I only bathed them in cool spring water and accompanied them to the sweat lodge."

"As an uncle would do," Stone Wolf observed. "It's good you stayed close. You will keep your camp nearby, I think."

"I would winter in your lodge."

"We'll make a place," Stone Wolf said, gripping the young white man's hand. "And we'll speak of my grandfather and your father. Those are good times to remember. Then the People were strong."

"They will be again."

"Will they?" Stone Wolf asked, gazing around him at the scarred, sickly people. How many had died? How many more would walk Hanging Road before spring arrived?

When he regained his feet, Stone Wolf discovered

half the band dead of the blister sickness. Those who survived walked solemnly across snow-covered hills, their mourning clothes and dour faces attesting to the heartache that had come to the People.

"This is what the white men have brought us," Stone Wolf told his wife. But although he spoke to her, his eyes were fixed on the empty space once occupied by their daughter.

"Leave the pain behind you, *Nah nih*," Younger Wolf advised. "Brave up! Difficult days are ahead of us, too."

"Yes," Stone Wolf readily agreed. But although he knew it was a bad thing for an Arrow-keeper to lose himself in sorrow, he was unable to cast his daughter's face from his thoughts.

Stone Wolf, as always when soured by despair, turned to *Mahuts*. He made the pipe ceremony and begged for the Arrows' council. Upon opening the sacred bundle, though, he discovered the stone points speckled with blood.

"What does it mean?" White Horn asked.

"The power of *Mahuts* is broken," Stone Wolf explained. "The People are in great peril. Defenseless against our enemies. *Ayyyy!* We must renew the Arrows."

"Nothing more?" the young man asked. "What of the stained points?"

"They must be purified," Stone Wolf explained. "When the snows melt, and the horses fatten themselves once again, we'll prepare new fletchings and points. I'll show you how so that you may know the old way it must be done. It will be a hard spring, for our enemies will find us, and our young men will be blind to their arrows. Game will elude our hunters."

"The Buffalo Shields will save us."

"Not even their power will overcome this disaster," Stone Wolf insisted. "Go to your brother, Thunder Coat, and warn him to keep guards among the ponies. Watch the little ones. Peril is at hand!"

Stone Wolf was right to voice concern. Even as the snow began to melt, and the ice on the streams broke apart and freed the waters, bands of Pawnees raided the horse herds. Men who rode off to hunt fresh meat didn't return.

"My husband is dead!" Blackbird lamented after her brother, Red Bird, returned with the grim news that Stands on the Mountain's mutilated corpse had been discovered on the bluff overlooking Shell River. Many Pawnee pony tracks were spotted nearby.

"Where is our protection?" other women cried. "Are our men all dead? Must we send boys out to bring in meat and chase the enemy?"

A council was called, and the men gathered to smoke and discuss the future.

"Maybe we should leave Shell River," Red Bird suggested. "Our brothers, the Oglala Lakotas, would welcome us."

"Yes," others agreed. "They have brave men. We should join them."

"Are we children to seek the protection of others?" Younger Wolf asked. "Hard times have come to us. That's true. But we're not naked or starving! We have our bows and our honor."

"You buried no sons under the hard face moons of winter," Red Bird objected. "You didn't see your sister's husband cut into pieces!"

"My brother's daughter died," Younger Wolf countered. "Wasn't she my blood? Who among you has led the fight as often as I have? Count the scars on my chest!" he shouted, tearing open his shirt. "Do you doubt my devotion to the People?"

"This isn't a time for quarrels," Stone Wolf said, rising slowly. "Disharmony only makes us weaker. Soon it will be summer, and we will renew *Mahuts*. Once the Arrows are restored to us, we will find our path straight and true again."

"It's a long time before we gather the ten bands," Red Bird said, swallowing hard. "Will any of us be alive to see that time, Stone Wolf? We respect your words and are thankful for your devotion to our welfare. Still, we're fearful of our enemies."

"There's reason," the Arrow-keeper admitted. "But to abandon our freedom and go to the Lakotas is to erase the *Tsis tsis tas* from the earth. We would no longer be ourselves!"

"Then what can we do?" Red Bird demanded.

"Seek the high places," Stone Wolf advised. "My dreams see me in the pines near *Noahvose,* the sacred center of our world. There the Crows and Pawnees can't find us. We can pick nuts and berries there, and small game is plentiful. As the other bands arrive, we will be stronger and stronger. Once we renew *Mahuts,* we will again stand tall."

"You're certain?" Thunder Coat asked.

"When hasn't he been?" White Horn cried. "It's not Stone Wolf's fault the blister sickness struck us down. He warned us of the danger the traders brought."

"He has a white man in his lodge," young Swallowtail pointed out."

94

"Corn Hair helped my sons," Stone Wolf explained. "And others beside."

"He brings us things we need," Younger Wolf added. "He walks the sacred road, too."

"Enough," Stone Wolf declared. "I go to the high country tomorrow? Who else?"

As murmurs of agreement spread among the men, most merged their voices with that of the Arrowkeeper. Finally it was decided, and preparations for the move were made.

"You must leave us for a time, Corn Hair," Stone Wolf told Freneau. "You have listened and walked quietly in my lodge, but we soon go to a place where only the People are welcome."

"It's time I returned to my work," Freneau said, clasping his host's hands. "I learned much from you, Stone Wolf. Maybe one day we will be brothers."

"We're different," Stone Wolf argued.

"In some ways, yes," Freneau agreed. "But not where it's important."

The young trader departed three days hence, and Stone Wolf directed his companions northward, toward the wooded hills where Sweet Medicine first brought *Mahuts* to the People.

By midsummer, *Noahvose* saw the ten bands gathered to its slopes.

"Here we are, in this sacred place where the People are taught," Stone Wolf told the others. "Always we come here when our trouble is great, for Man Above is close to this high place, and he hears our pleas."

"*Ayyyy!*" the men howled.

"Now we will renew the power of *Mahuts* and return the People to the straight path. First I admonish you all to heed the old prophecies. Beware of pale people. It was the hairy faces who brought sickness to us. Keep harmony in your lodges. See to the welfare of the defenseless ones, and make yourself strong and fearless when facing the enemy."

"*Ayyyy!*" the men shouted again.

In many ways the Arrow renewal resembled the New Life Lodge ceremony. It was performed periodically, as determined by the Arrow-keeper. Rarely, however, did the medicine Arrows require purification. It was that task which Stone Wolf concentrated his efforts upon.

No one knew the age of the arrow shafts, but they were weathered and hard. The fletchings had been changed before, but great care had been taken to twist the feather strips along the back of the shaft in the ancient manner rather than apply them to opposite sides of the shaft as was the current fashion.

New tips were made of stone from the summit of the butte. White Horn flaked them carefully until the new heads resembled the now tainted ones.

"They will do," Stone Wolf announced after turning the points over in his fingers.

After removing the old tips from each of the sacred Arrows, Stone Wolf attached the new points with deer sinew and performed the required prayers.

Each time the Arrow renewal was performed, the Arrows were exposed to the light, and the men filed by to gaze upon the wondrous Arrows and invite their blessings. Stone Wolf looked at the long line of men and boys, but he found little satisfaction on the faces. Too many had died. Even the youngsters appeared tired, tormented, haunted by the dead.

"They only remember the recent hardships," Younger Wolf said as he, Stone Wolf, and White Horn stood on the mountain with Arrow Dancer and Crow Boy after the renewal had been completed.

"They and the other young ones," Stone Wolf agreed. "There are other things they should know."

"We'll teach them, *Nah nih*," Younger Wolf vowed.

"Yes, and we'll return the People to the sacred path. Soon it will be too late, and all we know will be buffalo dust. We must begin soon."

Thereafter Stone Wolf summoned the young ones to the Arrow lodge and told them many stories. He spoke of the ancient ones, narrated the story of how man first came to the earth. He introduced the boys to Bull Buffalo and Red-tailed Hawk, taught them medicine cures and morning prayers.

"Uncle, my mother went to *Se yan'*," a boy called Gopher Foot, whispered. "Still, I hear her shade call to me."

"Those are only memories, little one," Stone Wolf insisted. "I heard my daughter's voice after she climbed Hanging Road, too, but such things aren't possible. Your ears hear things, and you listen, hoping to again feel the softness and know the comfort."

"Avoid shades," White Horn urged. "They draw you to them."

"Sometimes they foretell of a man's death," Stone Wolf explained. "But don't confuse shades with dreams."

"You hear voices in your dreams," Gopher Foot said, nodding. "My father told me how you learned to make Buffalo Shield. Will you show us how to invite a dream?"

"That," Stone Wolf agreed, "and more besides."

"*Ayyyy!*" the boys shouted as they crowded around.

Stone Wolf drew his own little ones to his side and warmed at their touch.

"Once, in the time before Horse came to the People," he began.

Nine

The pain of Dawn Dancer's passing never entirely left Stone Wolf's heart, but he had sons to raise and the obligations of an Arrow-keeper to fulfill. As seasons passed, and children grew fast as river reeds, the Wolf gave up his daughter's ghost and looked up toward the path his People would walk in the future.

Other men might have begun their twenty-eighth summer with a young man's step, drinking in the sweet scent of buffalo grass after a sudden rain. Stone Wolf walked cautiously, ever alert to peril and hardship.

Arrow Dancer, who at five could now ride at his father's side when the band moved its camp in pursuit of Bull Buffalo, observed his father had Raven's eyes.

"Raven studies the world before acting," the boy explained.

"Yes," Stone Wolf agreed. "He does nothing in haste, but always ponders the consequences. An Arrow-keeper, too, must consider his every action with great care. He holds in his hands the welfare of *Maahuts,* and must keep the People safe!"

Crow Boy, who was only three and had to bounce along in a travois or walk with Red Willow Woman, deemed his father slower than Box Turtle.

"Younger Wolf rides swiftly," the boy noted.

"Our uncle chases the wind," Arrow Dancer agreed. "He leads the young men."

The boys often dogged their uncle's heels or else attached themselves to White Horn. Both men tolerated, even welcomed the children. Only when Younger Wolf and White Horn took to the river walk, where maidens waited, did Stone Wolf hold his sons back.

"If you are ever to have cousins, leave your uncle time to himself," the Arrow-keeper demanded.

The boys would sit together by the cook fire for a time. Later, though, they would escape their father and stalk Younger Wolf.

"He shared a robe with Striped Basket," Arrow Dancer would whisper later. "It's strange! What use does a man have for a blanket in such heat!"

If their mother had spared time for them, Arrow Dancer and Crow Boy would likely have kept to the camp as other little ones. But French Pete Dumont had returned, and Star Eyes was often at the trader's camp.

"Isn't it enough she's brought death to your lodge, *Nah nih,*" Younger Wolf complained. "Set her belongings outside your lodge! Let her find a home with the traders."

"They wouldn't have her!" Red Willow Woman argued. "Each has two Pawnee women already. They have troubles enough!"

"You should send all the white traders away,"

Younger Wolf advised. "As before. The others would agree. They remember the blister sickness and the ones who brought it."

"Yes, they dislike Dumont," White Horn agreed. "But they enjoy his whiskey. Thunder Coat says some men trade the meat from their kills for this fire tongue. Their children cry with hunger, but no one hears."

"Some hear," Younger Wolf argued.

"I'll see the little ones are fed," Stone Wolf vowed.

"How?" Younger Wolf asked. "The scouts ride far, but they've found no buffalo sign."

"I will ask *Mahuts*," Stone Wolf explained. "And seek a dream."

"And the traders?" White Horn asked.

"We'll move camp soon," Stone Wolf said. "I'll speak to the chiefs and urge them to send these whites away. It's for them to do."

"Too many of the chiefs neglect their obligations," White Horn argued. "The Frenchman gives them whiskey to keep them happy. Even *Mahuts* could not convince these old whiskey men to send the traders away."

"Can we have turned so far from the sacred path?" Stone Wolf cried. "Why have I been so blind to these troubles?"

"Your heart is good, Uncle," White Horn observed, "and so you don't read the dark hearts of others."

No longer, Stone Wolf promised himself.

That very evening he set off into the hills with White Horn to seek a vision. Not since making the Buffalo Shields had he felt such a need among the People.

101

"They hunger for hope," White Horn had observed when he readied the horses.

"Then we must find some," Stone Wolf answered. "A man needs hope to feed his spirit as much as he needs turnips or buffalo meat to fill his belly."

Standing on the high bluffs above Shell River, Stone Wolf chanted and cut his flesh, inducing a fever. All the while White Horn stood alongside, keeping a fire burning and guarding the Arrow-keeper from prowling animals or curious enemies. As so many times before, Stone Wolf collapsed beside the fire and saw White Buffalo Cow emerge from the clouds. He saw a world swept clear of Bull Buffalo, covered by hungry white men.

"My children are dead," White Buffalo Cow lamented. "Soon you, too, will be gone, my brothers. Why couldn't you heed Sweet Medicine? Why did you accept these strange ones?"

Stone Wolf felt his heart ache, and he thrashed wildly in his sleep. White Buffalo Cow's voice grew softer, and she sadly led the way past familiar hills and streams to a great buffalo wallow three days to the west. There a great herd spread out on both banks of the river. Beyond, antelope bounded across the plain.

"Man Above sent you a vision," White Horn declared when Stone Wolf awoke the following morning.

"Yes," Stone Wolf replied. "We must make the morning prayers and return to the People. Soon we'll have game to hunt."

Even as Stone Wolf shared his dream with the council, he again voiced Sweet Medicine's warning.

102

"Leave these whites behind us," the Arrow-keeper urged.

"It's my task to keep order in the camp," Bear Claw, chief of the Bowstrings, pointed out. "The man Dumont does no harm. He brings me bullets for my gun and beads for my wife and three daughters."

"He buys your blindness," White Horn argued.

"I'm not the one here who is blind," Bear Claw answered angrily. "My wife keeps to my cook fire. Who are you, a boy who has yet to face the enemy, to speak hard words to me, a man who has counted seven coups?"

"Truth is truth," Thunder Coat insisted, rising to defend his brother. "Have you all forgotten the emptiness in our camp caused by the blister sickness? Who brought that among us? Dumont! We should look upon him as a blood enemy. He merits the slow death given the many children of our camp!"

There was a stir of support for the notion, but the chiefs quickly silenced it.

"We hunt Bull Buffalo on Shell River," Bear Claw said. "Stone Wolf says we will find game there. That is a land hunted by Crows and Snakes. Pawnees even ride there. To kill meat for our families and to fight our enemies, we need powder and lead for our guns. We dare not send the traders away."

"There's danger if they stay," Stone Wolf argued.

"For us?" Bear Claw asked. "Or for your wife?"

The Bowstrings laughed, and many urged Stone Wolf hunt Star Eyes and leave the buffalo to the young men.

"Tie her to a travois," Red Bird suggested. "Hamstring her so you can catch her."

Stone Wolf stared furiously at them and stalked off.

"Nah nih, they mean no insult," Younger Wolf called. "Return. There are prayers to make, and the pipe should be smoked."

"Leave the Bowstrings to do it," Stone Wolf suggested. "If they boast of such greatness, leave them to conduct the hunt."

"Uncle, please," White Horn pleaded.

"I go to my lodge," Stone Wolf told them. "Do as you will. I keep my own council hereafter."

"You are a man of the People," White Horn pointed out. "What of the children? The chiefs won't feed them. Nor the Bowstrings!"

"Bring back meat enough for them," Stone Wolf said, gazing intently into his brother's eyes. "Such an act of generosity may lesson Man Above's anger. Still, we must act to drive off the traders."

"How?" Younger Wolf asked.

Stone Wolf frowned. He had no notion.

As summer nights shortened, and the blazing sun relented, the People continued to search for game. The buffalo on Shell River filled bellies for a time, but a great storm swept the animals off in a tempest of dust and hail, leaving the People to wander north and east.

"Something must be done!" the young men demanded.

"Stone Wolf can seek a vision!" Bear Claw urged.

"Arrow-keeper, bring out the Buffalo Arrows," the chiefs pleaded.

"Their medicine would not swallow the anger Man Above feels for the People," Stone Wolf replied. "Again and again I have spoken the warning, but nothing is done. The white traders remain, and our medicine grows weaker. You say we need powder and lead! Before, when the grandfathers' grandfathers were small, the *Tsis tsis tas* killed with lance and arrow. We can do so again. Our power is in our hearts, brothers, and in the Buffalo Shield. You sell your souls for shiny beads and fire tongue!"

"Bring us to Bull Buffalo," the others demanded.

"Am I a small child to be told what to do?" Stone Wolf asked. "A camp dog to be whipped across the plain? Take care you don't turn my power against you."

The warning stunned even Stone Wolf, who regretted the words the instant they were spoken. Another time he would have swallowed them and done as they asked. But he was angry, and instead he turned and walked far from the camp circle. He remained there until dusk, when White Horn summoned him to the Arrow Lodge.

"Your sons miss their father," the young man explained.

"Then I must return," Stone Wolf said, sighing. "Once a man who spoke ill of an Arrow-keeper would have been whipped to his horse and sent from camp. Now chiefs speak such words!"

"Bear Claw fears the whole camp will starve," White Horn explained. "The Bowstrings are restless, and their anger is turning toward the traders. Uncle, once you told me that a man of the People must also hold their interests above his own. Can't you forget

105

the insult and lead us to meat? Just tell Younger Wolf, and we Foxes will hunt alone."

"A man's heart must be free of concern when he speaks to Man Above," Stone Wolf explained. "Mine is troubled. I have lost the far-seeing eye and must search inside myself to recover it."

As he had after Dawn Dancer's death, Stone Wolf kept to the camp. He invited the boys to come and listen to his stories, and he crafted bows for those without uncles or grandfathers to do it.

"Tell us again of how Cloud Dancer brought Horse to the People," some urged.

"Tell us of Sweet Medicine's dreams," others cried.

"No," another argued. "The Medicine Wheel."

Stone Wolf merely smiled and motioned them close. If there was time he would go from one story to another.

"Tie another on to that, *Ne' hyo,*" Arrow Dancer would say, and Stone Wolf did so.

While Stone Wolf remained in camp, Younger Wolf led the Foxes out in search of game. Sometimes they brought in a dove or a crow. Occasionally their ponies kept up with the fleet antelope, and a buck would fall prey to an arrow or rifle ball. Usually boys could catch fish in Shell River, and their mothers dug onions and turnips on nearby hillsides.

The children eased Stone Wolf's anger, but so long as the chiefs allowed the traders to remain, and the young men smelled of whiskey, Stone Wolf's heart was sour. A great bitterness toward Star Eyes threatened to explode into violence, and he carved bows or fashioned arrows in order to divert his feelings. Sometimes, though, when Star Eyes appeared at the lodge with a new cloth dress or silver bracelet, Stone Wolf angrily erupted.

"Woman, you neglect your children!" he shouted. "You bring shame onto our lodge. You don't cook or clean!"

"Why should I?" Star Eyes answered. "You don't bring in meat! I thought I wed a warrior, a great man, but you are lost to dreams!"

"And where is it you lose yourself?" Stone Wolf asked, wincing at the sting of her words. "Don't you see it's these traders who spoil the land, destroy our medicine, bring sickness and death?"

"So the dog people die. I laugh at the thought. Who killed my father and brothers? Why would I cry to see you all boil over in fever and perish?"

"Can you hate us so much?" Stone Wolf asked. "Your daughter? Your sons?"

"They were never mine," she growled. "Not from the time you first took them in your arms. They're Cheyenne. I have no more use for them than I would for the offspring of a wolf!"

"Leave my lodge," Stone Wolf said, glaring at her.

"And what will you do if I chose not to?" she asked. "Nothing. You call yourself a man, but you're weak. No Crow would give up a wife to strangers."

"And no woman of the *Tsis tsis tas* would weave such disharmony into her life. Man Above will punish you, Star Eyes, not for disdaining your husband but for ignoring your duties. And what will the traders bring you? Wealth? Love? Only shame in the end."

"The shame's yours, Stone Wolf. Mine was surviving my family.

"You might have found a new beginning," he told

her. "Love and happiness. But now I see you for what you are, the bitter fruit of a dying tree. It's good you've been no mother to my sons, for their hearts are free of your blight. Your behavior has turned me from my obligations and brought hunger to our people. No more. I will climb the hills and seek a dream. Man Above will tell me what must be done. I already know this much. You will no longer sleep at my side, and my sons are yours no longer. I am an Arrow-keeper and must not strike out in anger, so I won't cut your nose as is the custom when a woman behaves in such an outrageous manner."

For the first time her anger faded. Fear took its place.

"Obey my brother in my absence," Stone Wolf concluded. "And don't go to the trader camp. If you do, don't return."

"Am I free of you then?"

"As you've been since you came to live in my lodge. You once came willingly. Now go if that's your choice."

Stone Wolf turned and left her those words to consider. He half hoped she would leave. It was the only way he would be free of his obligation to her. Even a woman of low character could expect charity from an Arrow-keeper. And there were the boys to consider.

Stone Wolf summoned the chiefs to a council. There he again spoke against the traders and reminded them of Sweet Medicine's prophecies.

"We've heard these words before," Bear Claw replied. "We've told you what will be."

"Then I cry for the children who will hunger this winter," Stone Wolf said, scowling. "I will ask *Mahuts* to lead me to game, and we will provide for the defenseless ones. But so long as the whites remain, I fear we'll enjoy no prosperity."

Even though he built tall fires and slashed his arms and chest so that blood flowed freely, Stone Wolf received no dream. The buffalo hunt continued to fail, and the People grew thin and quarrelsome.

"It's my selfishness that's led us to this," Stone Wolf told White Horn. "I try to cast the anger from my heart, but it remains. I must empty myself."

"How?"

"Undergo a starving," Stone Wolf explained. "Speak the ancient prayers and hope Man Above can ignore our many wrongs. The children cry with hunger, and their voices will invite a dream too."

When Stone Wolf prepared to set out for the hills again, the boys of the camp gathered and made a blood sacrifice to aid him in his quest. Arrow Dancer and Crow Boy came along, for they worried their father needed their attentions in those difficult times.

"They fear you'll starve yourself to death," White Horn explained. "I share their concern."

"We'll find game," Stone Wolf insisted. "The berries are fat and the grass is thick. If not buffalo, then antelope and elk. If not deer, then rabbit. We'll fill bellies soon."

Stone Wolf dreamed of plentiful game, of wonderful cool springs and rich meadows. Later he led the people there, and for a time there was food enough for everyone.

"You've regained your medicine," Younger Wolf observed. "Now the chiefs will listen."

"Oh, the deer come here each year," Bear Claw argued when the council gathered to celebrate the successful hunt.

"It was nothing but memory brought us here," Red Bird added. "We killed these animals ourselves. You didn't slay them with your medicine, Stone Wolf!"

The Arrow-keeper didn't respond. There was no need. He simply turned from the council, and the game vanished once more. Hardship and sickness tormented young and old, and the first to die were set upon their scaffolds under the cherry ripening moon of late summer.

"Our need is great once more," White Horn observed. "What will you do, Uncle?"

"Swallow my anger, as I must," Stone Wolf answered. "Seek a vision. Pray Man Above hasn't hardened his heart to us."

Ten

Stone Wolf felt as if a storm were gathering around him. As he studied the discouraged faces of the men, the worried eyes of the women, and the thinning flesh of the children, he collected his medicine charms and powders in a carrying bag and prepared for a journey.

"You can't go away," Arrow Dancer protested. *"Ne' hyo,* many are sick here and need your cures."

"I know," Stone Wolf replied, motioning the boy closer. *"Naha',* sometimes a medicine man must heal all the People. The sickness that's come to us eats our hearts. I must go and find a path for us to walk."

"A path?" the boy asked with wide eyes. "What path?"

"One that brings us buffalo meat to cast the emptiness from our bellies. One that quiets the anger and restores laughter to the lodges."

"Can my brother and I come with you?"

"Another time," Stone Wolf said, touching Arrow Dancer's face . "I must go alone this time, with only White Horn to keep watch."

"I'll keep our lodge in order then," Arrow Dancer pledged. "You won't be gone long?"

"I hope not, *Naha'*, but only Man Above knows for certain. I must find the path."

The boy nodded, and Stone Wolf led him along a way, talking of other, better days. Then White Horn appeared with the horses, and Stone Wolf said his farewells. Little Crow Boy arrived to climb into his father's arms, and Red Willow Woman offered food for the journey.

"Star Eyes didn't come?" Stone Wolf asked, glancing around.

"Our mother is with the traders," Arrow Dancer grumbled. "She thinks her place is with strangers."

"It's a hard road we walk," Stone Wolf said, drawing the boys close. "I'll miss you."

"We, too," Arrow Dancer replied. "We'll go with Younger Wolf to make the morning prayers. Perhaps we'll kill a rabbit or shoot a bird."

"It would be a good idea," Stone Wolf whispered. "You're both too thin."

"You, too," Arrow Dancer pointed out. "Be careful, *Ne' hyo*. It's said there are Crows nearby."

"Ah, but I will be invisible to them," Stone Wolf boasted.

He held them to his side once more. Then he broke away, mounted the buckskin pony White Horn had readied for him, and departed the camp.

As Stone Wolf rode out onto the plain, he tried to clear his head of all the bitterness he'd felt in the camp. The fate of the People rested on his shoulders, and he would suffer anything, undergo whatever hardships were necessary, to bring harmony back to the *Tsis tsis tas*.

"Where do we ride, Uncle?" White Horn asked when they turned away from Shell River.

"Where Man Above waits to speak to me," Stone Wolf answered. "A high place maybe."

"Don't you know?"

"My heart will know," the Arrow-keeper declared. "When I see it."

The sun fell and rose again three times before Stone Wolf spoke again. White Horn asked their destination periodically, but Stone Wolf merely pointed toward the distant horizon.

"How can we find what we don't seek?" the young man muttered when the last of the food was gone. "We'll starve out here. Or be killed by Crows!"

Stone Wolf gazed at his companion with stern, scolding eyes. And the quest continued.

That fourth day Stone Wolf halted his horse and gazed across the sun-bleached grasses southward.

"There," he announced, pointing to the faint outline of a range of mountains. "Man Above will speak to me there."

"So far?" White Horn asked. "Will we find game first?"

"You may eat," Stone Wolf answered. "There are fish in Shell River. I will take nothing. The starving will hasten the vision."

"It's been a long time already, Uncle."

"It will be longer still," Stone Wolf explained. "You're no longer a boy eager to learn the healing cures, White Horn. You walk man's road, and you must soon choose to stay or go. If your heart's not with me, I must go on alone. You should return to the People."

"I'm hungry, Uncle, and tired, but I won't leave you to make this ride alone. It's only my weakness speaking. My heart is still strong."

Stone Wolf nodded. He understood. His own hunger was great, and he'd known difficult times before.

They were two days returning to Shell River, and another snaking their way into the hills beyond. White Horn had only two small rabbits and some fish to eat, and Stone Wolf accepted nothing. Weak with hunger and faint from exertion, Stone Wolf halted his horse beside a bubbling spring and rolled off his buckskin.

"Here we'll rest," Stone Wolf declared, dropping to his knees. He managed to remain there until White Horn had kindled a fire and made a bed of pine needles covered by a buffalo hide.

"We will smoke," Stone Wolf announced, and White Horn took out a pipe. Stone Wolf performed the pipe ceremony, then said a single prayer.

"Man Above, we are yours," the Arrow-keeper chanted. "All we know you have made. Only earth and mountain live long, and if our time has come to climb Hanging Road, we go willingly. If we are to stay, give me a dream. Show me the path we must walk."

He cried out and sang an ancient chant whose long-forgotten words White Horn could not comprehend. Stone Wolf next bared himself and cut strips of his flesh, wincing as the pain tormented his being. Finally the Arrow-keeper collapsed. White Horn affectionately rested the buffalo hide over Stone Wolf's emaciated frame and stoked the fire.

"Give him the dream," the young man pleaded, staring skyward. "Bring his suffering to an end."

Stone Wolf knew only the comfort of sleep for a long time. Peace seemed to wrap him in a soft cloud, and his troubles flowed from his heart.

"Sleep well, *Naha'*," the voice of White Buffalo Cow urged.

"You seek a path," Wolf told him. "It's been before you all this time. Set aside your anger and foreswear the new ways. You carry the Buffalo Shield to confuse your enemies. Wipe the mist from your eyes so that you can see your friends."

A dream came next. Stone Wolf sat alone beside the fire, smoking and praying, when a small boy appeared.

"I come to join you, Uncle," the young one said. "I carry only this shattered bow as a weapon and am thus harmless."

"No arrows?" Stone Wolf asked.

"They're useless without the bow," the boy explained.

"Why bring the bow then?"

"Because it was here Man Above brought it to me. I was small then, pitifully naked and helpless among all the creatures of the mountains. Man Above saw my need and gave me this bow."

"Ah," Stone Wolf said, recalling the ancient story. "It's the Medicine Bow."

"Yes," the young visitor sadly confessed. "With it I rose above all the four-legged creatures. My people clothed our bare flesh with the hides of Elk and Buffalo. Our bellies filled with good meat, and we sewed skins to make lodges. Arrows from this bow never failed to find their target."

"So long as the prayers were made and the heart of the hunter remained pure," Stone Wolf added.

"You know these things?" the boy asked. "Then you must also know my brother thought to take the bow and make himself a great man. But he didn't know the prayers and so shot an arrow whose flight was disturbed. It turned from its path and slew instead he who had thought to kill. It was then the bow cracked, and so its medicine is broken even now."

"What will you do?" Stone Wolf asked.

"Bury it in the earth. One day, perhaps, Man Above will send it back to us mended. When the need is great. And our hearts are free of greed and anger."

"Can such a time come?"

"All things are possible, it's said, Stone Wolf," the boy told him. "Yes, I know you. We've walked the high places together before. I've watched from the mountains as you rode with the young men, striking Bull Buffalo to feed the hungry. I saw the hard fights against the Crows, and I suffered with you when Dawn Dancer, your daughter, climbed Hanging Road."

"Who are you then?" Stone Wolf asked.

"Everyone," the boy answered. His face became old friends long dead. For a time he appeared as Cloud Dancer, Stone Wolf's grandfather. Later he was Stone Wolf himself.

"I came to seek a way back to the center of the sacred hoop," Stone Wolf explained. "The People have lost their way."

"They've forgotten the old power," the boy said, stretching himself tall. "Long before the pale people came to Shell River, the *Tsis tsis tas* had *Mahuts* to guide their hunters. Arrows brought down many buffalo, and there was food enough for the winter camps. Now rifles make the young men lazy. They don't silently stalk the prey, killing reluctantly and out of need. No, they strike with anger, inflicting suffering. They've lost the old kinship with the trees and rocks, with all creatures as I knew when I first lifted Medicine Bow in my hands."

"What can I do?" Stone Wolf cried.

"Much, if you can forget personal insult and pain. A man of the People must consider others first."

"As I have sought to do."

"Then take comfort, Stone Wolf, my brother. Man Above will visit your dreams and show you the way. Now I must bury the bow and return to my kin."

The boy melted into the blackness, and Stone Wolf slept once more.

He awoke to discover White Horn cooking a rabbit on the fire.

"Are you hungry, Uncle?" the young man asked. "Did the dream come."

"A dream came," Stone Wolf answered. "But I don't think it was the one which I seek."

"We'll return then."

"No, Man Above has yet to show me the way, White Horn."

"Will we ride on?"

"No, this is a sacred place, and the vision will be

117

given to me here. That is what the first dream told me."

"I don't understand."

"Yes, I know," Stone Wolf said, accepting food. "But you remember the old stories. These are the Medicine Bow Mountains. Here Man Above gave the gift of the bow to man, setting him above all the creatures. But man was foolish and broke the power of the bow."

"Yes, I know that story," White Horn said, grinning. "You share it with the camp boys, reminding them to keep the old ways and perform the necessary prayers."

"It's a good lesson for these times, don't you think? We have strayed from the sacred path, taking in all these new weapons and odd ways. Our arrows can't find Bull Buffalo, for we don't ask him to give up his children to feed our bellies. Too many hunt hides to trade with the whites."

"You've told the council they should send Dumont away," White Horn reminded the Arrow-keeper. "They won't agree. If this is the dream you carry back, our journey is wasted."

"No, this first dream only showed us the road we must seek," Stone Wolf argued. "Another dream will follow, showing me the way to bring the People back to the straight road."

"But you eat?" White Horn asked.

"Yes, but tomorrow I will suffer again. I must be strong enough to carry the dream home."

"It must give you great comfort, knowing what will come to be. I have dreams myself, but I'm never certain of their meaning. How does

118

a man know if he walks the true path?"

"His heart tells him," Stone Wolf said, forcing a smile to his face. "All a man must do is give himself up to be guided by the spirits. Accept what comes and brave up when difficult things await him."

"I try, Uncle."

"It's all anyone can do."

Stone Wolf resumed his fast next morning, and he again cut his flesh and invited a fever. He sang and danced and prayed for the vision. Soon he fell into a deep sleep once again, and he followed White Buffalo Cow onto a prairie split by a great swollen river.

The waters roared like thunder, and they reached like claws to tear at the bank. On one side stood the warriors and their women, gazing helplessly at the far bank where the children waited, pleading for help.

"Who can cross such a river?" a chief with many feathers tied in his hair asked.

Two men started across, but they were swept away in the violent torrent, each in turn. A small band of Elk Warriors next tried, but they were turned back by the raging stream.

"Man Above, save the little ones!" the People cried.

Overhead an eagle turned slow circles, and the People grew hopeful. Surely Eagle would fly down and carry the little ones over the river. But Eagle instead caught rocks in its beak and dropped them into the river, creating a precarious bridge.

"Who will try to cross?" the chiefs called, but no one stepped forward.

"Is there no one who will save the defenseless ones?" a woman screamed.

119

Finally a wolf howled on the far side of the stream, and he trotted to the children.

"Here," he suggested, "climb on my back. I'll get you across."

And so Wolf saved many children. But he alone could not manage it all. He grew weary, and his feet began to slip on the wet stones.

"Bring my child over," a chief pleaded.

"Bring mine!" another urged.

"Will no one help?" Wolf called.

Those whose little ones were rescued had left, and the others insisted Wolf might bring them all across.

"I'm but one," Wolf insisted. "You are many. Can't you make a bridge with your hands and help the children find their way?"

"We'll drown ourselves," the People argued.

Then, from behind the others, a shadow stepped forward.

"I'm a stranger," he said, but I won't see children drown because their fathers are faint of heart. Show me the stones, Wolf, and I will cross."

"*Ayyyy!*" the People cried. "He's brave. We'll go, too."

So it was that the strange one led the way across, and all the children were saved. A council was called, and Wolf was praised. The stranger was made a brother to the People, and though he brought strange ways to Shell River, the People grew in power and numbers.

Stone Wolf awoke from the dream in rare good humor.

"You were shown the way," White Horn observed

as he collected food and set it before the Arrow-keeper. "Now we'll return."

"Later," Stone Wolf explained. "I must seek the meaning of the dream first."

"Can you tell me of it?"

"Yes, it's time you share my medicine, White Horn," Stone Wolf declared. "You must choose your path soon, too. If you stay, you should begin to perform the ceremonies. If you go, you should take all the power I can give you as reward for great service."

"Thank you, Uncle," the young man said gratefully. "The dream?"

"Yes," Stone Wolf said, narrating the strange tale as he took food. White Horn nodded as the story of the river formed an image in his mind. He scowled at the cowardice of the men, but brightened when Wolf saved the first children. In the end he remained confused.

"What does it mean?" White Horn asked.

"Much," Stone Wolf explained. "What are children to us?"

"The young," White Horn answered. "The defenseless ones."

"More," Stone Wolf insisted. "Those who will be warriors when we are gone. The future."

"Why would they be left behind?"

"Because their fathers turn from the old ways," Stone Wolf explained. "You said yourself men forget their sons' hunger and trade meat for white man's whiskey."

"It's true."

"Wouldn't such a man let his son starve? Is it harder to let a boy drown?"

"You are Wolf, Uncle."

"My brother and I," Stone Wolf said, frowning. "But we were not enough."

"There was the strange one, though. Me?"

"You wouldn't be looked upon as a stranger, White Horn. You are one of us."

"When who . . ."

"Ah, that's the mystery," Stone Wolf said, shaking his head. "I must search for an answer to that question."

"Here? Won't we go back?" White Horn asked.

"Yes, it's time to return. I know I must wash anger and resentment from my heart and seek to restore the old power. When the need is greatest, perhaps the shadow will reveal itself."

"I hope so," White Horn said. "To lose the future is to die."

Eleven

Stone Wolf led White Horn back from the Medicine Bow Mountains toward the camp of the *Tsis tsis tas*. The return journey was always made at a brisker pace, for even the ponies hungered for home. They had been gone many days, though, and a summer camp was never idle. Even upon reaching Shell River, the Arrow-keeper was a considerable time locating the new camp of the People.

Stone Wolf never expected shouts and screams upon his return, but he was disappointed no one was eager to greet him.

"Have we done something wrong?" White Horn whispered. "The People shy from us as if we carried spotted sickness."

"I don't understand, either," Stone Wolf told his young companion. "Something has happened."

"The trader is gone," White Horn observed. "Maybe they blame his leaving on us."

Stone Wolf thought it possible, but Dumont rarely passed the entire summer with any one band. There

123

wouldn't be enough hides to compensate him for his trouble.

"Nah nih, you're back!" Younger Wolf called, and others also seemed to acknowledge the fact.

"We've been far," Stone Wolf said as he dismounted and left the buckskin in the care of his brother.

"Yes, you appear thin," Younger Wolf noted. "The little ones have missed you."

"I haven't been away so long before. The hunters haven't enjoyed success, I see. There's little meat on the drying racks."

"Bull Buffalo doesn't travel Shell River, it appears."

"Then we'll find game elsewhere," Stone Wolf declared. "Now I must greet my sons."

"I'll take you to them," Younger Wolf said, turning to White Horn. "Tend my brother's horse, if you will."

"We'll see to the animals," Thunder Coat said, joining his brother. "You have important matters to discuss."

Important matters? Stone Wolf wondered. *What has happened?*

He soon discovered the unspoken truth.

"Ne' hyo," Arrow Dancer said as he greeted his father, "my mother has gone."

"Gone?" Stone Wolf cried. "Gone where?"

"With the trader," Arrow Dancer explained.

"I should have spoken to her before leaving," Stone Wolf said, frowning. "We argued. I must restore the harmony in my lodge."

"She didn't leave because you were away," Younger Wolf said, gazing uneasily at the little ones.

"One of the Pawnee girls fell from her horse and was killed," Red Willow Woman explained. "Dumont

124

had a place for her in his lodge, and she took it."

"They left on a moonless night and traveled fast," Younger Wolf added. "She said nothing to anyone in our camp, but it's said she was to have a child."

"It would not have been your son," Red Willow Woman said, taking the boys in her arms. "I know you have not mated with her in many weeks. She could no longer hide her shame, and Dumont welcomed her help."

"She couldn't tell me," Stone Wolf muttered as he sat on an elk skin and swallowed the news. "I've not been a husband to her since Dawn Dancer died."

"Star Eyes was no wife to mourn," Younger Wolf argued.

"She was never a good woman, *Ne' hyo,*" Arrow Dancer added. "Other women cook and tend their camp, but Star Eyes kept to the trader camp. Often Crow Boy and I would need her help, and she would call us 'dog boys' and slap us away."

"It's true," Crow Boy agreed. "Red Willow Woman has been our mother."

"The others know?" Stone Wolf asked.

"Yes, and they worry such bad feeling in the Arrow Lodge may have brought on their suffering."

"It was the trader Dumont," Arrow Dancer complained.

"It's many things," Stone Wolf declared. "She was always a stranger to our ways, and I never made her road an easy one. But I wish no woman the life of a trader's woman. We must go and get her back."

"No, *Ne' hyo,*" Arrow Dancer objected. "Let her go. Hasn't she brought all of us enough pain?"

"Perhaps," Stone Wolf admitted. "But my dream

told me I must be a bridge to my people. How can I bring them together if I can't restore peace in my own lodge?"

"You're tired, *Nah nih*," Younger Wolf said, gazing intently into Stone Wolf's eyes. "You have words to share with the People. Star Eyes may be far from Shell River already."

"I must retrieve her," Stone Wolf insisted.

"I'll go and find her," Younger Wolf promised. "The traders may not wish to give her up, and the Arrow-keeper must not give himself over to anger."

"You're right," Stone Wolf agreed. "But don't strike them down if she wants to stay."

"She went, didn't she?" Red Willow Woman asked. "It's foolish to run after her this way. Let her go and be thankful she can no longer embarrass us."

Stone Wolf was tempted to agree with her, but already he faced the difficult challenge of leading the band back to the sacred path. So long as Star Eyes was with the traders, his anger at Dumont would be seen as a personal grudge and not fear born of prophecy.

While Younger Wolf was searching for Star Eyes, Stone Wolf prayed for his brother's safe return. In addition, the Arrow-keeper met with the chiefs and shared his vision with them.

"You say we are to return to the old ways, but I don't read such words in your dream," Bear Claw complained. "You say Wolf means to bring the future to the People, but also this shade was there. Can't this shade be our good new guns?"

Others murmured their agreement, and Stone Wolf argued they had misunderstood.

"It was a person," Stone Wolf growled. "Or will be. We haven't yet met him perhaps."

"You're just angry because your woman left with the traders," Bear Claw said, laughing. "Better you content yourselves with small children. They heed your words and enjoy your stories."

Stone Wolf controlled his anger, but his eyes betrayed a growing fury.

"I have pledged to keep *Mahuts*," Stone Wolf said, breathing deeply. "I'll take no revenge. Don't mistake restraint for cowardice, Bear Claw. I haven't forgotten who spoke for these traders, nor how they brought the blister sickness among us."

Bear Claw shrank from the fierce gaze of the other chiefs.

"We'll consider what you have told us," Red Bird told Stone Wolf. "But we must smoke and discuss among ourselves what must be done."

"Do what you wish," Stone Wolf answered. "But I will be a captive of your decisions no longer. You have led us to hunger and sickness! I will put up a sweat lodge and purify those wishing to be reborn. Then I will ask *Mahuts* to guide me back to the sacred path. Those who wish to live can follow where I ride. You may stay on Shell River and starve."

The chiefs were surprised at the power of Stone Wolf's words. Some nodded, deeming it wise that the Arrows should lead. Bear Claw and some others only smiled and whispered to each other. Their contempt was transparent.

As Stone Wolf walked about the camp, he saw others who held Bear Claw's opinion.

"There goes the one with the dirty nose wife," one

spoke. "How can he provide for the People when he can't keep a wife?"

"He's brought shame on all the People by taking this unfaithful Crow woman," an old woman called Burned Nose declared. "He should give the Arrows over to Thunder Coat's brother. It's said that boy knows the ceremonies."

"Don't listen to them," White Horn said as he helped build the sweat lodge. "They know nothing."

"They're right," Stone Wolf argued. "I should be held in low regard."

"You're a man of the People," White Horn said, lowering his eyes. "You devote yourself to the care of others and neglect your own heart. I will never be worthy of your friendship."

"You are already," Stone Wolf said, clasping the younger man's hands. "The world would be hollow if not for such friends."

"Younger Wolf was gone nine days. When he returned, a shout was raised, and the young Foxes raced out to greet their leader.

Stone Wolf welcomed his brother home with a more solemn gaze.

"You found them?" the Arrow-keeper asked.

"Dumont and his camp, yes," Younger Wolf answered.

"Star Eyes?" Stone Wolf asked.

"Her, too," Younger Wolf said, dismounting and accepting a cool drink. "It's hard news I have for you, *Nah nih.*"

"She didn't wish to stay," Stone Wolf muttered.

128

"I never had the chance to speak to her of it," Younger Wolf said, shuddering. "The Oglala were there. Our cousin, Long Walker, told me what had happened."

"Yes?" Stone Wolf asked.

"French Pete sold the Oglalas bad whiskey. Three young men drank it and died. Their fathers and brothers held great anger in their hearts, so they rode upon Dumont's camp and killed everyone."

"Star Eyes?"

"Scalped and cut," Younger Wolf said, sighing. "She was heavy with child, and some of our relatives recognized her for having a husband among the *Tsis tsis tas*. She was with Dumont, who was hacked into small pieces. She, too, had her limbs and head severed."

"I must make a scaffold to hold her body."

"Too late, *Nah nih*," Younger Wolf muttered. "The coyotes and birds have visited the trader camp."

"It's justice," Burned Nose declared. "The evil one's been punished."

"Yes," others agreed.

"Now you can put this woman behind you," White Horn suggested.

"She was my wife," Stone Wolf said, frowning. "Look at the way everyone looks at me."

"They are sad for your loss," White Horn said.

"No, they wonder how a man of power could come to such a low place in their eyes. They're right to hold me in contempt. A man with vision should see things."

"All men are blind where the heart is concerned," Younger Wolf responded.

Stone Wolf remained troubled by Star Eyes's death.

Gloom had settled over the camp, and it wasn't helped by hunger and sickness. The only change came when Marcel Freneau paddled his canoe to the bank of Shell River and entered the camp.

"Long Walker told me of your sadness," Freneau told Stone Wolf. "The little ones are well?"

"Growing taller each day, if hungrier," Stone Wolf confessed. "Their road is rocky."

"As is yours," Freneau observed. "They deserved more from a mother, though."

"Don't judge her too harshly. She was a stranger, and she never learned our ways."

"Adapting to new ways requires a strong heart," Freneau agreed.

Stone Wolf noticed a new seriousness in the young man's eyes. He recalled the dream, and for the first time studied the young white man's shadow. Was it Freneau who was to help the People step safely into the future? Could a pale one be the bridge that was needed?

"Once I sent you from my lodge," Stone Wolf said, taking the trader's hand in his own. "I held fear and anger in my heart for you because of the deeds of others. You've been a friend to us, Corn Hair, so I say now you are welcome. Soon my sons and I will go into the hills and rid ourselves of the pain we feel for Star Eyes. Then we set out on a new road."

"Alone?" Freneau asked.

"My brother and some others will follow. But many won't leave what they know."

"I did long ago," Freneau said. "If you'd have me, I'll come with you. I know little of your customs and laws, but I have a good eye with a rifle, and I'm not afraid of hard work."

130

"Then we will make you our brother," Stone Wolf said.

Stone Wolf broke down his tipi and the Arrow Lodge. They were carried out of the camp, as was the still incomplete sweat lodge, and reassembled on a bluff overlooking the river. There Stone Wolf and his sons fasted and chanted, wringing the sadness from their withered bodies. Together, naked as when they were born, the three gazed upon the moon and hurried Star Eyes along Hanging Road.

"You were not the wife I sought," Stone Wolf whispered, "nor the mother my sons needed, but we offer your ghost no curse that would hold you from finding peace on the other side."

"Rest easy, *Nah koa,*" Arrow Dancer said, making a shallow cut on his chest.

"Rest easy," Crow Boy added, making a like cut.

Afterward Stone Wolf readied the Sweat Lodge. He, Younger Wolf, Freneau, and the two boys sat inside together, purging their bitterness as they cast off every inharmonious notion.

"Once we sat in the sweat lodge with our grandfather, Cloud Dancer," Stone Wolf recounted.

"Yes, he was a great man," Younger Wolf agreed. "When our own father was killed, Cloud Dancer raised us."

"My father lived with Cloud Dancer for a time," Freneau explained. "There his life was saved, and he was made to feel as a member of the family."

"Cloud Dancer was also an Arrow-keeper," Stone Wolf told the boys. "He learned to keep *Mahuts* when

131

he went to live with his uncle, Touches the Sky. Ah, there was a man to remember. He was tall as a horse, it's said."

"But it was Cloud Dancer who brought Horse to the People," Younger Wolf declared. "I've heard the story told many times, but I don't tire of it. *Nah nih,* share it with us."

"Yes," Freneau added. "How did Cloud Dancer catch Horse?"

"It's well known," Arrow Dancer said, gazing up into his father's tired eyes. "But you'll tell us, won't you, *Ne' hyo?*"

"It's a remembered tale, yes," Stone Wolf agreed. "That was long before I was born, of course. Back then the Snakes and Pawnees rode Horse, but the People walked the earth like Bull Buffalo and Wolf."

"Only man used two feet instead of four," Arrow Dancer pointed out.

"He's right," Younger Wolf agreed.

"Who's telling this story?" Stone Wolf asked, pouring water on the stones so that fresh steam flooded the small lodge. "Horse came to Cloud Dancer in a dream, and the boy, for he was small then, set off across Shell River, south to Muddy River, and walked among the camps of the Pawnees."

"They were fierce in those times before white man's sickness killed many of them," Younger Wolf noted.

"And Foxes killed many others," Stone Wolf boasted. "Cloud Dancer wore elk horn paint which rendered him invisible, and he was able to come and go as he wished. When he discovered Horse, he didn't know what to think. These huge creatures could carry a man across the earth far and fast. 'The People must have

132

them,' Grandfather decided. So he went among the animals, speaking to them in whispers and telling them of the kind treatment they would find in the camps of the People."

"Pawnees can be hard on their horses," Freneau noted.

"So that night Cloud Dancer stole the ponies of the enemy and rode homeward, eager to be welcomed for his brave heart deed. He had other adventures on the way, for the Pawnees chased him. In the end Horse was brought to the People, though, and Cloud Dancer was recognized as a man by the Fox Warriors."

"It's a good story," Arrow Dancer declared.

"Tie another onto it, *Ne' hyo,*" Crow Boy urged.

"No, it's time we prayed," Stone Wolf said, gripping his sons' shoulders and pulling them close. "These things we've spoken of, they are the remembered tales of our family. Know them, and you can't forget who you are. Our men have never been rich in possessions, nor high among those wearing war honors. Ours is the hardest place in battle. Ours is the task of guarding the defenseless ones. We are men of the People, and we value others before ourselves."

"*Ayyyy!*" Younger Wolf howled.

"You are young, my sons, but remember those who have gone before you to make the road smooth. Your hard days, too, will come. Prepare yourself for them, and devote your efforts to helping all across."

"We will, *Ne' hyo,*" Arrow Dancer vowed.

"Yes, *Ne' hyo,*" Crow Boy agreed.

Stone Wolf concluded by chanting an ancient call and dancing a bit afterward. Then he led the way outside and rushed to Shell River to cool himself. The cool

133

water swept away the sweat and anxiety, leaving the Arrow-keeper refreshed.

"Look there," Freneau said when he splashed into the river alongside the others. The young man's finger pointed upstream to a line of pony drags headed for the bluff.

"Others are following," Younger Wolf observed. "Most."

"Nearly all," Freneau added. "They trust *Mahuts*."

"*Mahuts* is the heart of the People," Stone Wolf insisted. "It's good to see so many. We'll be a strong band once again."

"*Ayyyy!*" Younger Wolf howled.

Twelve

Stone Wolf greeted the People as a man reborn. The past bitterness was forgotten, and he gazed out past Shell River to a fresh horizon.

"We'll hunt Bull Buffalo," he told the chiefs of the soldier societies. All but Bear Claw's Bowstrings and a few others had rejoined the Arrow-keeper.

"We must kill many," Younger Wolf declared. "Our bellies are empty, and the little ones need winter coats."

A great council of all the men was held, and Stone Wolf shared his vision of the future. He spoke of the old as well as the new, and the men shouted their agreement.

"I'll lead the way with the Buffalo Arrows," Stone Wolf explained. "For three days we'll make the required prayers. Then, when the scouts find Bull Buffalo, those who lead the way will hunt in the old fashion, using stone-tipped arrows. Those who follow may use their guns or iron-tipped arrows, but each kill must be treated with reverence."

"We'll see it's done," Younger Wolf promised.

"It will be a remembered hunt," Thunder Coat added.

"It's good harmony has returned to the People, and we are on the straight road again."

Stone Wolf directed the tribe eastward, toward the place where Fat River joins Shell River to form one stream. White Buffalo Cow visited his dreams every night, guiding him to a great herd that would provide all the People needed.

"What manner of hunters are these?" Bear Claw asked when his Bowstrings passed the scouts. "Using stone arrows! You will all starve!"

But White Buffalo Cow led the Buffalo Arrows to her children, and the scouts brought word of a tremendous herd grazing nearby.

"Now we make the prayers," Stone Wolf told the anxious hunters, and they gathered to form a separate camp, allowing the women and children to trail behind. As Stone Wolf invoked the spirits and asked forgiveness for killing brother creatures, the others listened solemnly.

"This is the way my father hunted," one old man remarked. "The People were never hungry then."

Once the hunt began, even those few who still had doubts were convinced of their Arrow-keeper's power. Hundreds and hundreds of buffalo grazed along the banks of Fat River, and the hunters met with great success.

"Never will a buffalo steak taste better," White Horn declared after returning with his first kill. *"Ayyyy!* I'm truly a man now."

"You've been one many days," Stone Wolf observed. "Never shying from hard tasks, and sharing every danger. It's time you sought your own vision and found a name."

"Yes," Thunder Coat agreed.

Stone Wolf reluctantly gave White Horn over to his brother, wishing he could guide the boy's name quest. It was for a relative to do, though.

With White Horn gone, Stone Wolf found himself sharing his thoughts with Young Corn Hair, Marcel Freneau.

"You're right to favor the old ways," Freneau said when Stone Wolf showed how to affix the stone point to an arrow. "So much that's gone before has been lost. We who lost our fathers as young men know the importance of passing on the lore of our People. A man that knows who he is, from where he's come, can withstand almost anything."

"Yes," Stone Wolf agreed. "My sons have no mother now, but I'll give them all I can of their father."

"I hope my sons are as well rooted in their traditions."

"You have sons, Corn Hair?" Stone Wolf asked.

"Five," the young trader boasted. "And one daughter. They're in St. Louis with my brothers."

"And your wife?"

"Gone three long years," Freneau explained. "She disliked open country and returned East. It's what brought me back to the plains. I had to cast out my anger, as you did in the sweat lodge."

"And your children? They should walk at your side."

"Soon," Freneau declared. "When they have some size. Maybe I'll bring them to your camp, and we will all hunt elk and buffalo together."

"Yes, it's a good notion. Brothers' sons should share a hunt."

"Brothers?"

"When the hunting is over, and we have made our winter camp, Younger Wolf and I will call a council. We will give away presents and take you into our family."

"Adopt me?" Freneau asked. "I'm too old and too white."

"Only your skin," Stone Wolf said solemnly. "Your heart is one with the People, and so you should be known as *Tsis tsis tas.*"

"What changed your mind? Once, not so long ago, you wished me to leave."

"Now I know you. And I understand why you came."

"Oh?"

"Man Above sees you can help us to understand these strange new ways of your people. The time may come when we need a friend among the whites."

"Others would have far greater influence."

"That's not what we need," Stone Wolf said, sighing. "We need a man whose voice we can trust to speak the truth. This is Corn Hair, our brother."

The hunt came to an end as the hard face moons of winter arrived on the plains. Stone Wolf's band moved to the base of *Noahvose,* and a dance was held to celebrate the new prosperity of the People. It was there that Stone Wolf and his brother took Corn Hair into their family.

"It's strange how the Arrow-keeper has changed," Red Bird observed. "He who thought to flee the traders takes Corn Hair into his lodge, welcomes him into the family."

"It's not so odd," Younger Wolf argued. "Corn Hair has much in common with us. He cherishes the old ways, and his heart is of the mountains. Yes, he trades, but more than that he learns our words and our ways. He is one of us."

Stone Wolf allowed Arrow Dancer the honor of giving away the four ponies provided for the giveaway. Four times the boy led an animal to the lodge of an impoverished family as his father said, "We give this horse in honor of our new brother."

"*Ayyyy!*" the People shouted. "It's a great thing to be so honored by a family."

Other presents were made as well. Everything from buffalo hump roasts to fine skins were distributed among the People.

"You make me tall in the eyes of the *Tsis tsis tas,*" Corn Hair Freneau declared as he clasped his new brothers by the arms. "I'll never know greater belonging than I do this day."

"Yes, but your sons are far away," Stone Wolf said, sensing something unspoken in the yellow-haired trader's eyes.

"I should winter there, with them," Freneau said, dropping his gaze. "It's hard to leave you after so many fine things have been said of me."

"It's your rightful place," Stone Wolf told Freneau. "Hold them close to you. Let them learn what's in your heart. Then, if you wish it, come back to us. Your sons, too, will be welcome."

"I will come back," Freneau vowed.

"Yes, I think you will," Stone Wolf replied. *You were, after all, in my dream.*

By the time the first snow fell on the sacred center of the world, Freneau had departed. Stone Wolf felt the frigid bite of a north wind and swallowed the first bitter taste of winter.

"Once I feared you," Stone Wolf told the darkening skies. "But now I know you are only a clearing away of the old so that new grass may grow."

139

That winter was remembered as a hard time. The rivers froze, and deep snows smothered the land. Even in their new buffalo robes the little ones shivered and whined at night. Old people wandered into the snowdrifts and began the long climb up Hanging Road.

"Ne' hyo, why is it so cold?" Arrow Dancer asked. "I'll never be warm again."

"Come closer, *Naha',"* Stone Wolf suggested. Already Crow Boy was burrowed into one side, and now Arrow Dancer, too, shared his father's warmth. Before the Big Wheel Moon arrived to signal winter's close, the children were huddling between Stone Wolf, Younger Wolf, and Red Willow Woman. But even a blazing fire of oak logs didn't completely overpower the cold.

"Why does the world so torment the defenseless ones?" Red Willow Woman complained.

"It's these hard times that make the warm days so much better remembered," Younger Wolf declared.

"Hard?" Stone Wolf cried. "Have you so quickly forgotten the blister sickness? Hard? We have food enough and good hides. The enemy doesn't stalk our camp, and no blood stains *Mahuts."*

Winter wasn't finished yet, though. Even though the Big Wheel Moon had passed, a late snowstorm emptied a universe of white powder upon the land, freezing horse and man alike.

"Come close," Stone Wolf told the boys. "Even the warmest fire can't hold off this cold."

But even an Arrow-keeper couldn't keep all the People warm.

"My son is sick," Wood Snake, the Fox Warrior crier, said when he appeared with the child outside the Arrow Lodge. "He needs your help."

140

"Enter," Stone Wolf said, and the man stepped inside. Stone Wolf motioned to a blanket resting beside the fire, and Wood Snake placed his son there.

"Ferret Boy is my second son," Wood Snake explained as he presented the Arrow-keeper a pipe. "He's dear to my heart, and it hurts to see him in pain.

"Winter brings on illness," Stone Wolf noted as he accepted the pipe. The two men then smoked and invoked the healing spirits. Afterward Stone Wolf knelt beside the boy, peeled a hide shirt from the twelve-year-old's chest, and touched the Ferret Boy's flesh. It was cool, and the breathing was shallow.

"He's had food?" Stone Wolf asked.

"He ate well until the snows came," Wood Snake answered. "For two days he's kept nothing in his belly, and he now takes only water."

"There's fever," Stone Wolf observed after touching the boy's forehead. "Is he always this quiet?"

"Since he stopped eating."

"Ho ho' ta ma itsi hyo' ist, the ground people, have put illness in him," Stone Wolf declared. "You were right to bring him here."

"You'll make the cure?"

"Man Above does such things," Stone Wolf said solemnly. "I will invite the curing."

Stone Wolf then sent for Red Willow Woman, for a cure needed a woman's help. He smoked again, invoking the help of the spirits, and began drawing the poison the earth people had shot into Ferret Boy from his body.

Sometimes a small bone or splinter of wood would be drawn from the sick one. Other times the sickness was carried in other ways. Stone Wolf painted his face and began chanting, fighting off the evil odors. He pounded

141

horn and painted the boy's chest. Later, as the boy began to respond, Red Willow Woman boiled skunkweed leaves into a tea, which Ferret Boy drank slowly. It would cure the belly ache and restore appetite.

Stone Wolf also treated the boy with yellow cornflower tea, a good cure for the head and belly. The medicines and the chanting drew out the ill humors, and Ferret Boy revived.

"How have I come to be here?" the boy asked when his eyes detected the presence of *Mahuts*.

"Your father brought you to me," Stone Wolf explained.

"Have I been so sick to need the Arrow-keeper?" the boy asked in surprise.

"Here, see this?" Stone Wolf asked, holding up a particle of bone. "See how *Ho ho' ta ma itsi hyo' ist* put sickness into you?"

"Ah, the ground people," Ferret Boy said, nodding soberly. "I've heard of their tricks."

"Rest easy now, knowing you are whole again. Soon you'll return to your father's lodge."

"That's good," Ferret Boy said, drinking the tea. "There's much I must do there."

Later, as Ferret Boy regained his strength, Red Willow Woman fed him rock earth mint tea. Once the tea had brought him back to life, he was ready to chew buffalo meat and tubers.

"You've brought my son back to me," Wood Snake declared when Ferret Boy left the Arrow Lodge. "Accept these good horses for your efforts."

"They will serve me well many summers," Stone Wolf said, giving the horses over to Arrow Dancer's care.

Some cures came easier, and some were difficult to

bring about. Several children drank tea made from bad roots, and their throats swelled so they could hardly breathe. Stone Wolf made a tea of prairie clover that eased the discomfort and countered the swelling. When Charging Hawk, an Elk Warrior, was brought to him with an arrow wound in his chest, there was little to do.

"Bring the black bark medicine," Stone Wolf told Red Willow Woman. "I will examine the arrow."

"We were hunting," the Hawk's younger brother, Yellow Hand Pony, explained. "I saw a movement in the trees and thought it a deer."

"You couldn't know," Charging Hawk assured his brother.

Stone Wolf offered the medicine, and it eased the pain. He then gave the Elk Warrior a strong root to chew which left him to drift across the world while the arrow was withdrawn.

"It had an iron tip," Stone Wolf observed as he worked his stone knife deeper. "It is in the breastbone, and I can't take it out."

Stone Wolf withdrew the shaft and left the point, but the bleeding was great, and even black bark medicine had its limits. Men and women gathered to sing and pray, for Charging Hawk was a brave young man who would be much missed. Stone Wolf suffered, cutting flesh and going without food, and Yellow Hand Pony tore at his clothes and cut his chest many times.

"Man Above, return my brother to me," the young man pleaded. Man Above had other concerns, though, and Charging Hawk awoke in great pain.

"I can't feel my legs," the warrior cried. "Where is the world? My eyes can't see!"

Yellow Hand Pony clasped his brother's hand and

143

sang remembered songs of their young warrior days. But Charging Hawk heard nothing. He was already setting his feet on Hanging Road.

"I brought him to you so that the power of *Mahuts* could cure him," the Pony said afterward when Stone Wolf helped prepare the body for its scaffold. "But your power was spent."

"Sometimes I can bring a man back to the People," Stone Wolf said. "Other times the spirits call him to the other side. It's not for you or I to question. Yellow Hand Pony, we are nothing to the Great Mystery. Any of us."

"I killed him by my carelessness. My brother, who showed me man's road and did the things a father should do. *Ayyyy!* How will I find my way now?"

"Your feet are on man's road," Stone Wolf insisted. "Your brother had a wife and small son. His burden is now yours. Stand tall, and walk the world with far-seeing eyes. What Charging Hawk did for you, you must now do for his son."

Charging Hawk was the last of Stone Wolf's band to climb Hanging Road that winter. Spring came at last, and there was much to do to prepare the camp for the summer hunts. Women gave birth, and boys chased each other through streams, playing the games their fathers before them had played.

Arrow Dancer shot rabbits with his small bow, but his eyes were always fixed on the older boys.

"Soon I will join them," the boy told his father. "I, too, will be strong and tall. Then I will hold the horses for the young men on raids against the Crow ponies. Later I'll hunt Bull Buffalo with Younger Wolf."

144

"Yes, these things will come to be," Stone Wolf agreed. "But don't hurry your feet onto man's road. Your father enjoys your singing, and my lodge would miss you."

"I'm not yet old enough to take to the young man's lodge," Arrow Dancer said, laughing. "We'll have many summers yet, *Ne' hyo*."

The camp moved finally from *Noahvose* up the twisting river known for the People themselves. *Sahiyela,* the Lakota called it. *Cheyenne,* the hairy-faced whites wrote it on their skin maps. The river makes a wild turn around a rocky hill before descending onto the plain, and there the People favored making their spring camps. But as they neared the place, scouts returned with grim news.

"Bear Claw made his winter camp there," White Horn explained. "Now he calls it the place of the fifty dead."

"Fifty?" Stone Wolf cried. "How?"

"Hunger," Thunder Coat explained. "They found no game, and the hard face moons took the young and old. All but a few are gone, and those who remain are bitter with hatred."

"Soon we'll renew the Arrows," Stone Wolf declared. "Maybe then their spirits will recover."

"Maybe," Thunder Coat said. "But I don't think so. Their eyes are too full of death and suffering."

Thirteen

As spring painted the land green and bright, pipe carriers rode out to call the ten bands together for the Arrow Renewal.

"We've been strong before," Stone Wolf told the People. "We'll be strong again. As we replenish the power of *Mahuts,* the Arrows will protect us."

But even as the bands assembled to the south and prepared to begin the rituals, scouts brought word of another gathering.

"The Skidi Pawnees have come together," Thunder Coat announced.

"Ayyyy!" Bear Claw cried. "Let's go and destroy our old enemies!"

"Once and for always let's finish them!" a young man, Bull, urged.

"Yes, we'll paint ourselves and ride to war!" the Bowstrings shouted.

"Ayyyy!" the young men screamed.

"What madness is this?" Stone Wolf objected. "This is the time for prayer and renewal. Winter has thinned the horses, and they need fattening. Many

146

children have been born, and the women require rest."

"These things are true," Younger Wolf added. "Most of all, our safety depends on *Mahuts*. We must make the renewal."

"The Foxes are all old women," Bear Claw accused. "Where were they when the fifty starved? They once led the fight against the Crows, but now they rest in their lodges, telling stories and hiding from the enemy."

"Not all!" Red Bird shouted, rising angrily. "I will go and strike the enemy!"

"I, too," Thunder Coat announced.

"I will follow my brother," White Horn declared. "It's time I won a name."

Stone Wolf gazed solemnly at his young friend. A terrible sense of betrayal and despair filled the Arrowkeeper's heart.

"Wait," Stone Wolf pleaded. "Let me consult *Mahuts*. I'll seek a dream and . . ."

"There's no time for dreams," Bear Claw argued. "Never again will we have such a chance. Here are all the enemy in one place where we can rub them out. Many horses will fall into our hands, and the captives will fill the lodges emptied by winter's hard time."

Many of the younger men had not gone to war, and their passions were stirred by Bear Claw. Others, long bent by suffering, wished only to strike back at someone.

"Quiet your war cries and listen," Stone Wolf said, studying the faces of the others. "Once before I spoke caution to the young men, but my words were ignored. Who remembers Snake Eater, who led the

147

young men against the Crows? Ah, he was going to bring back good horses, but he found only death at the hands of the enemy, and he led others to share his fate."

"The Crows are many, and they are good fighters," Bear Claw declared. "The Pawnees have grown weak. Remember how we chased them down and rescued our captives?"

"We?" Younger Wolf asked. "I don't recall any Bowstrings riding that day."

"No, it was the Foxes," Thunder Coat boasted. "But it was a hard fight."

"My brother won his shield that day," White Horn recounted. "When he killed the Pawnee lance carrier."

"His hair decorates my shield even now," Thunder Coat added.

"It was their chief, Raven Eyes, who stole the women," Bear Claw pointed out. "This same chief is among the Skidi now."

"Yes," Thunder Coat agreed. "I saw him there."

"There are few grown men among these Pawnees," Bear Claw argued. "They, too, have had the blister sickness in their camps. Small boys tend the horses and hunt game. If we kill them, the Skidi will be no more."

"Yes, but will you?" Stone Wolf asked. "They are many, young or not. What power will you use against them? You've won no shield to turn the bullets! You couldn't find meat for your winter camp. How will you feed a war party?"

"*Mahuts* will lead us," Bear Claw demanded. "The Arrows will lead the way, blinding the enemy. We'll

148

fall upon them unawares and strike them down!"

"First you interfere with the renewal," Stone Wolf said sternly. "And now you would use what power remains to make this attack? You risk more than is wise, Bear Claw. It's a foolish adventure. You must not go."

"We will go!" Bear Claw insisted. "Who would follow me?"

"*Ayyyy!*" many shouted.

Stone Wolf searched the men for others who would argue caution, who would hold back the young men. No one rose to speak.

"It's decided then," Bear Claw said, stepping close to the Arrow-keeper and glaring into Stone Wolf's eyes. "Will you help us, or will we whip you around the camp until you give us your support?"

Stone Wolf didn't flinch, and Bear Claw took out a quirt and lashed the Arrow-keeper.

"Stop!" Younger Wolf shouted. "What cause have you to strike a man of the People?"

Others restrained Younger Wolf, though, and Bear Claw again quirted the Arrow-keeper.

"Are you all determined to do this thing?" Stone Wolf shouted angrily. "Can you be so foolish to have learned nothing?"

"Fool, you feed on dreams," Bear Claw muttered. "What truth have your dreams brought you? You didn't even see a wife's unfaithfulness when all the camp spoke of it. Fear not. One of the young men will carry the Arrows into the fight. You may remain safely behind where the Pawnees can't find you."

"Yes, stay back in safety," others echoed.

149

"You're all fools," Younger Wolf charged. *"Nah nih* bears battle scars won while many of you were still wetting yourselves. He's bled for the People more times than I can recount. Wood Snake, who suffered so your son would find his health? Yellow Hand Pony, can you so quickly forget Stone Wolf's help? And who hasn't received meat from his kill or medicine prayers when there was need?"

"Our need is for war," Bear Claw argued. "We won't win honor counting the People or dancing beside a council fire. If we're to be strong again, we must strike the enemy!"

"Yes!" the others agreed. "Strike the Pawnees!"

Bear Claw again raised his quirt, but White Horn stilled the Bowstring's hand.

"It's hopeless, Uncle," the young man insisted. "We will fight these Pawnees. Give us power to keep us safe. Ask *Mahuts* to lead the fight."

"Yes," Bear Claw added. "It's the obligation of an Arrow-keeper to lend his power to the fighters. It's right you should do so, for the disharmony you brought to the Arrow Lodge has too long tormented the People."

"Yes," others agreed.

"Am I the blame for your ignorance?" Stone Wolf cried. "Was I the one who led the Bowstrings off to starve?"

The other stirred uneasily, and Stone Wolf grew cold. Yes, they blamed him for that misfortune and others.

"Help us win back the honor of the People," White Horn pleaded. Stone Wolf studied his young friend's

150

determined face and knew he would comply. Any other save Younger Wolf could have been refused. Stone Wolf remembered the seven scars White Horn bore from the Crow horse raiders. Such courage and the devoted service the boy had provided since merited protection.

"I'll offer what power I possess," Stone Wolf answered. "But it may not be enough to prevent disaster. Consider well the strength you would possess after the Arrows are renewed."

"The Pawnees will not keep their camp so close forever," Bear Claw declared. "No, we must strike now."

"Yes, but no good will come of it," Stone Wolf predicted. "You'll come to a bad end, Bear Claw, and the birds will pick at your bones!"

While the soldier societies met to organize war parties, Stone Wolf prayed and sang and made medicine. His dreams clouded with visions of death and despair. In one he saw himself standing alone on Shell River, a great hole in his chest where his heart might have been.

"Man Above, if this raid must bring my death, let it be that way," Stone Wolf said as he made the morning prayers. "Keep safe the helpless, and let my sons grow tall in the old ways."

The Bowstrings complained Stone Wolf was delaying the raid with his prayers, and one band of them set upon him with quirts, whipping him to the river.

"Coward," they mumbled. "You don't even defend yourself."

"You have no honor!" Younger Wolf shouted at the

tormentors. "Don't you know he will never strike back at one of us? His vow is to protect you, and his power grows from devotion. The prayers he makes are to keep you safe!"

"My rifle keeps me safe," Bear Claw insisted. "I'm no believer in dreams!"

"No, you believe in starving," Stone Wolf grumbled. "What coup have you counted? You fight with insults and accusations. Even so, I won't strike back. Accept what protection I can give you and be satisfied."

Bear Claw merely laughed and stalked off with his companions, laughing.

"Nah nih, the People are foolish to heed such a man," Younger Wolf declared.

"No, they hunger to regain their lost honor," Stone Wolf argued. "I can only pray it's not won with our own blood. Grandfather spoke of old fights when our fathers stood to protect the defenseless ones. Theirs was an honored death, but it was death. I wish life for the People."

"You're only one man," Younger Wolf reminded his brother.

"Yes, and that isn't enough," Stone Wolf admitted.

The next morning scouting parties spread out along both banks of Shell River, searching for Pawnees. The main band followed them slowly, keeping the ten circles close for mutual defense. *Mahuts* led each movement of the camps, and the Suhtai carried the sacred Buffalo Hat alongside.

"Look at them, leading the way!" White Horn declared as he rode in with news a Skidi hunting party had been located. "Our power is great. Many Pawnees will die!"

That night other scouts returned, bringing word of more hunters. Most were northeast, and Bear Claw announced his plans when the men gathered in council.

"We'll begin by striking these hunters," Bear Claw explained. "They are north and east, so we will move our camp in that direction. Small parties will attack the Pawnee hunters, and the enemy will send word for the rest to come fight. Then we will kill the warriors and strike the camp."

Stone Wolf thought it a good enough plan, but he worried there were too many young men in the war parties. Their blood would be up, and they were sure to race ahead, endangering themselves and their companions. What if the weight of the Skidis fell on the raiding parties? Many were sure to die.

"I've considered this raid long," Stone Wolf told the others when he was invited to offer his views. "I've smoked and prayed, and my dreams continue to warn of peril. Even so, I will give you what medicine I have to keep you safe. I have elk tooth charms and much bittersweet for you to chew and make the red paint which will keep you from the paths of bullets and arrows."

"And *Mahuts?*" Thunder Coat asked.

"Will you carry the Arrows into battle, Uncle?" White Horn added.

"It's not for an Arrow-keeper to do," Stone Wolf explained. "There should be a young man who will tie them to his lance. He should be a brave heart, for the

153

enemy will see him leading the way."

"I would do it," White Horn volunteered.

"No, you've yet to count coup," Younger Wolf argued.

"I will do it," Bull said, stepping forward. "It's right one who has spoken loud for this attack should carry the Arrows."

"Listen to me, brothers," Stone Wolf said as the men shouted their approval at Bull's offer. "Guard Bull well, for he carries the heart of the People. I've kept *Mahuts* safe many moons now, but my power will not hold back the Pawnees. You must do that."

"We will!" Bear Claw promised.

Stone Wolf then busied himself preparing medicine for the young men. Much of that night and early the following morning he crafted elk tooth charms and tied them behind the ears of unblooded young men. Boys as young as fourteen summers had been chosen to join the war parties, and their eager eyes and strong hearts would bring them into grave danger.

"Chew this," Stone Wolf instructed each boy who came to him. "Bittersweet makes strong medicine. The red paint you make should cover your body. No bullet can pass through it."

"I'll paint my chest," Yellow Hand Pony declared. "A wound elsewhere won't bring much harm."

"I'll paint myself all over," a young Bowstring named Iron Wood said. "I've seen what bullets do to a man, and I wish all my arms and legs to accompany me on man's road."

When White Horn arrived, Stone Wolf led the young man away from the others and gazed seriously

154

into his eyes.

"Uncle, you still believe we're foolish to strike the Pawnees," White Horn observed. "I've read the stars, and they seem favorable. No sign have I glimpsed to forewarn us of calamity."

"Do you dream?" the Arrow-keeper asked.

"Only of battle, and the hard fighting that will find us. Men will fall, true, but what honor can be won without blood?"

"In the old days, men would be content to strike the enemy with the flat head of their lances. We had enemies then as now, but there was respect among us. Now war is only killing. Men strike each others' camps, slaying the innocents. Before, young ones would be taken into our lodges, adopted as our own. Now there's talk of rubbing out all the Pawnees, even the smallest child. This has never been our way."

"Remember, Uncle, Bear Claw isn't the only one riding against the enemy. Younger Wolf and Thunder Coat will allow no such slaughter. They carry the Buffalo Shields, too, and will protect the others."

"If my dreams hold the truth, there will be no protecting," Stone Wolf said, frowning.

"What do they tell you?"

"I saw the heart of the People cut from my body."

"You are the heart of the People, Stone Wolf," White Horn argued. "Stay in the Arrow Lodge. No harm will come to you there."

"I'm a man of the People," Stone Wolf objected. "My place is with the others."

"Ride with the Foxes then, Uncle. We won't allow

harm to touch you."

"You will have peril enough," Stone Wolf said as he painted the young man's chest. In addition to the red bulletproofing, Stone Wolf dabbed on lightning bolts and hailstones, his personal medicine, and gave White Horn a necklace of bear claws to ward off injury.

"Thank you," White Horn said, clasping the Arrow-keeper's wrists.

"I have more," Stone Wolf said, tying an owl feather in the young man's hair. "Owl will give you eyes to find the enemy. Bear will lend you strength. Elk will provide endurance," he added, tying an elk tooth behind White Horn's ear. "And eagle will guide you down sacred road," Stone Wolf concluded, tying a second feather in his young friend's hair. "Be watchful, and remember all I've shown you."

"I always remember," White Horn declared. "Though sometimes I forget to acknowledge my gratitude."

"It's not what's required," Stone Wolf said. "You've been a brother to me, and I can see you no other way."

"*Ayyyy!*" White Horn cried. "It's a father I see when I look in your eyes."

The young man then departed, and Stone Wolf returned to the others. There were so many, and they were so young.

"What brings them to hurry themselves so?" Stone Wolf asked his brother.

"The same urges that sent us along man's road, *Nah nih,*" Younger Wolf suggested. "They remember the stories of their fathers and grandfathers. How can they be otherwise? They are *Tsis tsis tas!*"

Yes, Stone Wolf thought. *And they have Mahuts to lead them.* Still his heart remained heavy, and his eyes clouded with misgivings.

"Ne' hyo, you should rest," Arrow Dancer said when he found Stone Wolf wandering about the camp in the predawn stillness. "You'll need your strength for the battle."

"Yes," Stone Wolf said, smiling as the boy led him homeward. *Rest. Sleep. Dreams.* How could one explain the fear of seeing the future unfolded?

"I know," Arrow Dancer whispered. "But even a troubled sleep is better than none at all."

Fourteen

Stone Wolf slept uneasily, though, as shadowy figures visited his dreams.

"I gave into your hands the greatest trust," Cloud Dancer's shade said. "Don't neglect your obligations. *Mahuts* is in danger."

White Buffalo Cow lamented the end of the old ways.

"All I've predicted has come to pass," Sweet Medicine's shade whispered as it floated by on a cloud. "My People, you haven't listened!"

Star Eyes's dismembered body reassembled and laughed at her husband.

"You thought to have power! You're nothing!"

Finally little Dawn Dancer reached out a small hand.

"Ne' hyo, all is quiet on the other side. Come, find your peace."

He rose even before dawn and sought the freshness of the early morning air. Others were also about, seeing to their horses or freeing themselves of concerns. Many young men sat together, singing the brave heart songs and making medicine.

"Battle's for younger men," Wood Snake declared as he joined the Arrow-keeper. "Soon our sons will stand in our place when the charge is made."

"Not for a time," Stone Wolf argued. "But the winter does bring on a weariness."

"It's said you dream of ill fortunes. Even as a boy you had far-seeing eyes. What do you see, Stone Wolf?"

"Hunger," Stone Wolf said, sighing. "Death. The heart of the People carved from me."

"Will the Pawnees find our camp then?"

"I don't know," Stone Wolf admitted. "We'll keep men behind to guard the defenseless ones, though. In truth, I know nothing. Still, I sense disaster. How it will come or why I don't know. But it's there."

"If the worst comes to pass, know we Foxes will see your sons put upon man's road. Even if Younger Wolf, too, climbs Hanging Road, you have brothers among us."

"It's not for myself I fear," Stone Wolf insisted. "Death is no stranger to run from. It's the comforting hand of the grandfathers. Dawn Dancer waits on the other side, as does my father, Iron Wolf, and old Cloud Dancer, who showed me the straight path."

"For us then," Wood Snake said, frowning. "Make strong medicine, today and tomorrow. Those who lead us have never practiced caution, and my fears are now yours."

"Then there are two men who will be watchful,"

Stone Wolf said, smiling hopefully. *But would it be enough?* He wondered.

When he made the morning prayers, Stone Wolf invoked every spirit known to favor the People.

"Bring our young men success," Stone Wolf pleaded. "Keep safe the reckless ones."

Thereafter he made medicine for the chiefs and drew *Mahuts* from the Arrow Lodge.

"Here is Bull, who will carry the sacred lance," Bear Claw said, urging the young warrior forward. Stone Wolf accepted Bull's lance and tied the bundle near the point.

"You undertake a grave responsibility," Stone Wolf warned. "Here is *Mahuts,* the greatest of our medicine powers. Other than the Suhtai, who bring the Medicine Hat to battle, we are the most trusted band. Guard these Arrows with your life, Bull, for they above all must be kept safe."

"They can be in no danger on my lance," Bull boasted. "Come, brothers, let's ride!"

The young men howled and mounted their horses. Stone Wolf tried to hold them back, hoping to add other prayers to heighten the Arrows' power. But Bull was in great haste to bring on the fighting, and Stone Wolf scrambled to finish preparing himself for the coming conflict. Finally he mounted his horse and joined the Foxes.

Scouts brought word the Skidi Pawnees were assembled in a great camp, preparing to sacrifice the life of a captive to the Morning Star.

"It's a bad thing," Stone Wolf muttered when he heard. "Captives should be protected from all harm.

Have the Pawnees become like the Snakes, eager to cut apart their prisoners, adding torment to humiliation?"

"It's said the captive is a Snake," White Horn explained. "If it's true, perhaps they mean to return cruelty with cruelty."

"Maybe," Stone Wolf said, knowing how among the People the life of a captive was guarded as that of a son. To harm the defenseless was unpardonable.

The Foxes and Bowstrings found themselves riding together northeast from Fat River. The Skidi camp was near now, and the buffalo hunting party even closer.

"We'll strike the hunters first," Bear Claw declared after the lead riders reported Pawnees on the far hillside, skinning their kills.

"Shall I lead the way?" Bull asked eagerly.

"If we charge the enemy," Stone Wolf said. "Never go far from the main band, though."

"Stay with me," Bear Claw urged. "I'll tell you when to use the Arrow medicine."

The other Bowstrings interposed themselves between Arrow-keeper and Arrows, and Stone Wolf was forced into the third rank of riders. His buckskin was thin from the hard winter, and it carried him slowly so that he fell behind ever more.

"Man Above, watch over the young ones," Stone Wolf prayed as he heard shouts from the first line. There, near the top of a low hill, a group of Bowstrings had put the Pawnee hunters to flight.

"Leave the men to run!" Younger Wolf shouted.

"Ignore these Skidi," Wood Snake added. "Take the pony herd!"

But the Bowstrings had no ears to hear. Their blood was up, and they doggedly pursued the hunters, striking down two before a long line of Pawnees appeared to counter the charge.

"Ayyyy!" White Horn shouted. "See how we've run them!"

"They're not running," Stone Wolf objected. "Forming. They'll give us a fight."

"Then I must not be left behind," the young man said, kicking his horse into a gallop.

"They won't fight us," Younger Wolf declared as he pointed to Pawnees breaking down their lodges.

But all the Pawnees weren't running away. No, bands of young men lined up on the nearby hillsides, and the two lines taunted and derided each other.

"Who will follow me and strike the enemy?" Bear Claw called at last.

"I!" Thunder Coat cried.

"I!" Bull added.

"I!" another and another shouted.

Bear Claw raised his lance, and the young men rode forward. Pawnees rode down the hill to meet them, but it wasn't much of a fight. Men on horseback, waving lances, had a hard time gaining much advantage. Only when the rest of the *Tsis tsis tas* surged forward did the Pawnees break and run.

Not all fell back, though. One old Pawnee jumped down from his horse and sat on the ground, singing his death chant.

162

"Who will go and count coup on this ancient one?" Bear Claw asked.

"I go," Bull said, slapping his pony and charging toward the lone man. The Pawnee ignored the frothing horse and its frenzied rider. Even when Bull struck the Pawnee's shoulder, the Skidi failed to respond.

"He's clever like coyote," Wood Snake observed as the old one dodged Bull's lance again and again. The Pawnees screamed their admiration, and for a time it seemed they would charge to rescue the old warrior.

"How can this be?" Younger Wolf cried. *"Mahuts* should blind the enemy!"

Stone Wolf, too, was growing uneasy. The Arrow power was spoiled by rashness, and now Bull remained alone and far in front of the others. *Mahuts* was in danger.

Then the unthinkable occurred. The old Pawnee reached up and tore the lance from Bull's hands. Bull steadied his horse and tried to retrieve the lance, but now the Pawnee held it, and its sharp point opened a gash in Bull's pony's side.

"No!" the older men screamed when the Pawnee discovered the medicine bundle. He held it high overhead and showed his companions.

"Mahuts is lost," Bear Claw said, dropping his chin onto his chest. "We are defeated."

"No!" Stone Wolf shouted. "We must recover our heart!"

"Foxes, brave up!" Younger Wolf cried as Bull managed to kick his wounded horse to safety. "We must recover the Arrows."

The Foxes drove themselves toward the old Pawnee,

163

but the remainder of the Skidi, encouraged by the capture of the *Tsis tsis tas* medicine Arrows, came to the old one's aid. By threes and fours they threw themselves with great force at the enemy. Soon the Foxes found their charge met and repulsed. The fighting was fierce and bloody. Brave men on both sides fell, and others retreated, wounded. But the courage of the Foxes could do nothing to retrieve what was lost. The red bulletproof medicine had no effect on the Pawnee lances, and the Buffalo Shields failed to catch the blinding light.

Stone Wolf found himself confronted by two Pawnees. They were young, but the hair on the sides of their heads had been shaved, leaving a solitary strip in the center. These were blooded men, and they balanced their lances lightly in both hands.

"Ayyyy!" Stone Wolf screamed. "Nothing lives long!"

He wheeled his horse around, and the animal collided with the first Pawnee's mount with a force that sent the Pawnee pony reeling. Stone Wolf then lashed out at the young Skidi with his stringless bow, slapping him hard in the belly and knocking him from the horse.

"Haaa!" the second Pawnee yelled as he swung his lance at Stone Wolf. The Buffalo Shield blunted the point, and the lance shaft snapped like a twig.

"You're lucky this day," Stone Wolf called to the stunned Pawnee as he rammed the point of his bow into the young man's ribs, stealing the breath from his lungs. The Pawnee bent over his horse's neck, gasping for air.

164

"Mahuts!" Stone Wolf screamed as he charged onward. Three more Pawnees raced over to block his path. A fourth joined them, and Stone Wolf turned and searched for help. Four were too many, and these weren't young men. Raven Eyes himself was among them, and all four bore battle scars on arms and shoulders.

"Come, brothers, carry the fight to the enemy!" Stone Wolf urged. "Strike hard and save the day!"

To his dismay, Stone Wolf saw Bear Claw and the Bowstrings withdraw. The Claw, who had pressed the fight at every council, retired to safety, lamenting the lost chance to rub out the Skidi.

"Brave up!" Stone Wolf shouted to the embattled Foxes. "It's for us to do now."

But one man or twenty could not hope to break the Skidi line. Stone Wolf charged, determined to save the Arrows or fall on that hillside. It was what a man of the People did.

"Man Above, guide my sons down man's road," he prayed as he met the four Pawnees. Three moved aside, leaving Raven Eyes to fight the Arrow-keeper alone.

Raven Eyes struck first, using a brightly painted lance, but the Buffalo Shield was too strong, and again a lance snapped.

"Call all your Pawnee medicine," Stone Wolf urged as he struck the chief's shoulder. "Remember the man who slew you!"

But the others interceded, and Raven Eyes escaped. Stone Wolf blunted their lances with his shield, but the stringless bow lacked the power to knock these others from their horses.

"*Ayyyy!*" White Horn shouted. "Look at how Stone Wolf fights!"

Other Foxes, too, recognized the fury of the Arrow-keeper and rode to his side. The three Pawnees were driven back, and White Horn killed one and took his painted lance.

"*Ayyyy!*" the young man screamed. "I've driven the enemy!"

But even as they routed one line of Pawnees, a second appeared. Raven Eyes had recovered, and he directed these men to charge the Foxes.

"We can't fight so many alone," Younger Wolf argued as he urged his pony alongside Stone Wolf. "We must cover the retreat of the wounded. Come away, *Nah nih*. We'll fight another day."

"No," Stone Wolf objected.

"We can't stop them," Thunder Coat declared.

"Look at us, Uncle," White Horn added. "We've shot all our arrows, and blood flows from our veins, stealing our strength."

"*Nah nih*, it's finished!" Younger Wolf shouted as Thunder Coat and White Horn turned away.

"*Mahuts!*" Stone Wolf shouted.

"The Arrows are lost," Younger Wolf said, grabbing his brother's horse and drawing it away as Wood Snake covered their retreat. "The Pawnees have broken our power."

"Then we are lost," Stone Wolf said, bowing his head. "The heart of the People is gone from us!"

If the fight was over, its effects were scarcely beginning. Stone Wolf and the Foxes returned to find the camp astir with panic.

"The Pawnees have taken *Mahuts!*" the women cried. Children collected their family's possessions, and lodges were broken down.

"What's this?" Younger Wolf asked. "We must make a council and decide how best to attack the Pawnees."

"We must recover *Mahuts!*" Stone Wolf shouted.

"Our medicine is broken," Bear Claw said, flinging his lance aside. "We must flee. The enemy is close upon us."

"This was the brave heart who you followed," Stone Wolf muttered. "See how he has led you to ignore the medicine trail? The Arrows should have been renewed. Instead their power is broken, and they are lost."

"Was this my doing?" Bear Claw asked. "No, it was our Arrow-keeper who brought us to this end. He pledged to keep the heart of the people safe!"

"You had no ears for my words!" Stone Wolf argued. "And when the fight turned against us, you who might have won the day ran away."

"Stop this quarreling!" Younger Wolf cried. "We must make a council and decide."

"I've decided," Bear Claw said, hurrying his woman toward his lodge. "I will take my people to safety."

"As you did last winter?" Stone Wolf asked. "Hear me, brothers, the Arrows may yet be recovered and their power restored."

167

"No, we are beaten," Bull said, lowering his head. "It's as you said, Stone Wolf. We broke the medicine, and now we are run by our enemies."

"Not all of us," Wood Snake argued. "The Foxes fought well. *Ayyyy!* Stone Wolf led a remembered fight. The Pawnees will remember him."

"We, too, will remember," Red Bird said, frowning. "This is the day we lost *Mahuts*. It's the death of our power, and the beginning of the long walk toward Hanging Road."

Stone Wolf dismounted and made his way around the camp, urging the men to find courage and mount a fresh attack. The People had lost their heart, though. Their faces reflected their despair, and they broke down their lodges and scattered to the winds.

"Nah nih, it's hopeless," Younger Wolf declared. "We must decide where to go."

"Will nobody follow me?" Stone Wolf cried.

"Our horses are weak," Thunder Coat observed. "Many require time to mend their wounds. We need your medicine to make us whole, Stone Wolf, and to celebrate my brother's coup."

"Uncle, we must go," White Horn agreed. "The Pawnees will recover and strike our trail. A man of the People must remember the defenseless ones. You taught me that."

Stone Wolf gazed into the shaken faces of the children. Yes, they were in peril. But to leave *Mahuts* . . .

"We must go," Younger Wolf said, placing a heavy hand on the Arrow-keeper's shoulder and leading the way to the Arrow Lodge. "There's much to do. Later, when our ponies are fat and the men are well, we'll make the required prayers and fall upon the Paw-nees."

"Yes," others agreed. "We'll return when we're strong again."

"When we're strong again?" Stone Wolf whispered. *"Mahuts* is gone. Strong again? Our power is broken! We won't be strong again until it's restored to us."

Fifteen

The People were lost, bewildered.

"How can we perform the Arrow renewal when *Ma-huts* is lost to us?" some cried.

Others set off into the hills to set their dead on scaffolds and mourn their passing.

"We should all of us mourn this time," Stone Wolf declared. "The heart of the People has been torn from us. We are without life, all of us."

But even as some were mourned, the Foxes gathered to welcome into their ranks boys who had proven themselves in the fight against the Pawnees and the flight that followed. Some as young as thirteen summers, like Ferret Boy, were brought forth by their fathers and uncles.

It was also the time White Horn received the name won in battle.

"Brothers, look on this young man," Thunder Coat said as he led his brother to the fire. White Horn was stripped to the waist so that his battle scars danced in the firelight. Aside from the marks left by the crow raiders long ago, new, fresh marks left by Pawnee lances drew his elders' attention.

"Long has he ridden among us," Red Bird observed. "His trail has been full of brave heart deeds."

"Ayyyy!" the other howled.

"He has learned the medicine trail, too," Wood Snake observed. "He will be a man to follow."

"Ayyyy!" the younger Foxes shouted.

"Look here!" Thunder Coat cried, holding up the painted lance taken from the Pawnees. "When others ran, he fought on."

"Yes," Younger Wolf agreed, rising to face the young man. "You've carried a good name, White Horn, but now I ask you. Is it the one you wish to carry?"

"I've earned another name," White Horn declared. "This old one is useless now, and I give it away to any who would have it."

"Ayyyy!" the Foxes yelled. "Who will give the nameless one a suitable present?"

"It's for me to do," Stone Wolf said, stepping to his young friend's side and resting both hands on his shoulders. "Long you have followed the straight road, Nephew, and always your eyes have seen the truth. This stick you've taken," he added, touching the trophy lance, "speaks loudly of your courage. Let it be that you be called Talking Stick."

"Yes," the others agreed. "It's a brave heart name."

"Here," Thunder Coat said, bringing three ponies to the council. "I give these presents in honor of my brother, Talking Stick."

171

The horses were given those with the greatest need, and all considered the naming well done.

"Once you told me I would have to make a choice one day," Talking Stick told Stone Wolf afterward. "My brother wishes me to ride with him the soldier road."

"It's a good, straight road, and Thunder Coat is a fine man to follow."

"My heart calls me to the medicine trail, though," Talking Stick explained. "I have learned the many cures, and I understand the ceremonies. If I come to you, one day perhaps I will come to be Arrow-keeper."

"That was before," Stone Wolf lamented. *"Mahuts* is gone from us."

"It's been said nothing is ever lost from a man who searches hard enough. Maybe we can find the Arrows and restore the heart of the People."

"It would be a good thing," Stone Wolf agreed. "Come. We'll smoke and consider it."

But although there was much talk of going to *Noahvose* and remaking the medicine Arrows, no hint of it came to Stone Wolf's dreams. The Arrow Lodge remained empty, and the bands continued to break apart and seek their own way.

"Many have turned to the Suhtai, the old ones, for Medicine Hat remains in the hands of the People," Younger Wolf noted. "Our band grows ever smaller."

"Yes," Stone Wolf admitted. "The others blame me for our misfortunes."

"Bear Claw talks loudly, and his voice carries in whispers through the lodges. Some have forgotten it

172

was he who led us to the Pawnees before the Arrows were renewed. He, too, hurried the attack before prayers could be completed."

"If I had spoken louder and stronger, the People would never have followed him."

"*Nah nih,* they followed their hearts," Younger Wolf argued. "Now they blame you because they know they themselves brought this dark time upon us."

"But it was my obligation to lead them away from such dangers," Stone Wolf insisted. "I failed."

In those first days, the loss of *Mahuts* tore at the soul of the People, but it was later that the true impact was seen.

"How will we find Bull Buffalo?" Wood Snake asked. "Last summer we knew hunger, but *Mahuts* was with us. Now what will we do?"

"Send out scouts," Younger Wolf suggested. "Keep the old ceremonies with great care. Make medicine and trust that Man Above will not forget our needs."

All those things were done, but Bull Buffalo proved elusive. Signs were everywhere, and other tribes boasted of their successful hunts while passing the camps of the *Tsis tsis tas*.

"Come, hunt with us," Stone Wolf's Oglala cousin Long Walker suggested. "Our medicine remains strong."

"No," Stone Wolf answered. "If we are ever to regain our heart, we must practice the old ways. I will suffer and make prayers. Perhaps then we'll find meat."

But summer passed, and only game enough to fill the bellies of the people fell into their hands. There was no buffalo meat smoked for winter, and few deer fell to arrows in the hard face moons. When snow covered the country, the children cried out in hunger. And the dying began.

"You've brought us to this!" Red Bird screamed when his youngest son climbed Hanging Road. *"Ayyyy!* How can we have given *Mahuts* into the care of such a foolish person!"

"Maybe it's time for me to give up my obligations and give the Arrow Lodge over to the care of another," Stone Wolf said. "A dream might come to someone else."

"No, you have always been a man of the People, *Nah nih,"* Younger Wolf argued. "If the medicine ceremonies come into the hands of another, how can we be certain the welfare of the defenseless ones will remain foremost? Bear Claw would leave the helpless behind him as so much dung."

"Talking Stick knows the rituals," Stone Wolf suggested. "He would do well."

"Our family has always been trusted with *Mahuts,"* Younger Wolf pointed out. "Talking Stick is young, and his dreams are full of confusion. How can he direct others when he cannot find his own way?"

"You must remain Arrow-keeper," Yellow Hand Pony added, stepping to Stone Wolf's side. "It was you who foresaw these terrible times and warned us of our mistake. If we had listened, the People would have kept *Mahuts,* and we would enjoy harmony and prosperity."

"It's so," Wood Snake agreed. "Brave up, Stone Wolf. We've known worse winters."

But winter had scarcely begun. As the snows deepened, and the scarcity of game grew worse, few remembered harder times. Old people gazed into the hungry eyes of children and gave up their food. With skin stretched tightly over bones, and winter's torment striking hard, the grandfathers and grandmothers walked off into the snow and let the cold carry their shades across to the other side.

"Will the big wheel moon find any of us still alive?" Arrow Dancer asked his father.

"Your uncle has gone to kill a deer," Stone Wolf told the boys. "Soon we'll have meat."

But when Younger Wolf did kill a buck, Stone Wolf meted out ribs and shoulder slices to others so that little meat remained for the Arrow-keeper's family.

"You should put the needs of your own sons first," Talking Stick complained when he noticed how gaunt Crow Boy had become.

"If I did," Stone Wolf explained, "do you think Man Above would give my brother's arrow the true aim? No, it's our suffering that brings us success."

But even that often failed to bring in game. Stone Wolf listened to the whining children and searched the empty, hungry eyes of his own sons.

"Man Above, haven't we suffered enough?" Stone Wolf called to the midnight sky. "Guide us safely through these new trials."

Stone Wolf bared his breast and cut his flesh, but the blood failed to flow. The cold air coated his brown

175

skin with white frost, and he felt a terrible fist grip his heart.

"Gladly would I give up my life for the defenseless ones," Stone Wolf told the stars shining overhead. *"Mahuts* is lost. Are we all to die?"

The wind seemed to whine a promise of better days. When Stone Wolf could bear the cold no longer, he returned inside the lodge and wrapped himself in his buffalo hides. It was then White Buffalo Cow visited his dreams, showing him a rich valley where her children endured the winter starving.

"Awake, Brother," Stone Wolf said when he arose the next morning. "Younger Wolf, we must break down camp and move north."

"Why?" Younger Wolf asked. "The wind is bitter and harsh there, and we've found shelter from it here."

"I've had a dream," Stone Wolf explained.

So it was the remaining lodges were torn down, and the People again journeyed. The promised valley was as foreseen, and the men hurried to slay buffalo.

"Wait!" Stone Wolf called. "Remember the prayers."

But desperate men have no ears and no patience. The buffalo stampeded out onto the plain, all but two, who were killed and skinned. But where the herd would have fattened even the frailest child by spring, the two solitary bulls merely revived the appetite of the little ones.

"What can we do now?" Younger Wolf asked in despair.

"Send parties out into the snowdrifts," Stone Wolf

suggested. First warn the People to eat sparingly. What meat we have must last many days."

The criers went from lodge to lodge, warning the People, but many ate all they had anyway.

"We may starve tomorrow," one woman said. "What use would meat put aside be then?"

Stone Wolf himself took little, leaving more for his sons. Younger Wolf also took a small share. But it was Red Willow Woman who most sacrificed herself for the little ones.

"She who has been as a mother is sick," Arrow Dancer told Stone Wolf. "Her eyes are empty, and her breathing short."

Stone Wolf hurried to examine the Oglala woman, but she had left the lodge. Together with Arrow Dancer and Crow Boy, he traced her tracks in the snow to a rocky outcropping. There, wrapped in a thick elk robe, lay Red Willow Woman.

"She's gone from us," Stone Wolf said as he felt her icy wrist. "She knew death was near, so she took the long walk alone to spare us the sadness."

"She's started the climb up Hanging Road then," Arrow Dancer said solemnly. "Our sister is there to show her the way. I won't cry for her. She's in a better place."

"Yes," Stone Wolf agreed. "But our lodge will miss her touch."

"And her cooking," Younger Wolf noted when he returned from the buffalo hunt. "She was a woman to know."

"And to remember," Stone Wolf added.

They mourned her as an aunt and set aside her few

belongings until it was time to give them and the ghost up, as was Oglala custom, a year from the day of her death.

The Horse Fattening Moon found Stone Wolf's band in the mountains near *Noahvose.* Deer and rabbits flourished in that place, and the hunters were returning with much meat. Soon tubers could be dug from the earth, and many good plants would green themselves.

"Nah nih, this is Dove Woman," Younger Wolf said when returning from the hunt one afternoon. "She and her son, Porcupine, have no one to provide them food. I've brought them to share my kill."

"Ah, that's a good thing," Stone Wolf said, welcoming the young woman. "Your son and my youngest are much the same age."

"I'm older," Crow Boy declared.

"Only one year," the boy, who was called Porcupine, said. "I'm nearly as tall."

"Open your heart, *Naha',* and see he has no father," Stone Wolf said. "Go and bring your brother. Perhaps you three may find some game to join."

"Ayyyy!" Crow Boy cried. "It's a good idea."

As the boys raced off, Dove Woman took charge of the cooking and chased the men away.

"I cook good venison," she assured them. "It's a woman's task, and you men will only get in the way."

Younger Wolf led his brother a short distance away. Then the two of them halted and watched Dove Woman put the camp in order.

"She works hard," Younger Wolf observed. "And she's lonely, with a son to raise. *Nah nih,* you have

178

been too long without a wife. The healing cures require a woman's touch, and your sons need a mother."

"I'm too long unmarried?" Stone Wolf cried. "You have never taken a wife, Brother."

"I thought to ask her, *Nah nih,* but she spoke only of you. Her eyes have long been on you, I think. She's pretty, and she walks the straight road. She would not bring suffering like the Crow woman."

"Has her husband long been dead?" Stone Wolf asked. "I don't recall her traveling with our band."

"She married a Bowstring who was slain when the Pawnees took *Mahuts,*" Younger Wolf explained. "She came to us when Bear Claw would not find food for her son."

"It's a heartless man who would allow a boy to suffer."

"There's been much starving among the Claw's band," Younger Wolf said. "Two days ago I left a whole deer with them, and all that remained when I returned was bone."

"And you say this woman thinks well of me?"

"Yes," Younger Wolf said, grinning. "She's young and can give you more sons. *Ayyyy,* it would be good to rebuild our People with my brother's blood!"

Stone Wolf nodded. He felt a rare longing for a woman's touch, for a quiet smile, for comforting words he'd rarely heard.

"I'll talk to her," Stone Wolf agreed. "Maybe tonight we'll walk the river."

"You remember how it's done?" Younger Wolf asked, grinning. "You've been old a long time."

"Not so long as to have forgotten everything,"

Stone Wolf insisted. "Not important things."

After eating, Younger Wolf led the boys off, and Stone Wolf watched Dove Woman put the camp in order again.

"You cook well," he told her. "You have brightened our camp. Where is your lodge?"

"I have no lodge," she explained. "The Bowstrings broke it down and made a giveaway when my husband fell. Porcupine and I make a shelter of buffalo hides when some old one doesn't invite us into his lodge."

"You should have shelter," Stone Wolf grumbled. "My wife is dead, and the woman who cooked for us, too. I would invite you to stay here with us if you consider it appropriate."

"You would adopt me as a sister then," she said, sighing. "Or as a daughter even."

"Am I so old?" Stone Wolf asked.

"You don't mean to dishonor me surely."

"No, I thought perhaps you would consider being my wife."

"You don't know me," Dove Woman declared. "Not now."

"Did I once before?"

"Once, long ago, before I started to walk woman's road, we swam the rivers together. You called me Little Fish."

"I remember," Stone Wolf said, grinning. "You were forever diving under and surprising us."

"It was a girl's game."

"We all of us loved those fine days," Stone Wolf declared. "But then we grew older. You took a husband among the Bowstrings and left our camp."

180

"Yes," she said, sighing.

"I've missed the remembering of those good summers," he said, taking her hand. "I'm older, and much has happened. Some wouldn't consider me a proper husband for anyone. I know I stand low in the eyes of many."

"Higher in the eyes of others," she assured him.

"My sons need a mother, and yours needs a father. I would make the match if only to bring our sons comfort."

"My heart holds more, Stone Wolf," she said, touching his cheek. "Others may see the Arrowkeeper, but I know, too, the boy who swam Shell River and walked with dreams. You will bring the People back to better times. I would help make the road you walk an easy one."

"I have need of woman's hands," Stone Wolf said. "With the curing and the prayers."

"And I need a man's strength," she said. "For Porcupine. And for myself."

"We'll consider it well," Stone Wolf promised. "You can stay with us while the hunt is organized. Then, if you decide it's the place you seek, I would have you walk the land as my wife."

"It's a fine idea," she told him.

"Little Fish, you surprise me still," he said, holding her close.

Sixteen

Stone Wolf had never known a woman's love. He'd passed his boyhood with old Cloud Dancer in the Arrow Lodge, standing tall early as an Arrow-keeper's grandson was destined to do. He was in his twentieth summer when he took Star Eyes into his lodge. She had never been a true wife. Her mating had been a captive's compliance, and her face had never told the lie that it was otherwise.

Dove Woman did, indeed, surprise him. She was a mother to the children, offering kind words and encouragement. She sang to them on nights when Thunderbird shook the heavens, and she fashioned good clothes from the skins Stone Wolf provided.

Stone Wolf approached her cautiously, displaying great respect. She merely laughed and drew him close.

"I'm Little Fish no longer," she said, laughing as she overwhelmed him. The warmth flowed from her as a great flood, and Stone Wolf felt himself revived from a long, cold sleep.

"I never imagined such a thing possible," Stone Wolf told his brother. "We've been together only days, but I would give up my arms before I would lose her. She's the warming fire my heart has searched for."

"Yes, I see it in your eyes," Younger Wolf replied. "And in hers. It's a good thing you've found each other."

Dove Woman didn't come alone to Stone Wolf's lodge. Her small son Porcupine, a boy of four summers, spread his hides beside Crow Boy.

"It's good you've come to us," Arrow Dancer told the boy. *"Ne' hyo* is a good man to show you the way."

"Soon we'll help you make arrows," Crow Boy said, helping Porcupine make his bed. "When you're taller, maybe you can come when we make the morning prayers."

Porcupine nodded solemnly. He spoke only with his mother then, and he shrank from Stone Wolf's gaze.

"Give him time," Dove Woman urged. "He's known many men, but always they've gone away."

"Silence shows respect," Stone Wolf told the child. "If more men kept quiet when they step onto unfamiliar country, they would fare better."

Porcupine nodded soberly, but he uttered no word.

On days when the men rested from the hunt, Stone Wolf collected the three boys and led them to the river to join the swimming. They were small to go into the deep water where the young men splashed about, but Stone Wolf invited them to bathe and swim as he did.

"It's good a man washes off yesterday's memories and greets the day new," Stone Wolf explained. "My grandfather waited until Younger Wolf and I were older before bringing us to the river, but the world has changed. We are few, and it may be that boys will walk man's road at an early age."

"Yes, *Ne' hyo,*" Arrow Dancer agreed. "Already boys of twelve hunt Bull Buffalo. I, too, will join them when four summers have passed."

"Don't hurry them, *Naha',*" Stone Wolf pleaded. "These good times will pass fast enough. I have need of my sons' laughter."

They climbed onto his back and fought to pull him under, but they were small, and he was too strong. Only when Younger Wolf joined the attack did the Arrow-keeper sink beneath the surface. And then he emerged, thrashing his arms and driving the little ones to the bank.

"*Ne' hyo,* you're not angry?" Arrow Dancer asked.

"Angry?" Stone Wolf asked, scratching his head. "How can a father be angry at his sons for being boys? I might as well expect my horse to fly or an eagle to grow scales."

That notion brought a cackle from Crow Boy, and even Porcupine grinned.

"Come, dress yourselves," Stone Wolf urged. "We'll ride today."

"Not far, *Nah nih,*" Younger Wolf cautioned. "The horses need rest."

"Then we should catch some fresh ones," Stone Wolf declared. "It's time we raided the Crows again. They have the best horses."

"And the worst guards," Younger Wolf noted. "First we must shoot game. The little ones are far too thin, and we should smoke some against the future need."

184

"Yes," Stone Wolf agreed. "It will be a short ride. Even a boy needs to feel himself mounted, though."

"I remember my first ride," Younger Wolf began, and the boys paused to listen. It was an often told tale, and even Porcupine had heard it. But there was joy in the sharing of such things, and Younger Wolf stood tall in his nephews' eyes.

It was a long summer, that second year when the People hunted Bull Buffalo without the help of *Mahuts*. The bands were scattered, and when the pipe carriers rode out to gather the People, few responded.

"We'll make the New Life Lodge," Stone Wolf insisted. "Those who are absent must walk their own road."

Unspoken was the fear that many had climbed Hanging Road. But once the world was reborn, and the hunt organized, word came from other bands that life continued.

"Many have joined their camps to the Lakotas," Younger Wolf explained. "Others rode too far south last winter to arrive in time for the gathering. Maybe they will come for the hunting."

Stone Wolf hoped so, but he thought it unlikely.

Wood Snake, Thunder Coat, and Red Bird made the New Life Lodge that summer, and as Stone Wolf oversaw the prayers and the singing, he sensed the People's pain was passing.

"If we can find Bull Buffalo and hunt as before, we may recover our spirits," Thunder Coat declared. "The children are hungry, and too many lack good coats to keep winter's bite from their ribs."

Stone Wolf nodded his agreement. The next day he left camp with Younger Wolf and rode into the low hills to the west. There he starved himself to bring on a dream. He cut flesh from his arms, prayed, and danced, but the vision didn't come. In despair he made strong medicine and drank tea made of jimsonweed. Afterward his head floated through clouds of gray mist, and voices called to him from the other side.

"Ne' hyo, the People need you," Dawn Dancer told him sadly. "You must stay to guide them."

"Nothing lives long," Cloud Dancer chanted.

Finally White Buffalo Cow led him off across broken country toward Shell River. The buffalo were thick as reeds along the banks.

"Go there, but hunt in the old manner," she instructed. "Make the required prayers, and take only what the People need. Keep the young men in hand, and guard your ponies."

Stone Wolf tried to answer, but he had no voice. His throat was dry, and his lips were cracked.

Man Above, lead me back, Stone Wolf prayed. *I have work to do.*

He awoke in a sweat. Younger Wolf covered him with a buffalo hide and tried to steady his shivering shoulders.

"Nah nih, you're cold and hot at the same time!" Younger Wolf exclaimed. "What must I do?"

"Keep me awake," Stone Wolf muttered. "Bring me closer to the fire and cover me. It's the chill I fear, not the fever."

All through the night and well into the following morning Younger Wolf knelt beside his brother, fighting off the shade that threatened to steal Stone Wolf's consciousness. Dawn painted the land yellow-orange, and its warming rays spread a glow through Stone's Wolf's chest.

"The chills have passed," he told his brother. "It's time we returned. White Buffalo Cow has shown me where to find Bull Buffalo. It's time we made the prayers and began the hunt."

When Stone Wolf told the council of his vision, many urged the chiefs to send out scouts and hasten the hunt.

"The little ones are still hungry from winter's scarcity," Red Bird declared. "We must waste no time."

"You've learned nothing," Talking Stick argued. "We must make the medicine prayers as Stone Wolf says. His medicine will bring us success. If you ignore his counsel, more will surely die."

"Prayers are important," Wood Snake agreed. "Let's make the proper ceremonies and begin. The little ones have suffered long enough."

"*Ayyyy!*" the young men shouted. "We go to hunt Bull Buffalo!"

Stone Wolf took great care with the rituals that summer. He carefully made the required prayers, and when singing was needed, he saw to it that the correct songs were performed. There was dancing, too, and the young men engaged in mock battles and hunts.

Later Stone Wolf marked the hunters with the white powder made of pounded buffalo horn and led them in an ancient prayer.

187

"Remember," Stone Wolf told them, "use only stone-tipped arrows this first day, and strike only those cows and bulls we need to feed the People."

There was grumbling about the old arrows, for some of the younger men required three or four shots to kill a buffalo with the blunt-pointed projectiles.

"How will we manage to kill enough to feed the hungry?" Yellow Hand Pony asked. "My brother's son is hungry."

"Do it as I've instructed," Stone Wolf replied. "You often talk of how you would like to have known how the old ones hunted. Now you will see for yourself."

The Pony still appeared confused, but he accepted the words for the truth they held. He, more than some others had come to trust the medicine of the Arrow-keeper, and he respected the wisdom Stone Wolf's words had always possessed.

After making the final medicine prayers, Stone Wolf followed his brother south toward Shell River. Young and old, the men formed small bands to locate the buffalo. Where before the beasts were dispersed over a vast area, now Bull Buffalo seemingly awaited the killing lances with great patience.

"There they are," Younger Wolf declared, waving at the black sea of animals.

"Man Above, we thank you for driving the hunger from our camp," Stone Wolf said, gazing skyward. "*Ayyyy!* Now we must brave up and begin the hunt."

The others nodded somberly and formed a line. Then they charged the buffalo, shrieking as they notched arrows and drove them deep into the hairy creatures. The hunters whipped their horses and pressed themselves closer. The stone-tipped arrows cut deep into the buffaloes' vitals, and one after another fell.

"*Nah nih,* it's a good day to be alive!" Younger Wolf shouted after dropping a huge bull. "Here's meat to make the little ones strong."

"*Ayyyy!*" Stone Wolf howled. "It's good you've made such a clean kill."

As buffalo collapsed and died, the women appeared with their pony drags. Soon the butchering had commenced, and meat was prepared for smoking.

"You should kill one yourself," Younger Wolf urged after a time. "*Nah nih,* your aim is true. Kill one."

"Our needs are satisfied already," Stone Wolf objected. "Leave our brother buffalo to flee unhurt."

"Today we'll have plenty," Younger Wolf agreed, "but what of tomorrow? Winter's not far away."

"We'll hunt again in autumn," Stone Wolf said. "Then we'll take more meat, and the hides will be thick and haired over, fit for winter coats."

That first day White Buffalo Cow gave generously of her children. Even using the old arrows, the People struck down many buffalo. And in the two days that followed, hunters had greater success using the iron-tipped arrows and what rifles were available.

"Now we will turn away from Bull Buffalo," Stone Wolf announced the third day. "Man Above, you've been generous. We will grow strong again while respecting the life of our brother, Bull Buffalo."

"Yes," Talking Stick cried. "Food enough has been

collected. Let the herd go."

There were some who argued the People should ride in Bull Buffalo's shadow, but most followed their Arrow-keeper's lead.

"It's best we make camp in a safe place," Stone Wolf told them. "Then there will be time for boys' games, courtship, and plant gathering."

"It's good to think of those good things," Younger Wolf noted. "They will breathe new life into the young ones and give cause for laughter."

"It's been too often absent from our lodges."

"And our hearts," Younger Wolf declared. "You've brought back the old remembered times to me, *Nah nih*. It's good. I've missed them."

When not hunting, the brothers passed the warm days of summer crafting arrows and bows of willow and green ash for the little ones. As Stone Wolf fixed small flint points to the shafts, he spoke of old ways and time long past.

"Ne' hyo, we'll remember these tales," Arrow Dancer vowed.

"It's good to hold these things close to your heart," Stone Wolf said, drawing the boys close. "A man who is rooted in the traditions of the People is like the strong oak which stands on the hillside. Even the strongest wind may bend him to its will, but it can't tear him from the earth. No, he will endure, even as we will."

Stone Wolf smiled. He knew, even as the dream had promised, that these young ones would be the future.

190

In sharing the past, he was the bridge which would insure their survival, and that of the *Tsis tsis tas*.

The future glowed brighter now with each sunrise. Making the dawn prayers with the boys at his side, Stone Wolf thanked Man Above for hanging the sun in the sky and greening the earth.

"Thank you, Grandfather, for breathing life into these small ones," the Arrow-keeper added. "Their eyes shine with new life, and they will grow tall and walk man's road in the old way, with respect."

"*Ne' hyo,* does Man Above hear our words?" Arrow Dancer asked one morning as they headed to the river to join in the morning swim.

"Man Above is all things," Stone Wolf explained. "He is earth and rocks and trees. He sees with eagle's eyes, and he dams the streams with beaver's tail. Don't you feel him always with you when the cold winds cut into your flesh, or when the sun burns in the summer sky? *Ayyyy!* The Great Mystery is always with us, *Naha'.*"

"Man Above wouldn't have time to watch boys' pranks, though," Crow Boy said, his eyes nervously glancing around.

"Man Above sees everything," Stone Wolf answered. "But his heart is often young, and he remembers a boy's laughter and the need for games."

"And if he doesn't, there's always Trickster," Younger Wolf added. "Ah, he's the one to watch for. When you think you have a clear shot at a deer, he will send a hawk to stir the birds to flight and disturb your prey. It's Trickster who plays the coyote games on the scouts, washing away Bull Buffalo's trail or swelling a

191

river so it can't be crossed. Trickster made ants to visit our camps and sting our flesh. He's always the one who insists we remain watchful."

But Trickster appeared to be occupied elsewhere that summer. Buffalo steaks and tubers, turnips and onions, they all drove the hungry eyes from the children and restored health. No longer could Stone Wolf trace boys' ribs outlined by skin stretched too tightly over bone. Watching them wrestle and race each other, a man's heart grew strong with hope.

"It's a good time to be alive!" Younger Wolf boasted.

Stone Wolf tried to echo his brother's cry, but *Mahuts* haunted his every moment.

"Ne' hyo, are you sick?" Arrow Dancer asked.

"My heart aches for what we have lost," Stone Wolf told his son. "We can not long enjoy prosperity when the Arrows remain in the hands of others."

"Talking Stick says the Arrows are gone, but their power remains," Arrow Dancer replied. "He says you hold the medicine cures and the ceremonies in your head, and when you make the appropriate prayers, *Mahuts* gives the power."

"Maybe," Stone Wolf said, wishing he could accept such a notion.

"Younger Wolf is right," Arrow Dancer argued. "It's a good time. When have the People been so strong? See how the women grow fat! Even Porcupine is becoming taller."

"Yes," Crow Boy said, nudging the silent child. "And his mother's grown fat as a melon."

"It's not fat," Porcupine said, stunning them with

his words. "It's the child she carries."

"Is it so, *Ne' hyo?* She is giving us a brother?" Arrow Dancer cried.

"Soon," Stone Wolf told them. "A brother or a sister. It would be a good thing to have a girl again in this lodge."

"I miss Dawn Dancer, too," Arrow Dancer said, wrapping an arm around his father. "But sons are good also."

"Yes," Stone Wolf said, touching each boy in turn. "But I have three already."

"Girls are troublesome," Crow Boy grumbled. "But one could help Dove Woman with the cooking."

"Yes, our mother works too hard," Arrow Dancer agreed. "You could take another wife, *Ne' hyo.*"

Stone Wolf laughed at them. The warmth flowed through the lodge and chased even the sadness and loss away for a time. Yes, it was a good time to be alive. And better days still lay ahead.

Seventeen

The Dirt in the Face moon of late autumn found Stone Wolf's band camped in the shadow of *Noahvose* once more. The buffalo hunting had been good, and women had filled baskets with plums and chokecherries. For once there was plenty to eat and good coats to keep the People warm when the snows arrived.

Stone Wolf nevertheless prayed hard for a mild winter. Dove Woman's child would not see light before snow fell, and a winter child's road was always hard.

"A son of Stone Wolf will not fear the cold," Dove Woman assured him. "Already he stirs inside me, fighting to join his father and hunt Bull Buffalo."

"It may be a daughter," he argued.

"No, he's far too disagreeable," she said, laughing. "And the People need strong young men to walk the sacred path."

The boys also wanted a brother, as did Younger Wolf.

"Dove Woman is young," Younger Wolf noted.

"She will give you other children. It's always best the son comes first."

"I have three good sons," Stone Wolf insisted.

"Yes, but this child you have made with a good wife. *Ayyyy,* he will have a father's strength and a mother's love to start him on man's road."

Stone Wolf laughed. Could anyone show greater love than Red Willow Woman? And now that Porcupine was talking, the boy seemed always to have been in his father's lodge.

For a time, though, Stone Wolf had other concerns. The hard days since the loss of *Mahuts* had brought much illness, and if the winter need was great, he had few medicines to offer the sick.

"I must collect what's needed," Stone Wolf announced. "I'll go into the hills and gather leaves and berries. I'll dig roots from Mother Earth."

"I'll go to keep watch," Younger Wolf offered.

"No, it's best you stay to watch the little ones," Stone Wolf replied. "There are Crow raiders nearby, and Pawnees to the south."

"I'll go," Arrow Dancer volunteered.

"Yes, you can learn how it's done," Stone Wolf said, nodding at his son.

"He's too small to help in a fight," Younger Wolf argued.

"We'll invite Talking Stick," Arrow Dancer suggested. "He knows the medicine cures, and he's brave. He would run the enemy in a fight."

"It's a good choice," Younger Wolf admitted. "But will he come? More and more he seeks his own way."

"He's no longer a boy to learn the cures or help

with singing," Stone Wolf pointed out. "He rides with his brother as a man, and he must be approached with respect."

"I'll take a pipe to him," Younger Wolf said, frowning.

"No, that's for me to do," Stone Wolf insisted. "Arrow Dancer, prepare our belongings and bring horses. I will speak to the Stick."

Stone Wolf found Talking Stick much changed. Even with the first chills of winter on the wind, the young man walked the camp bare-chested, revealing the many scars that marked his flesh. Here was the boy who had once made his bed at Stone Wolf's elbow, who had suffered in New Life Lodge, who had won a shield in the fight against the Pawnees when *Mahuts* was lost. Now he'd grown tall, and his arms were iron.

"Why bring a pipe to me?" the young man asked. "You don't mean to ride to war?"

"No, I go to gather medicine," Stone Wolf explained. "My oldest son and I. We need a watcher."

"There are others," Talking Stick grumbled.

"It's best to choose a man with far-seeing eyes," Stone Wolf answered. "And one I trust my life and that of my son with. You were always a good companion, Talking Stick, and I've missed your questions."

"I've found the answers now, Uncle."

"To all of them?"

"I've walked man's road a long time. Was it so different for you?"

196

"I've never found all the answers," Stone Wolf said, drawing back the pipe. "Not to the important questions. You're right to walk your own road, though. We all do that in time. Soon you'll lead the young men."

"Many follow me already."

"Then it's good you know the medicine trail," Stone Wolf said, clasping his young friend's hand. "Remember you always stand tall in my eyes."

"I know, Uncle," Talking Stick said, holding Stone Wolf's fingers a moment before releasing them.

Stone Wolf turned back toward the Arrow Lodge, but was met by Wood Snake first.

"I've heard of your need," the Snake said. "My older son, Whirlwind, now walks man's road. He's killed his first buffalo, and he stole ponies from the Crows."

"He's young, but serious," Stone Wolf observed. "I would welcome him."

"I'll send him to you," Wood Snake said, nodding. "His brother, Ferret Boy, who you once made well, asks to come also."

"It's good brothers ride together," Stone Wolf said, recalling the many journeys undertaken with Younger Wolf. "Send them both."

And so, after making the dawn prayers that next morning, Stone Wolf led the three young men toward *Noahvose*. There, where the wind blew solemn, whispering a mournful melody through the trees, Stone Wolf collected the medicine leaves. He showed Arrow Dancer which ones to dig or cut, but insisted the boy take no more than two each day.

"As my grandfather once told me, a young man must be patient and show respect for the world," Stone Wolf explained. *"Naha'*, one day you will share your knowledge with others, but now it's for you to learn."

Ferret Boy, too, chose to dig roots.

"My brother watches," Ferret Boy said, pointing to where Whirlwind stood high on the mountainside. "I remember the power of your medicine, Uncle, and would learn the healing cures."

"Consider it well," Stone Wolf told the young man. "It's not a thing learned like the crafting of arrows or the stalking of a deer. A man must devote his whole heart and mind. There's suffering to endure, and much effort."

"Yes, but to bring the sick back to the People. *Ayyyy!* That's a great thing."

Great? Stone Wolf wondered. *Hard, yes, but great?*

Ten days they were together on *Noahvose,* collecting what was needed to fill the medicine pouches. Long days of boiling leaves and pounding berries remained to make the medicine ready, but winter afforded such time.

"You've done well," Stone Wolf told his young helpers at last. "There's but one thing left to do."

"Yes?" Whirlwind asked. The young man had passed just sixteen summers, and his voice was only now making man's sounds. He was small, too, but his flesh was taut as stretched rawhide, and he seemed always to seek the hard things to do.

"My dreams told me nearby there's a spring," Stone Wolf explained. "There, where wolf comes to drink,

198

lives a great bull elk. This old one, who bears the scars of many hard fights, seeks a brave death, and my stone-tipped arrows would grant him that death. On his hide I'll paint my winter count, and his teeth and horns will make strong medicine to protect the young men when it's time to fight the enemy again."

"I'll kill the elk for you," Whirlwind offered.

"It's for me to do, but you are all welcome to come," Stone Wolf told them. "See how the old ones hunted. If this elk gives his life up to us, I will make you three the first charms. *Ayyyy!* Their medicine will be strong."

"I'll come, *Ne' hyo,*" Arrow Dancer declared, and the sons of Wood Snake added their requests.

"Then come and learn," Stone Wolf told them.

First they made a camp near the spring. Ferret Boy built a fire, and Stone Wolf filled a pipe.

"We make this smoke to show our respect," Stone Wolf explained. "Then we will make prayers to Bull Elk."

As Stone Wolf passed the pipe, Arrow Dancer touched it but briefly to his lips, for he was unaccustomed to the taste of tobacco. Ferret Boy took but a little smoke in, and Whirlwind took care not to swallow any. Stone Wolf emptied the pipe beside the fire and made the required prayers.

"Bull Elk, we seek the strength of your brother," he cried. "Hear my words, and know we come in the old fashion, with pure hearts, to ask this life."

He then added cedar logs to the fire and stripped. As the sweet smoke drifted skyward, Stone Wolf stepped close and brought the smoke over his flesh.

199

He was thus purified and made ready for the hunt. Whirlwind likewise stripped and stepped to the smoke. Stone Wolf waved the smoke over the young man with a feather fan and softly chanted an invocation.

"Next you, Brother," Whirlwind whispered, and Ferret Boy nodded. Bare, the boy seemed too small for the burdens his life had brought, and his slight frame already bore scars won on man's road.

"Man Above, keep this brave heart safe," Stone Wolf whispered as the smoke enveloped Ferret Boy.

Arrow Dancer came last. He seemed oddly out of place among his scarred and solemn elders, but he stood straight as the smoke curled upwards, sweeping over him as a cloud. His eyes watered, but he never flinched.

"It's well," Stone Wolf said as he pulled his son back.

Stone Wolf told them to dress.

"Tomorrow I'll paint your chests. Then we'll hunt the elk."

That night the fire glowed like a thousand stars amid the blackness all around them. The young ones slept uneasily, for the spirits of that sacred place visited their dreams. Stone Wolf himself received a vision of Bull Elk.

"It's good you came," Bull Elk said, dipping his antlered head toward the old elk. The enormous creature towered over the spring. His antlers showed signs of hard fights, and one branch was broken off where a younger bull had overpowered him.

"We come in the old way," Stone Wolf had explained as he stepped out from the trees. Barefoot, naked save for a breechclout, the Wolf drew up alongside the elk and notched an arrow.

"Brother elk, I come to give you rest," Stone Wolf whispered. The elk turned slowly, exposing his shiny breast. Stone Wolf released his arrow, and the stone point drove its way deep into the old elk's heart.

"It's well," Bull Elk proclaimed. The dream faded, and Stone Wolf awoke to find the sun peering over the distant horizon.

"Ne' hyo, did your dream show you the way?" Arrow Dancer asked as he crept to his father's side.

"Yes," Stone Wolf told them. "Leave your moccasins and shirts behind," he added. "Tie up your hair, and come close so I can paint you."

Each in turn did as instructed, and Stone Wolf marked their faces and chests with the ancient symbols of fire and lightning.

"Is there danger?" Arrow Dancer asked when Stone Wolf gripped his son tightly.

"No, only sadness," Stone Wolf explained. "It's always hard to take a brave heart's life. But the People need its strength to make medicine, and so I'll do it."

Stone Wolf had dreamed often, but rarely had a vision been so clear as that of the elk. As he led his young companions through the tall pines, he saw each scene re-enacted. Again he made the brave heart prayers and sang to Bull Elk.

"Give us your power, brother elk," Stone Wolf prayed. "We come in the old way."

As they emerged from the trees, the old elk appeared as in the dream. The boys sighed at the sight of such power and beauty. Yes, it was wonderful to read the respect and awe in their eyes.

"Brother elk, I come to bring you rest," Stone Wolf whispered. The elk stared at the Arrow-keeper and seemed to dip its head in acknowledgment. Then the arrow flew, piercing the tough hide and striking deep and quick. The elk dropped onto one side and died.

"*Ayyyy!*" the boys howled. "It was a brave heart thing!"

"Was there ever such an elk?" Whirlwind cried.

"Once the world was rich with elk," Stone Wolf said, approaching the animal. He made the throat cut and began the skinning.

"It would make a fine robe," Whirlwind observed. "Many make the winter count on deerskins."

"Ah, but they're often old and don't remember it all," Stone Wolf said. "I will paint this old one's hide with all I recall, and it will help my sons remember."

"What could we forget, *Ne' hyo?*" Arrow Dancer asked. "You've told us everything."

"No, I've forgotten myself," Stone Wolf lamented. "So much my grandfather told me. Before him, Touches the Sky knew things, remembered Sweet Medicine's warnings. Today I showed you the old manner of hunting, even as Boy did when he first accepted the Medicine Bow from Man Above. Remember what you've seen so when the People have need of medicine you can come to *Noahvose* and gain power."

"Who could forget such a thing?" Whirlwind asked. "I've hunted Bull Buffalo, and I've fought the

202

Crows, but I never thought to make such prayers or put aside my good rifle and use a bow."

"Once we walked the earth naked, with only stones to use to defend ourselves," Stone Wolf said. "Man Above has brought us many gifts since that time, but often we've forgotten all we owe to our brother creatures and to the spirits around us. No man lives long who can't walk in harmony. Remember, man's road is filled with traps, and only the far-seeing man can keep the People strong and safe."

Chapter Eighteen

Winter painted the world white with snow and ice, freezing the rivers and chasing the birds south. Stone Wolf's band kept its camp beside *Noahvose,* relying on the protection of that sacred place and the abundant game in the hills beyond to keep the People strong in the hard face moons of deepest winter.

Stone Wolf occupied himself making medicine and telling stories to the young ones. Often Arrow Dancer led other boys into the lodge to watch Stone Wolf record the events of his life on the winter count.

"This is the year the blister sickness came," Stone Wolf explained as he pointed to a sketch of Dawn Dancer's burial scaffold. "This is when the People ran the Crows from Shell River."

The other years were there, too, each marked by a remembered event. Last were sketches of the Arrow bundle torn from Bull's lance and the dove that symbolized Stone Wolf's second wife and the peace she had brought to his life.

"Thirty winters is not a long life," Stone Wolf told his brother, "but it often feels long."

"Yes," Younger Wolf agreed. "But you have sons to mark your life and to remember."

"They'll remember Younger Wolf, too," Stone Wolf assured his brother. "As will the young men you've led."

"Ah, but Talking Stick leads the young Foxes now."

"There are women who would share your path. And time to bring sons of your own into the world."

"I'm too old to walk the river road."

"No older than I when you brought Dove Woman to me," Stone Wolf argued. "It would be strong medicine if the People had sons of Younger Wolf to lead the way."

The children, too, encouraged their uncle.

"Ferret Boy has a cousin," Arrow Dancer said. "She doesn't cook well, but she's pretty."

"Talks too much," Crow Boy complained.

"Keep her busy," Arrow Dancer suggested. "She won't have time to talk."

Stone Wolf couldn't help laughing at his sons as they discussed the unmarried women in the band. Later they spoke of Oglala and Sicangu girls.

"If he married a Lakota woman, he would live with her relatives," Arrow Dancer complained. "Who would lead us to hunt Bull Buffalo then?"

"Yes, we'd miss him," Crow Boy agreed. "You must choose from among our band, Uncle."

They soon occupied every waking moment inviting one girl or another to visit Younger Wolf. Finally he drew the boys aside.

"I can find my own woman," Younger Wolf told them. "This Water Basket girl is only fourteen!"

205

"Perhaps," Stone Wolf suggested, "they thought you were used to children in your lodge. Water Basket has seven small brothers, though. You would find the obligations of her family great."

"But you would surely have sons," Arrow Dancer declared. "Her family is known for them."

Talk of children naturally turned to the expected arrival of Dove Woman's child. Her swollen belly was a constant reminder the child would come soon, and her sleeping moans often tore Stone Wolf from his sleep.

"Has time come for you to go to woman's lodge?" he asked.

"Not yet," Dove Woman said. "I'll know when."

Finally one morning she declared it was time.

"I go to be tended by my cousins," she explained. "Be mindful of your obligations to your brothers. Obey your father."

"We will," the boys promised.

Little Wren, who nursed Crow Boy, came to look after the children while their mother awaited the new child. Stone Wolf and Younger Wolf climbed *Noahvose* and made the required prayers.

"Winter's a cruel time to bear children," Younger Wolf observed as they huddled beside a small fire. "You made medicine for her?"

"I've done what I can," Stone Wolf assured his brother. "Now I'll make prayers and suffer in hopes of finding a name."

"*Nah nih,* do you, too, feel it's a boy?"

"I would welcome a son," Stone Wolf replied. "But I still hope for a girl."

"The dream will tell you," Younger Wolf said confidently.

Stone Wolf hoped so. And, in truth, he saw that and much more. As a cloud formed in his mind, Stone Wolf saw old Touches the Sky, his grandfather's uncle. It was the tall one who gave *Mahuts* over to the care of Cloud Dancer, who in turn taught Stone Wolf the obligations of an Arrow-keeper.

"It's good you came to this sacred place," Touches the Sky said solemnly. "The needs of the People are great, and brave hearts will be needed to lead the way."

Wolves howled, and feathers danced in the wind.

"Look," Touches the Sky urged, pointing to a small boy waddling beside the Arrow Lodge. "He is small now, but he, too, will walk the medicine trail."

"Ayyyy!" the wolves howled. "Cloud Dancer is born again to us."

"Here is joined the sacred circle," Touches the Sky explained. "From the beginning our blood has flowed through my brother to Cloud Dancer, through your father, you, and now on to your sons. It's a good thing, Nephew, for all life is a circle, and the completion of a man's path marks the beginning of another."

Stone Wolf warmed. He saw even clearer how he was the bridge to his People's future. Prosperity was sure to find the *Tsis tsis tas* so long as they kept to the straight road.

He awoke to find Ferret Boy standing beside Younger Wolf on the snow-covered slope.

"Dove Woman has given you a son," Younger Wolf said, smiling.

"He waits for you in the camp," Ferret Boy added. "Arrow Dancer sent me to bring you."

"Dove Woman?" Stone Wolf said anxiously. "She is well?"

"Everyone is well," Ferret Boy said, dropping his chin. "It's only your sons want to share their new brother with his father."

"Stone Wolf would have returned when the dreaming was over," Younger Wolf grumbled. "Boys should leave such matters to their elders."

"Yes," Ferret Boy agreed. "But all the camp celebrates this birth."

"Oh?" Stone Wolf asked. "Why?"

"Stone Wolf has another son," Ferret Boy said, confused. "Why? The birth of a brave heart is always cause for gladness."

"He's right," Younger Wolf said as he collected the horses. "A new son of Stone Wolf makes the People stronger."

Stone Wolf himself viewed his companions as snow-crazed. To make such a stir about a child was to tempt disaster. Winter births were rarely blessed.

After extinguishing the fire and packing up their belongings, Stone Wolf followed his brother and Ferret Boy back to the camp. The young Foxes sang brave songs around a council fire, and others shouted a welcome to the returning riders.

"*Ayyyy!*" Whirlwind called. "You have a son!"

Again Stone Wolf frowned. He nodded a greeting, dismounted, and hurried to Dove Woman.

"Here's your father now," Lark Woman said as she brought the child from woman's lodge. "See how big he is? He will be a man to remember."

Stone Wolf accepted the bundle and held the squirming infant. The child didn't seem large at all. He was surprisingly quiet, though, and his large brown eyes seemed unimpressed with the noise in the camp around them.

"Does he have a name?" Lark Woman asked.

"He'll carry his grandfather's boyhood name," Stone Wolf said. "Even as he completes the sacred circle of life, so he begins anew our family."

"Ayyyy!" Younger Wolf shouted. "He is Dreamer."

Stone Wolf passed the infant into Younger Wolf's arms and stepped back to watch the two.

"Never has my cousin been happier," Lark Woman declared. "You are a good husband to her. Some doubted the wisdom of the match, knowing you found no happiness in Star Eyes, but no one can mistake the shine in your eyes, or hers."

"When can I see her?" Stone Wolf asked.

"Soon," Lark Woman promised. "She rests now, but she's young and strong. There was no bleeding, for the birthing went well. Now I should take the child in from the cold."

"Yes," Stone Wolf agreed.

Lark Woman accepted Dreamer from his uncle and returned inside woman's lodge. And Stone Wolf went to share his happiness with his other sons.

"It's a fine thing we've done," Dove Woman said later when she returned to Stone Wolf's lodge. "He'll be a fine boy."

"He's winter born," Stone Wolf said nervously. "His road will be a hard one."

"Hard paths make strong hearts," she whispered. "Don't worry. He'll make his father proud."

Stone Wolf painted four boys on the elk hide, for the birth of Dreamer was considered a remembered thing. A year later, with the child now walking, Stone Wolf sketched a wolf and a painted hoop, for Younger Wolf had taken a wife.

"We'll miss your brother in our lodge," Dove Woman said, "but he'll find Hoop Woman a good choice."

Stone Wolf managed a smile. He was dismayed by the choice. The girl was younger than Whirlwind — just sixteen — and he blamed Star Eyes's weakness on her youth. Later, when their small son was stillborn, it seemed proof of poor judgment.

"She's young," Younger Wolf insisted. "She'll give me a son yet."

Stone Wolf himself was much occupied with his growing family. The boys were becoming taller. Story telling and arrow-making could no longer occupy them. They ran and rode like wind itself, and when they attacked their father at the river, he could no longer fight them off.

"Soon you'll walk man's road," he whispered to them after they were asleep. "That will be a hard turn in my road. Yes, the hardest."

* * *

Four winters had now passed since the Pawnees stole *Mahuts,* and still the loss of the Arrows weighed heavily upon Stone Wolf's soul. Buffalo hunts were successful, and the People were regaining their strength, but the heart of the people remained empty.

Three summers men had gone to the Pawnees to negotiate the Arrows' return, but the enemy knew *Mahuts'* power and refused to bargain. Even though the People didn't bother the Pawnee horse herds or raid their camps, no agreement was reached.

"Something must be done," the chiefs argued. "We've been without *Mahuts* too long."

"Yes," Stone Wolf agreed. "I'll go to *Noahvose* and seek a dream. It was there Sweet Medicine first received the sacred Arrows. Perhaps Man Above will favor the People again."

"This has been a time of new beginnings," Younger Wolf declared. *"Nah nih,* I'll ride with you. Perhaps we can restore *Mahuts* to the People."

"Yes!" the young men shouted. "Bring the Arrows back!"

When Stone Wolf set out, he was unsure how to bring about such a thing. Even a man with far-seeing eyes couldn't perform such a miracle. Stone Wolf, for all his power, wasn't Sweet Medicine!

"They expect great things of us," Younger Wolf observed as they departed. "Look how the young ones watch."

Stone Wolf turned and gazed into the eyes of Arrow Dancer and Crow Boy. Other boys stood with the Arrow-keeper's eldest sons, calling out encouragement or singing brave heart songs.

"We've done the hard things before," Stone Wolf said. "But this?"

"We'll make prayers and suffer. Man Above will show the way."

The People were far south of *Noahvose* that summer, hunting along Shell River where Bull Buffalo painted the land black with his brothers. Days of hard riding passed, and still *Noahvose* lay far ahead.

"Often we've climbed that mountain together," Younger Wolf said when they paused to let their horses drink from a stream. "But today I remember the time I went there with Cloud Dancer, our grandfather."

"He'd given up the Arrows into my care," Stone Wolf said, sighing as the memory weighed him down. "He climbed that mountain to die."

"He wished to be near his uncle and the other old ones," Younger Wolf explained. "It's a place of powerful medicine. If you seek a vision there, it will come."

"I saw the Buffalo Shield there."

"And you will see how *Mahuts* can be brought back," Younger Wolf insisted. "I know my brother well. He's always done the hard things. He will again.

Stone Wolf thought it was easier to trust another than to manage such a difficult task. Even so he cast doubt from his mind and concentrated on the journey. Once they finally arrived at the butte, Stone Wolf let his brother lead the way.

"Take us to the place where Cloud Dancer climbed Hanging Road," Stone Wolf suggested. It was at that place the Arrow-keeper thought to begin his starving.

Little remained to mark the burial place. Only bits of hide and one scaffold pole could be located.

"His bones have returned to the earth," Younger Wolf observed. "That's how it should be."

"Yes," Stone Wolf agreed. "But perhaps his spirit looks down on us. If so, his shade may visit my dreams and tell what we must do."

Younger Wolf tended the horses while Stone Wolf built a fire. Then, after spreading hides out to make beds and erecting a small shelter to ward off the rain, Stone Wolf performed the pipe ceremony. As the brothers smoked and considered their actions, the wind seemed to sigh across the mountainside.

"Yes," Stone Wolf concluded. "We've come to the right place."

For three days he ate nothing. Aside from small cups of water, he rejected everything Younger Wolf offered. All that time he sang and danced, cutting the flesh of his arms, his thighs, his chest. Blood and hunger gradually induced a fever, and when he collapsed, Younger Wolf covered the emaciated Arrowkeeper with an elk robe and waited for the dreaming to begin.

From the first Stone Wolf knew this vision was different. There were no clouds, no familiar creatures. Instead he walked in a world of shadows, hearing old songs sung by somber voices.

"Why have you called me from my sleep?" Cloud Dancer asked, stepping out of a fiery light. He was only shade, and Stone Wolf felt the chill of his touch.

"Grandfather, I'm lost," Stone Wolf answered. "I

213

don't know where next to go. The People have lost their heart."

"You were to keep *Mahuts* safe!" the ghost cried.

"Yes, I failed you. Punish me if you wish, but restore the heart of the People. Bring *Mahuts* back to them."

It was then that the earth shook. Touches the Sky appeared, as did other Arrow-keepers long dead. They sang and prayed, and finally Sweet Medicine's shade appeared.

"Once I was given great power," the old one said. "I brought *Mahuts* to the People. Now it's time to restore that power. I will tell you what has to be done."

Two days Stone Wolf slept deeply. Once Younger Wolf thought his brother dead, he moved so little. Then finally the Arrow-keeper stirred.

"You were far away," Younger Wolf noted.

"Mine was the deep sleep," Stone Wolf explained. "I have been to the other side, Brother, and seen the old ones. They have shown me the path."

"Where do we go?"

"We're here already," Stone Wolf said, waving his arms at the trees and rocks all around them. "Here we'll remake the Arrows."

"This won't deceive the People," Younger Wolf argued. *"Mahuts* was much more than four stone-tipped Arrows."

"Yes, but it was the Arrows the Pawnees took. They can be replaced. The power was always renewed. We'll gather the ten bands and restore *Mahuts*, even as we did when the points were bloodied or the feathers ruined."

Younger Wolf remained doubtful, but when Stone Wolf prayed and smoked, his brother watched hopefully. While fashioning the tips, Stone Wolf sang in the old long-forgotten tongue. The prayers, also, were ancient. The shafts were cut from sacred ash and worked until they were straight and smooth. Lastly Stone Wolf wrapped feathers around the shafts and fixed them with hoof glue.

"Come," Stone Wolf said at last. "Look upon *Mahuts* reborn."

"*Ayyyy!*" Younger Wolf shouted as he felt the power of their medicine. "You've done well, *Nah nih*. Now we must return."

The hardest task remained. Even as pipe carriers sped to the other bands with word the renewal would be made, Stone Wolf faced the doubts of the chiefs.

"How can this be?" Thunder Coat asked. "These are simply arrows. They possess no power."

"The Pawnees hold *Mahuts*," Bear Claw agreed.

"Do they?" Stone Wolf asked. "I've walked *Noahvose*. There Sweet Medicine spoke in my dreams. 'It's not the power of physical things that guards our welfare,' sweet Medicine told me. '*Mahuts* is the gift of the Great Mystery.' Can we doubt the truth of these words? No, Sweet Medicine is right. We'll celebrate the renewal, and the power of *Mahuts* will be restored."

"*Ayyyy!*" the chiefs cried. "The heart of the People has returned."

Nineteen

Once the Arrow renewal was conducted, *Mahuts* again led the hunt and protected the People from their enemies. Any ill feelings lingering in the hearts of the People toward their Arrow-keeper seemed to pass, and Stone Wolf was recognized as a man of high standing once more.

"That's Stone Wolf," boys would whisper. "He brought *Mahuts* back to the People."

That summer and the next Stone Wolf passed making the healing cures, sharing stories of the old ways with the children of his camp, and instructing his sons in the things they would need to know before setting their feet on man's road. Each dawn he took Arrow Dancer, Crow Boy, and Porcupine to the river to make the morning prayers. Afterward they would join the men and swim for a time. Most days the boys would remain at the river, wrestling with their age mates or joining in mock combat. Even little Porcupine, only seven, eagerly tested himself against the others.

Once the summer hunt was finished, and camp established above Shell River, Stone Wolf would take his elder sons on a short hunt. Sometimes Porcupine came along, bringing his small bow and bird arrows. Dreamer often squawked at being left behind, but he was far too small for such adventures.

"We'd never find game with him along," Arrow Dancer declared. "He makes too much noise."

Stone Wolf felt no small pride watching Arrow Dancer and Crow Boy stalk rabbits or porcupines. Sometimes they would even track a small deer. The Dancer now carried a good willow bow, and he loosed his arrows with killing power. Twice he brought down bucks in the woodlands south of the river.

"Next summer, when I'm twelve, I'll ride to the buffalo hunt," the boy boasted. "Ferret Boy says I may ride with him. If we kill a bull, the Foxes may invite us to join them."

"Ne' hyo is a Fox," Crow Boy said, eyeing his brother with admiration. "As is Younger Wolf. It would be good to join the council of our fathers."

"It requires a brave deed," Arrow Dancer said, pondering the notion. "I hope I can perform one. Some boys wait until they have seen fifteen or sixteen summers before joining a soldier society. That would be hard, being left behind for so long a time."

"Yes," Crow Boy agreed as he followed his brother into a deer thicket. "Maybe the Crows will strike our camp again. Soldiers will be needed then, and they will seek out even young ones."

"I wouldn't welcome a raid," Arrow Dancer said, dropping his eyes earthward. "Our mother and small brother would be in danger. *Ne' hyo,* also. He always hurries to protect the defenseless ones. Already his body is scarred from war wounds and sacrifice cuts. I hope I, too, will be a man of the People one day."

"I imagined you would follow *Ne' hyo* on the medicine trail. Who will keep the Arrows?"

"Dreamer perhaps. He senses things. It's good to know the healing cures, and I'm glad when *Ne' hyo* asks us along when gathering roots or pounding the powders. My heart calls me to hunt, though."

"Yes, Dreamer should do it," Crow Boy agreed. "Or our uncle's son. We carry our mother's blood, and an Arrow-keeper should be of the People."

"What do we know of the Crows, Brother? Except how to fight them. Not since our mother ran to the traders' camp has anyone called me a Crow."

"It's less easily put behind me. My name reminds them."

"When you start down man's road, you'll win another name. Then it will be forgotten."

"By everyone but me," Crow Boy grumbled. "And some others."

"Pay them no mind," Arrow Dancer said as he quietly stepped under a low limb and drew an arrow. Silently he prayed to the spirit of the doe twenty feet away. Then he notched the arrow, drew back the bowstring, and fired his arrow. It struck below the right shoulder and pierced the heart. The deer died swiftly, painlessly.

Stone Wolf heard all this, for he was trailing the boys that day. Porcupine was a stone's throw to the right, and when he saw the deer fall, he shouted his praise.

"My brother has the true aim!" Porcupine yelled. *"Ayyyy!* He's killed a deer."

Stone Wolf proudly helped the boys carry the deer to camp, and he proclaimed to all with ears the skillful manner in which his son had tracked and slain the animal.

"Nah koa, here's meat for the fire," Arrow Dancer declared when he reached his father's lodge.

"Ah," Dove Woman said as Dreamer hurried to inspect the carcass. "I've been hungry for venison. Perhaps some of the old people would like some."

"Ne' hyo?" Arrow Dancer asked. "How can I share my good fortune without insulting anyone?"

"Come, we'll cut up the deer first," Stone Wolf suggested. "Then I'll show you."

After butchering the doe, Stone Wolf cut sections of rump and ribs, then brought them to those in need.

"Man Above has given my son a deer, Grandfather," Stone Wolf told an old man named Beaded Moccasin. *"Ayyyy!* His true aim has provided meat, but we are a small family and have too much. Do you have any use for this?"

Stone Wolf offered a roast, and the old man accepted it.

"I'll see it's eaten, Nephew," Beaded Moccasin said. "Your son should stand tall, knowing he feeds the hungry."

"It's good to know he has helped someone," Stone Wolf replied as he turned to leave.

"I see," Arrow Dancer said, grinning. "I only offer."

"Suggest they do you a favor by accepting it," Stone

219

Wolf suggested. "Never hint it's for them. Often they pass the meat on to someone who needs it more."

"Porcupine has told us of the time when he and our mother moved among the bands, having no lodge of their own and relying on the gifts of relatives. It was a hungry time for them."

"Those were hard days for many," Stone Wolf noted. "But now we've put them behind us."

"It's your doing, *Ne' hyo,*" Arrow Dancer said. "You returned *Mahuts* to the People."

"Ah, but more importantly they returned to *Mahuts.* So long as we keep the rituals and perform the correct prayers, we should avoid such days. Soon you'll be old enough to help with the ceremonies."

"I'll help with the cures, *Ne' hyo,* but you should choose another to show the Arrow rituals."

"I thought to teach you as my grandfather taught me," Stone Wolf explained. "It doesn't mean you would be given the burden of *Mahuts.*"

"It's warrior's road that calls me," Arrow Dancer said, avoiding his father's probing eyes. "It's best. Many would remember my mother and think it improper for a man with Crow blood to hold so honored a position among the People."

"Many among us have mothers born of another tribe," Stone Wolf argued. "Or fathers. It's a man's heart that's important."

"His family matters, too," Arrow Dancer argued. "I remember how the women whispered about my mother. They would always have doubts."

"You're young to worry over such matters," Stone

220

Wolf argued. "You have yet to hunt Bull Buffalo, and here we plan your old age."

"I'm eleven, *Ne' hyo*. Soon I'll have hairs to pluck from my chin."

"Soon?" Stone Wolf said, feeling the side of the boy's face. "There's time yet."

Stone Wolf found it easier to carve spinning tops or fashion throwing sticks than to consider such grave matters as who should next keep the Arrows. Often he would show Porcupine how to aim his small bow, and the two would shoot rabbits or small birds.

"See how I, too, bring meat to our lodge!" Porcupine boasted each time he presented Dove Woman with a rabbit.

"You've done well, *Naha',*" she replied. "This rabbit will make a good dinner."

As for little Dreamer, the boy was quick-witted. He spoke early, and he seemed to remember everything.

"He's small, but he understands horses," Crow Boy noted. "This morning when I was seeing to our animals, I looked up and saw Dreamer atop the buckskin stallion. How he managed it, I don't know. That buckskin won't allow most of us to touch him."

"It's a good talent to have," Stone Wolf observed. "Cloud Dancer, my grandfather, spoke to animals. It's said when he first brought Horse to the People, he invited the animals to follow him to our camp."

"Tell the story, *Ne' hyo,*" Crow Boy pleaded. "Share with us the remembered tale."

"Ah, you've heard it too many times before," Stone Wolf objected. "We have work to do."

221

"How can we remember what came before if you don't share the stories?" Arrow Dancer asked. The others grinned, knowing Stone Wolf was never one to miss a chance to recount the adventures of his grandfather.

"Ah, then, I'll tell you," the Arrow-keeper said, leading them to the cook fire. As he sat beside the embers, the boys gathered close. He began, and other young ones from the camp walked over and joined them. Soon fifty were gathered in a circle, and their storyteller's eyes brightened as the remembered tale flowed from his lips.

That summer was also remembered as the time Trickster came to the blue coat soldiers. White men had become a common sight on Shell River, but memories of the blister sickness and other diseases kept the People cautious. Traders who were known as Corn Hair's brothers were invited to camp nearby, but many of the hairy faces were sent away.

"We don't want your whiskey!" Stone Wolf told them. "Keep your bad ways to yourself, or go and visit the Crows and Pawnees. Make our enemies sick!"

The blue coats were different. They came as a band of twenty men, and they left their women and little ones behind.

"How can you say you're no war party?" the People demanded. "Why else do men travel alone onto the buffalo range?"

"We come to find out what is here," the young soldier chief explained.

"We are here!" Thunder Coat, who understood the blue coats' words, answered. "If you want to learn what is here, ask. We'll tell you."

The blue coats trusted only their own eyes, though. Worse, they made no prayers before killing game, and they shot Bull Buffalo for his hides and left the meat to the birds and coyotes.

"These are strange men who come to us," Stone Wolf told the chiefs. "They walk with heavy steps, burying sticks in the sacred earth to mark their trail. With glad hearts they kill!"

"Yes, these are strange ones," Talking Stick agreed. "They have no harmony in their camp but shout and fight among themselves."

"The whiskey they buy from the hairy face traders brings on madness," Wood Snake declared. "They have no place on Shell River, where we have always hunted and camped. I've heard how the whites come and see a place. Soon it's theirs. Once Muddy River was a good place to hunt, but now it's lost to us."

"What can we do?" Red Bird asked. "Should we ride down and kill them?"

"They have many good guns," Younger Wolf warned. "They would kill many of us in a fight."

"Ask the Arrows," Talking Stick suggested. "Make medicine. *Mahuts* can instruct us, and our medicine will protect us from the blue coat soldiers."

"Yes, we'll ask *Mahuts*," Stone Wolf agreed. "Who will bring a pipe? Who will offer eagle feathers to find an answer to this hard question?"

"I'll do both," Thunder Coat said. "But it's appropriate other chiefs enter the Arrow Lodge to hear the

223

answer. We must be as one in dealing with these soldiers."

"Yes," the others agreed.

And so the chiefs came to the Arrow Lodge. Stone Wolf took the pipe and led the way inside. They then smoked and talked a considerable time before making *Mahuts* a present of the feathers. Then the question was posed.

"Do we fight these strangers?" Thunder Coat asked.

The smoke curled toward the Arrow bundle, and it seemed to move.

"There can be no fighting them," Stone Wolf answered.

"Then are we to leave them alone?" Talking Stick asked.

Again the Arrows moved, and Stone Wolf frowned.

"We can't do that, either," Stone Wolf said, sighing.

"Then what?" Thunder Coat asked. "Surely we must do one of these things."

"No, *Mahuts* can't be mistaken," Stone Wolf told the others. "There's another way. I'll smoke some more and invite a vision. Then we'll do what is best."

When the dream came, it surprised Stone Wolf that no one else had suggested such a plan. Weren't the People horse stealers from the time of Cloud Dancer? How far could the blue coats go on foot?

The chiefs howled their approval when Stone Wolf shared the dream in council.

"Yes, we'll do this!" Wood Snake cried. "They have many good horses, these blue coat soldiers, and they tie them all together with only two men to watch."

224

"We'll come by night," Talking Stick suggested.

"No, that's when the guard watches most carefully," Stone Wolf argued. "It's when they'll expect raiders."

"We're to come by light?" Thunder Coat asked. "When they can see us clearly?"

"Ah, but will they?" Stone Wolf said, laughing. "We're not the only ones to bathe in Shell River. When the sun stands high overhead, the whites grow weary. They strip their soldier coats and jump naked into the river. That's when we'll strike, for even the guards join the swimmers."

"They'll know it's us," Wood Snake objected.

"We'll paint ourselves as the Crows do," Stone Wolf said, laughing. "We'll leave our good clothes behind and ride only in breechclouts."

"Without the protection of the Buffalo Shields?" Younger Wolf asked.

"They'll have no guns in Shell River," Stone Wolf explained.

"And can we take their rifles, too?" Talking Stick asked. "Or only the horses?"

"We'll take everything," Stone Wolf replied. "Horses, blankets, guns, soldier coats . . . leaving them naked to burn in the summer sun."

"*Ayyyy!*" the young men howled. "It will be a re-membered day!"

"But hard on the eyes," Younger Wolf said, laughing. "So many hairy faces with no clothes to hide their ugliness!"

The People danced and sang and imagined the raid. Eager young men who had done nothing to distinguish themselves begged to join the raiding party.

225

"I would strike the enemy!" Ferret Boy announced.

"No one must hurt these blue coats," Stone Wolf cautioned. "Many times a hasty act has spoiled the medicine and brought death to the People. We only steal their possessions. Any harm that comes to these strangers must come from the sun and the wind. Insects may sting and bite them, but we must not notch our arrows or fire our guns."

"And if they shoot first?" Talking Stick asked.

"They won't if we do as instructed," Stone Wolf said sternly. "Success depends on doing so."

The chiefs discussed the raid and decided it was best only ten men strike the camp. Another ten would take the horses, and ten others would collect the rifles and other belongings.

"Only the first ten will be armed," Wood Smoke told the others.

"I won't strike the enemy then." Ferret Boy complained.

"You can strike the enemy's coat," Younger Wolf said, grinning. "It's enough. Now paint yourselves and get your ponies ready. The blue coats are waiting!"

Yes, the raid was long remembered. This time the men did as instructed, and when the soldiers stepped naked into Shell River, the People fell upon the camp with an unearthly cry.

"They're stealing the horses!" one hairy face shouted as he ran out of the river. Wood Snake drove his horse at the man, and the soldier splashed back into the river.

"Crows!" one of the swimmers hollered. "Crows! I

recognize the paint. They've always been friendly!"

"They love to steal horses," another said. "Rest easy, lieutenant. Likely they'll sell 'em back to us."

It was only later, when they discovered their clothes gone, that the whites angrily shouted at the retiring raiders.

"Come back!" they howled. "You can't leave us this way!"

Yes, it was a remembered day. Trickster had visited the blue coats, and the People had many fine horses and good guns.

Twenty

That winter many young men wore the captured blue shirts to remember the trick played on the hairy face soldiers. It proved to be poor cloth, and was easily torn by thorns or rubbed into shreds. By the next summer only the shiny yellow buttons remained to commemorate the raid.

That year, once the New Life Lodge was made, preparations began for the buffalo hunt.

"Ne' hyo, this time I should join the hunt," Arrow Dancer declared when his father and Younger Wolf readied their ponies.

"Come closer, *Naha',"* Stone Wolf said.

Arrow Dancer stretched himself tall and approached slowly. Stone Wolf rested his hands on the boy's shoulders and studied the boy's eyes. Determination overflowed Arrow Dancer's face. Stone Wolf felt his son's shoulders and arms, noting the new iron in the muscles.

"It's no small thing, riding with the men," Stone

Wolf warned. "Once you begin, there's no going back."

"I've waited long enough," Arrow Dancer insisted. "Others my age are going. Some are even smaller."

"Many wait longer," Stone Wolf observed.

"When did *Ne' hyo* ever hold himself back?" Arrow Dancer asked Younger Wolf. "Always he was the first. I'm his son. Can I be different?"

"Our father was dead," Younger Wolf explained. "There was need to hurry ourselves onto man's road."

"It's not possible to stay behind, *Ne' hyo*," the boy said, gripping his father's hands. "I will make what medicine prayers you suggest, and if you ask, I'll ride at your side. I have to go, though. To remain behind, keeping myself safe among the women, isn't in my heart."

"Then you'll come with us," Stone Wolf said somberly. "Younger Wolf and I will ride with the Foxes, and you are welcome to follow us."

"I'll make you a strong bow," Younger Wolf offered. "Of iron wood. The white face mare will carry you."

"She's fast," Arrow Dancer said, smiling.

"Many try the difficult things when they ride on their first hunt," Stone Wolf cautioned his son. "Choose a calf to kill and aim well. There are summers ahead when you can slay Bull Buffalo."

"I understand, *Ne' hyo*," Arrow Dancer said respectfully. "Tell me what I should do, and I'll do it."

"Come with us and take a sweat, *Naha'*," Stone Wolf urged. "Later we'll make the buffalo prayers and prepare for the hunt. Listen, learn, and do as we do."

229

The boy smiled brightly, and Stone Wolf drew him close.

"A man feels great pride, seeing his son begin the long walk down man's road," the Arrow-keeper said. "But I know sadness, too, for soon you'll leave to enter the young men's lodge."

"I won't be far, *Ne' hyo*," Arrow Dancer said, gazing up into his father's eyes. "Now that I'm coming to be a man, we will share the hunt. We can raid Crow ponies and strike the enemy."

"Yes, *Naha'*, but in these things you see only adventure. I know them for the dangers they carry."

"Your medicine is strong," Arrow Dancer argued. "I'll make mine strong also."

On the winter counts of the plains peoples, that year would be remembered as the time Firebird crossed the heavens. Never did anyone recall such a momentous event. Each night the great ball of fire blazed across the sky, scattering sparks across Hanging Road.

"Great things are sure to happen," the chiefs declared.

Stone Wolf was concerned. The heavens seemed disturbed, and the animals took note. Bull Buffalo stampeded through one camp, trampling seven lodges. Two women and seven children were killed, and many others required healing.

The horses acted strangely. Ponies who were used to man's touch grew skittish, and others raced off into the hills and were lost.

"What does it mean, *Ne' hyo?*" Arrow Dancer asked.

"I don't know," the Arrow-keeper confessed. "Never have I seen anything like this. It may be a warning, or it may be a sign. Who can say? My dreams tell me nothing."

"You'll ask *Mahuts?*" Arrow Dancer asked.

"Ah, maybe the Arrows know."

But though he smoked and talked with the Arrows, *Mahuts* led him to no conclusions. In his dreams he saw a successful hunt, so he told the chiefs it was best to organize the men.

"We'll hunt Bull Buffalo," Thunder Coat told the young men. "With meat and hides, we'll have nothing to fear."

Stone Wolf didn't argue although he knew food and shelter could not ward off all dangers.

"Remember the blister sickness," he told Younger Wolf.

"I know why the sky is burning, *Ne' hyo,*" Crow Boy declared.

"Yes?" Stone Wolf asked.

"It's to mark our brother's first hunt," the boy said.

Stone Wolf managed a grin, but so long as Firebird remained overhead, there was reason to worry. The People debated its meaning, but they gradually became accustomed to the sight.

"Firebird will soon finish his flight," Wood Snake declared. After all, the fire was creeping across the sky. Soon it, too, would pass into memory.

"Yes," Thunder Coat agreed. "The buffalo hunt should begin. Already it's been too long delayed."

231

Stone Wolf considered their words. Yes, it was time to hunt.

"Organize the men," Stone Wolf said. "I'll prepare to make the medicine prayers."

Stone Wolf's camp broke down their lodges and headed out onto the plain. The men made a hunting camp a short distance from the main body. It was there Stone Wolf called the men together to make the prayers.

"Bull Buffalo, we have come weak with hunger, and you have given us your meat to make us strong again. We came naked, and you gave your skin to warm us in the deep snows of winter. *Ayyyy!* All we need to live you give us."

The other men echoed the words and howled their agreement.

It was then the Arrow-keeper brought out the Buffalo Arrows and performed the required rituals. The men and boys passed by, invoking the aid of the sacred Arrows and offering presents. Then food was brought out, and the hunters sang and danced in the old way.

"Soon the scouts depart," Stone Wolf explained to Arrow Dancer. "Hunting parties will follow, waiting for news a herd has been sighted. When the scouts locate Bull Buffalo, we'll pray again and dance. Then we can hunt."

"I'll ride at your side, *Ne' hyo?*" Arrow Dancer asked.

"As was promised," Stone Wolf agreed. "We'll make medicine and paint our bodies. Then we'll begin the killing."

That summer Bull Buffalo was plentiful, but the fireball in the heavens had driven the herds from their accustomed range. The scouts rode four days before striking sign, and it was two days more before they brought word they had found a herd.

Ayyyy !" the Foxes cried when Whirlwind arrived with the word. "Soon we will strike Bull Buffalo."

First, though, Stone Wolf made prayers. The Arrows were moved farther so that they faced the herd. Then the medicine men sang and suffered, bringing their power to lances and arrows, for Stone Wolf insisted no rifle be used the first day. Finally the men painted themselves and danced.

Stone Wolf watched nervously when Arrow Dancer joined the dance. He and Ferret Boy paired off and engaged in mock combat. Other young men then donned horns and pretended to be Bull Buffalo. Hunters whirled wildly as they tried to strike the buffalo. Each time the ceremonial lances struck a bull, the others howled loudly.

"The People are strong once more," Wood Snake observed. "See how the young men dance! *Ayyyy!* They'll be good hunters, these young ones."

"It's good they test themselves," Stone Wolf agreed. "But the heavens are strange. We must guard against peril."

"I sent men to watch our camp," Wood Snake whispered. "Later I'll send men who have killed their buffalo back to take the place of the watchers."

"It's wise to guard the defenseless ones," Stone Wolf said, nodding. "And good all will have a turn at hunting."

233

"No one wishes to be left behind," the Snake noted. "Not even our sons."

"No young man ever had the patience to wait, old friend. The brave heart stories we share hurries them onto man's road."

"They'll be needed if the Crows come," Wood Snake said, locating his sons on the far side of the council fire. "Who can tell where Firebird has sent them?"

One party of Crows did approach the hunters' camp, but it was a small band and rode off when a line of Bowstrings rode out to meet them.

"Here's an enemy we can strike!" Bear Claw shouted.

"We have Bull Buffalo to hunt, and the Crows have fast horses," Stone Wolf argued. "Let them run!"

The other chiefs agreed, and Bear Claw found only three young men willing to follow him against the Crows.

"Where is your courage?" the Claw stormed.

"We remember you," Thunder Coat replied. "You led us once against the Pawnees, but when the fighting began, where were you? Far from danger!"

Thunder Coat imitated a whipped dog fleeing with its tail between its legs, and the men laughed. The Bowstring chief glared angrily, but even the other Bowstrings would not follow him to war.

Indeed, the men busied themselves forming bands to hunt. Men would pair off with friends so that one might charge the herd while the other waited. In such a way if a horse went down, its rider was assured of a rescue.

Stone Wolf and Younger Wolf had ridden together since their youth. They now invited Arrow Dancer and Ferret Boy to come along.

"I have a brother to go with," Ferret Boy said, nodding toward Whirlwind.

"And a father," Stone Wolf pointed out. "Which one would you have ride alone?"

The boy nodded his understanding and accepted the offer.

Next morning the scouts struck out early. They located the herd and turned them back toward the hunters. The Elks and the Bowstrings struck first, but the Foxes soon followed.

"Ayyyy!" the young men screamed as they drove themselves at the herd. Lances pierced hide again and again. Even when a killing blow wasn't struck, the animals soon lost strength from bleeding and slowed. The cripples were finished with arrows.

Younger Wolf led one half of the Foxes, but when the time to strike the herd arrived, he waved Ferret Boy in. The young one rode a raven black pony, and the two raced in like a falcon diving on its prey. Ferret Boy notched an arrow and waited for a clear shot. Then, from mere feet away, he fired his arrow into a large cow's chest. The animal spun in the dust and died.

"Ayyyy!" his elders shouted.

Stone Wolf now motioned Arrow Dancer toward a calf stumbling along the fringe of the herd. The boy's face paled with disappointment, but Stone Wolf waved a second time, and Arrow Dancer held high his lance.

"Guide his aim, Man Above," Stone Wolf prayed as the boy kicked his horse into a gallop and raced toward the calf. A bull tried to block the white-faced mare and its reckless rider, but Arrow Dancer was too quick. The horse swept around the bull and darted at the calf. Arrow Dancer rammed the stone point through the buffalo calf's side, and the animal stumbled. A second and third thrust were necessary to make the kill, but afterward the calf lay very still.

"*Ayyyy!*" Arrow Dancer screamed. "I've killed a calf!"

"*Ayyyy!*" Stone Wolf shouted in answer. "My son has taken his first steps on man's road."

That night there was more singing and dancing around the council fire as brave hunts of the past were recounted and young men described their first kills. When it was Arrow Dancer's turn, he spoke of the defending bull and then described the killing of the calf."

"It's a good thing, this first kill," Younger Wolf said, lifting his nephew up so even those in back could see Arrow Dancer. "Here's one who will also be a man of the People!"

Other young men clasped Arrow Dancer's hands and sang brave songs with him. There was good meat to eat and wild onions to chew. Only when the last song had died out and the food was finished did the council fire burn down. The hunters took to their beds and awaited the resumption of the hunt at dawn.

When the men again rode toward the herd that next morning, those who hadn't made a kill were particularly determined to have their chance. Even Stone Wolf felt an urgency in his movements, and Younger Wolf galloped ahead. He, too, was a father now, and he needed meat for his family. Reaching the herd, Younger Wolf shouted a brave heart cry and charged the largest bull in sight.

By then the approaching hunters had set the buffalo in motion, and the thundering bull was frothing with exertion.

"Ayyyy!" Younger Wolf shouted as he leaned across his horse and jabbed the bull below its shoulder. He plunged the lance in twice more, then drove the point deep through the buffalo's vitals. The bull dropped its chin and rolled over as it grunted out its life.

Now Younger Wolf found himself in peril. The herd began to turn, and Younger Wolf was caught in its midst. Stone Wolf kicked his horse into a gallop, but the herd turned a second time, and he was forced away.

"Ne' hyo, it's for me to do!" Arrow Dancer shouted, whipping the white-faced mare into a gallop. As if guided by some invisible force, the Dancer wove his way between the onrushing beasts to where his uncle fought to swing free of the horned monsters.

"Follow me!" Arrow Dancer shouted, and Younger Wolf swung behind his young rescuer. The two then threaded their way free of the buffalo and reached safety.

"That was a brave heart deed!" Ferret Boy shouted as he greeted his young friend.

"Yes, but I struck no bull," Arrow Dancer complained.

"There's time left to us, *Naha',*" Stone Wolf said, motioning to the spare ponies behind them. "I'll bring you another mount."

"I'll need a horse also, *Nah nih,*" Younger Wolf said, climbing down from his pony. Only now did the others notice the animal's wounds. Two horns had pierced the horse's flank, and blood ran down the creature's tortured flesh.

"He was a good horse," Stone Wolf noted before turning to bring the other ponies. Behind him he knew Younger Wolf was cutting the pony's throat, for to allow a brave animal to suffer was contrary to a horseman's nature.

Remounted and revived by water and smoked meat, the brothers and their young companions rejoined the hunt. Arrow Dancer made a brave charge and killed a full-grown bull. Younger Wolf struck down a second bull, pledging its meat to the defenseless ones.

"You've done well," Stone Wolf told his son when they turned back to the hunters' camp.

"I've never been so frightened," the boy confessed. *"Ne' hyo,* when the buffalo raced on all sides of me, I thought I would find my death. Then I remembered a brave heart song, and I saw my uncle struggling on. I was more afraid for him than for myself."

"That's how it is with the best men," Stone Wolf said. "They make no boasts nor lead war parties. Their courage is saved for when it's needed."

"I don't feel brave, *Ne' hyo.*"

"That's less important," Stone Wolf said. "What matters on man's road is that a man acts. Often there's not time to consider things or ponder the danger. A man either charges or watches."

On their way back to the hunters' camp, they passed the women and children. Already many were butchering the dead buffalos, and others had pony drags waiting to carry meat back to camp for smoking.

"There are my brothers!" Arrow Dancer called, and Stone Wolf waved the boy toward them. A brave deed merited a celebration, and the young ones wouldn't be invited to the council that night.

Nevertheless, when the men assembled to recount their exploits that night, Younger Wolf rose to tell the others of his rescue. The Wolf lent great drama to the event by holding up his bloodstained saddle. The story concluded at last when Stone Wolf led three good horses out and gave them away in honor of the brave deed performed by his son.

"*Ayyyy!*" the men cried. "Arrow Dancer is welcome among us. The Arrow-keeper has a brave heart son!"

Arrow Dancer was greeted by young and old, and it appeared to his father as if the boy stood suddenly taller.

"Soon he'll be invited by the Foxes to join them," Younger Wolf observed.

"Yes," Stone Wolf agreed. "We'll need to choose a brave name for him."

"I'm proud he walks man's road, *Nah nih,* but I'll miss the boy I knew."

"Yes," Stone Wolf agreed. "As I will."

Twenty-one

Stone Wolf felt himself walking a new path that autumn. His sons were growing into men, and the People were once more coming to be prosperous. More and more children were born, and each band saw its lodges increase.

"*Mahuts* has returned to lead the People along the sacred path," many declared.

Even so, the People were not without concerns. For a long time white traders and trappers had traveled up the rivers to collect beaver. The Frenchmen who had come first would live among the People, learn their ways, and bargain fairly. Now many came to trap their own animals. These were hard men who would shoot anyone who challenged their passage. Some of these newcomers stole hides from others, or from the tribes that hunted Shell River. Others sold bad whiskey or brought disease.

Most worrisome were the forts the traders and trappers built in *Tsis tsis tas* country. One such, called Ft. William, stood where a smaller stream emptied into

Shell River. The men who lived there called the stream Laramie River, and many who visited there knew the fort by this same Frenchman's name. Shell River they called the North Platte.

"Men who build stone forts and place their own names on rivers have come to stay," Stone Wolf told the chiefs. "The Lakota tell of how white men came to Muddy River this way. Now that country is full of hairy faces, and game has grown scarce. More and more these strange ones push us west toward the Shining Mountains, into the land of our old enemies, the Crows. Once we made long journeys west to reach *Noahvose*. Now our winter camps are spread west of the sacred butte."

"This is true," Thunder Coat admitted, "but the Fort William traders offer many fine things. We trade beaver and buffalo hides for iron pots and good guns, lead and powder. We can't make these things ourselves, and they trade them for hides we have in great numbers."

"It's not the trade that worries me," Stone Wolf told the others. "It's the way they walk the land. Already they speak as if it's their place, and we are mere visitors. Soon Shell River will be lost to us, and Bull Buffalo will grow hungry."

"Bull Buffalo blackens the prairies," Bear Claw argued. "He has been here always. He will still chew the grass on Shell River when our bones are dust."

"You're a fool, Bear Claw, who sees only a man's presents and not his motives. *Ayyyy!*" Stone Wolf shouted. "There are too many among us who have forgotten the old country we once roamed. Too many have been born long since the last hunt was made on

Muddy River. These places were once ours. Now they are gone. The day the People rode the wide earth is passing."

"Maybe Man Above is showing us a better way," Talking Stick suggested. "I've visited Fort William. Its walls are thick and cool in summer, and warming fires fend off winter's chills. Many of our people camp there. Lakotas, too. Some work for the traders, trapping beaver or bringing meat."

"A man might as well sell his heart," Stone Wolf lamented.

"Your brother is there," Talking Stick said, studying Stone Wolf's reaction. "The one you call Corn Hair. Freneau, the whites call him. He's come to stay, bringing his family."

Stone Wolf frowned. How could this be? Not so long ago he'd adopted this yellow-haired pale one into his family, hoping he would help build a bridge to a better future. Now Freneau had returned, but he hadn't bothered to visit his brothers!

"Brothers, what is to be done?" Wood Snake asked.

"What can we decide?" Talking Stick asked in turn. "Whether we wish the fort to stay or not, it will stay. Would you attack your brother, Stone Wolf? No, you can't do that, and it would be unwise to bring down the whites and their many friends upon us. What use is talking? The hard face moons are coming, and we need to make ourselves ready. Let's tend to important matters and be finished here."

The other chiefs rose and wiped their hands as if to say the talking was over. Only Younger Wolf remained, and even he saw no use arguing.

"Did you know our brother had come to Shell

River?" Stone Wolf asked as the two of them rode back to their camp.

"I heard he'd come to the fort," Younger Wolf answered.

"He should have visited us."

"Ah, we're the wind in summer, *Nah nih.* How would he have found us? He has little ones to look after. When the snows melt, we'll send word to him. He'll come, and we'll meet his sons. *Ayyyy!* Maybe we'll all hunt together."

"You expect it will be like riding with our Lakota cousins," Stone Wolf grumbled, "but it won't be. Corn Hair has been among the whites many moons, and he'll bring odd ways to us."

"His heart won't change, *Nah nih,*" Younger Wolf assured his brother. "You've read his eyes. No, he's still our brother, and it will be a good thing for his sons to learn our ways. White men, too, should walk the earth with understanding."

Even when winter froze the earth, Stone Wolf never entirely erased Corn Hair Freneau from his mind. Often the Arrow-keeper dreamed of walking Shell River with his white brother. Other dreams revealed yellow-haired boys swimming and wrestling with Crow Boy, Porcupine, and Dreamer. Sometimes, when Stone Wolf drew his sons around him and shared the old tales, he spoke of how the first Corn Hair came among the People. Dove Woman blushed at the notion of the naked white man, and the boys laughed to hear of it.

"Husband, is it true the white men don't pluck their whiskers?" she asked.

"I've seen some who are hairy like Bull Buffalo,"

Arrow Dancer said. "Ferret Boy says they aren't men at all but large rabbits."

"Soon you can decide yourself, *Naha'*," Stone Wolf said. "We will invite Corn Hair to visit us. Perhaps we'll hunt Bull Buffalo together."

"Will his sons come?" Crow Boy asked.

"I hope so," Stone Wolf replied. "We can teach them much."

"And we can take them to the river and swim," Porcupine declared. "There we'll learn if they are really rabbits."

Stone Wolf grinned as Porcupine imitated Rabbit. Maybe there was no danger in the coming of the white men. So long as children could laugh at them, they couldn't be all bad.

"It's hard for you to welcome a white man to your lodge," Dove Woman observed one night after Stone Wolf awoke from a fitful sleep.

"This one is different," he explained. "I've seen him in my dreams. Often. He'll help the People understand."

"Even so, you remember Sweet Medicine's warnings. And, too, there's the trouble Dumont brought to your camp."

"I have many reasons to hate the white men," Stone Wolf admitted. "But I have obligations, and so I cast such hatred from my heart. An Arrow-keeper must place the needs of his People high, and so I walk in harmony, forgiving the bad things the whites have done."

Even before Stone Wolf could send word to Fort

William that next spring, Long Walker appeared with a thin-faced young man of fourteen. The moment the visitor removed his hat Stone Wolf recognized the amber hair of a Freneau.

"He's called Peter," Long Walker said, motioning to his companion. "Cousin, he is the son of Corn Hair. His father sent him to learn from you. When you have finished making the Sun Dance, perhaps you'll come to Shell River and trade. I keep my band there now, and you have many relatives to meet. Corn Hair wishes you to meet his other young ones."

"I hoped he would come to me," Stone Wolf said, sighing.

"He will, in time," Peter said, surprising Stone Wolf with a command of the *Tsis tsis tas* tongue. "But there are things to do at the fort first. You understand. All people have work to do when winter passes."

"Yes," Stone Wolf agreed. "Come. The son of my brother is also my son."

"It's good to know, *Ne' hyo*," young Freneau replied. "My father said you'll teach me many things. I hope so. Before, living among my mother's people, I was never happy. Here, with the mountains near, I feel at home."

"I'm to teach you?" Stone Wolf asked. "Already you know our words. Share our food, and learn what you choose. Our ways may be strange, but I think maybe you know more than the word we use for father. Corn Hair's done well to send you. My sons, I think, will be the ones to learn, and you will be our teacher."

Indeed, that's how it seemed to Stone Wolf. Peter

Freneau was quiet most times, and he showed great respect toward the People's traditions. He didn't sleep well on the ground, and when Arrow Dancer provided him with breechclout and shirt, the young visitor eyed them with suspicion.

"It must be cold in winter," Peter said, touching his bare, pinkish thighs.

"Cooler in summer," Arrow Dancer argued.

"Maybe," Peter replied.

It had other disadvantages, too, for one unaccustomed to buckskin. Parts of Peter were rubbed raw and required a medicine cure.

"My father said I might suffer some," Peter said as Stone Wolf applied a soothing ointment to the boy's blistered flesh. "I never thought it would be this part of me, though."

"You will wear your old clothes," Stone Wolf said. "I'll see these others are chewed soft. You should have spoken up. I read the pain on your face."

"It's not half as bad as plucking whiskers," Peter remarked. "Arrow Dancer showed me how, but I think I'll shave them off instead. Your people don't grow much of a beard, but my family is famous for hair. I've got a razor with me, and soap, too."

"I don't know these things," Stone Wolf said, puzzled.

"I'll show you when I'm able to walk again," Peter promised. And he did.

Half the band gathered to watch Peter Freneau cut away the whiskers from his chin and upper lip. For a boy of fourteen, he had a rather remarkable growth.

"Some white men don't grow whiskers until they're much older," Peter explained. "Freneaus beard over

247

early, though. Even my little brother Charlie's got a whisker or two, and he's just eleven."

The boys among the crowd touched their chins and gazed in wonder at such a thing. The girls hid their embarrassed smiles.

When he was whole again, Peter joined in boys' games and contests. The young *Tsis tsis tas* tested his merits at every opportunity, and often Peter was thrashed. But he earned the respect of his age-mates by swallowing his pain and holding no grudge.

"Well done," he told Ferret Boy after losing a wrestling match. "Show me how you threw me over your hip. It's a useful trick. I hear Crows are fond of flying, and I might need to toss one or two into the stars some time."

By the time the pipe carriers went out to collect the bands for the making of New Life Lodge—the Sun Dance Long Walker had spoken of, Peter had burrowed his way into the heart of Stone Wolf's band. He was a natural leader, a fine rifle shot, and a loyal friend and son.

"He's not a rabbit," Porcupine observed one morning after the older boys departed. "But he's not a man like we are, *Ne' hyo*. What makes us different? Not skin color."

"No, that's not so much," Stone Wolf agreed. "White mare or brown, it's her speed that makes her a good choice on a hunt. No, the difference is there, though. We walk in harmony, hoping the balance Man Above made in the beginning will remain as it was. The pale people always watch for an opportunity to change things. They expect the world to grow better, easier, when we know life is what it's always been,

248

a hard road we must walk, winning honor for ourselves and keeping the People strong."

"Peter says you should accept his new rifle as a present, but I told him you wouldn't take it."

"No, I hunt with bow and lance," Stone Wolf said, nodding to the boy approvingly. "I draw my medicine from the stone points on my arrows. The whites will never understand such a thing. Many among the People don't, either. They've opened their eyes to so much, but in seeing, they've closed their hearts to the truth all around them."

But although Stone Wolf suspected young Peter would never comprehend the harmony that preserved the wonderful balance that was life, the Arrow-keeper recognized the young man's merits. When it was time to erect the New Life Lodge, Peter appeared in his breechclout, accompanied by Whirlwind.

"Ne' hyo, I have come to suffer," the yellow-haired boy explained. "Whirlwind will show me what's to be done."

"You're too young," Stone Wolf argued. "Have you made a vow to undertake such an ordeal? What sick person needs healing? What wrong must be made right?"

"None," Peter admitted. "But Whirlwind says a man can sometimes undergo this torture to give the People strength. I would hang from the pole so that no misfortune visits the People."

"You don't understand," Stone Wolf said, resting a fatherly hand on the slight-shouldered boy. "It's a severe test for anyone, and you're not born to such hardships."

"I won't disappoint you," Peter promised. "Your

cousin, Long Walker, told me of hanging from the pole in the Lakota Sun Dance Ceremony. He wasn't so much older. I know soon my father will come. Maybe we'll hunt buffalo together, and maybe he'll camp here for a time. But when he returns to the fort, he'll insist I come along.

"You celebrate the remaking of the earth here. You've remade me, *Ne' hyo*. When I came, I was sad and alone. Now I have brothers and belonging. Let me suffer. In doing so, I'll repay all the People who have given so much to me."

Stone Wolf nodded, and so Peter undertook the torture of the New Life Lodge. As others before him had done, he allowed his chest to be pierced. Bound by the rawhide strap, he danced and bled, blowing his eagle whistle until the shine left his eyes. The boy's pain was enough to soften the hardest heart, and when he broke free of the strap, a great howl rose from the onlookers.

"*Ayyyy!*" Whirlwind shouted. "Here's a good man to know."

Other young men lifted him in their arms and carried him to the river to bathe his wounds. Dove Women tended the tears in his chest and offered food to restore his strength.

"You've done well," Stone Wolf observed after the cuts were healed. "I know of no white man with torture scars on his chest."

"Perhaps *Ne' hyo* might now consider me worthy of a name," the young man suggested. "I know I should hunt Bull Buffalo first and kill a bull, but if I do, will you give me a name?"

"You'd then be one of us," Stone Wolf cautioned.

"The soldiers would invite you to join them. You thought to leave once. Have you forgotten?"

"I don't belong on Shell River," Peter insisted. "I've earned a place here."

"Come, walk with me," Stone Wolf urged, and they set off from camp together. For a long time they meandered along, watching a hawk fly by overhead or gazing at a pair of boys racing their ponies.

"I don't want to go back," Peter said, gripping his adopted father's wrist.

"Your father will expect it, though."

"He'll expect it, but he'll respect my choice to remain. We have the same love, *Ne' hyo*. Open skies, the wind, and good friends. I won't find them at Fort William, selling whiskey and buying pelts."

"And if you stay?" Stone Wolf asked. "There are those who will hate your pale skin. Many remember relatives rubbed out by the blister sickness. Others blame our misfortunes on the traders who came to us before. Your road here has been hard, but it would grow worse."

"What will I do?"

"Climb the hills with me and seek a dream," Stone Wolf explained. "Let Man Above reveal your path."

And so Stone Wolf journeyed to *Noahvose* once more, for he thought Peter's need great, and the power of Bear Butte was needed. A fire was kindled, and the two of them smoked and prayed while Arrow Dancer and Ferret Boy kept watch.

"Man Above, send this young man a dream," Stone Wolf pleaded. "Help him put his feet on the true road."

They bared themselves and allowed cedar smoke to

251

purify their spirits. Then they prayed and sang and cut their flesh.

"*Heammawihio,* grant me a visión," Peter cried as he allowed the blood to flow down his chest, over his belly, and down his legs.

"Man Above, he's suffered," Stone Wolf whispered. "Give him a dream. Help him walk the medicine trail this night."

The two of them went on singing and praying most of the night. They collapsed together, and Stone Wolf slept the sound sleep of exhaustion. He awoke to Younger Wolf's touch.

"Peter's had his dream, *Nah nih,*" Younger Wolf explained. "And a party of Crows is nearby."

"Peter?" Stone Wolf called.

"I saw the path I must walk," the young man explained. "I'll leave with my father, but it won't be to the fort I go. No, I'll journey past Shining Mountains and find the wide water beyond. Man Above has shown me how."

"Then you must do it," Stone Wolf said sadly. "Know, *Naha',* as long as I walk the earth, you will be welcome to return to my lodge."

"That knowledge will be a comfort to me, *Ne' hyo.*"

Twenty-two

Stone Wolf's band was hunting Bull Buffalo north of Shell River when Marcel Freneau arrived with his family. The trader greeted the People warmly, making signs and using words learned in the camp of the *Tsis tsis tas*.

"It's good brothers are together," Younger Wolf noted as he gripped the trader's hands. "Your son's grown tall in *Nah nih's* lodge. Come, see him."

Corn Hair didn't seem surprised that Peter had adopted the People's dress and manner. No, it was the younger Freneaus who were impressed by their elder brother's scarred chest and long hair.

John, at twelve the next eldest, ran his fingers along the scars won suffering in New Life Lodge.

"He asks if you did this, *Ne' hvo?*" Peter said, translating his brother's question for Stone Wolf. "He suspects I've been taken captive!"

"You have," Corn Hair Freneau declared. "They've won your heart. It will be hard going back."

"I'll come, though," Peter said, nodding sadly to Stone Wolf. "As the dream instructed."

253

But that was later. The summer sun still hung high in the sky, and there was hunting to do.

Peter now rode with Arrow Dancer and the other young Foxes, and only rarely did either boy visit Stone Wolf's lodge. Their place was in the hunters' camp, where they boasted of their kills with the other young men, swam away their afternoon weariness, and sang the brave heart songs as the western mountains ate the evening sun.

Corn Hair made a camp nearby in the beginning, but gradually Stone Wolf coaxed the trader inside the circle. The Arrow-keeper studied the hesitant eyes of Crow Boy and Porcupine when the young yellow-haired Freneaus joined them to eat and talk. The Freneau youngsters were no less shy. Soon, though, using signs and then creating a new mixed language, the children put aside their fears and joined in swims and games.

Besides John, there were three other boys. Charles, eleven, was quick-witted and sharp-tongued. Louis, like Porcupine passing his ninth summer, was solemn and moody.

"You don't talk much," Porcupine observed.

"You do?" Louis asked.

Porcupine grinned, and thereafter the two age-mates were rarely apart.

The younger Freneaus, seven-year-old Mary and Tom, just six, kept to the camp most times. They enjoyed the old women's stories and accompanied Dreamer when he allowed it.

"Girls help with the cooking," he announced when Mary followed him to the river one morning.

"I didn't know," Mary told him as she gazed at the

older boys racing in the river. "I have no sister to show me what to do."

"Dove Woman, my mother, will help you," Dreamer told her. And, indeed, Dove Woman was delighted to have a daughter's help.

Gradually the Freneaus forgot their shyness. They set aside their wool trousers in favor of buckskin breechclouts and vests.

"Don't worry," Crow Boy told the boys. "*Nah koa* chewed the skins soft so they won't rub you."

"That's good," John said, grinning. "I don't want to be called 'Blistered Thighs' like my brother."

"He's called worse things," Crow Boy whispered. "But he's grown tall in our eyes after undergoing the suffering."

"Maybe we, too, will hang from the pole," John told Crow Boy.

"Only when it's appropriate," Crow Boy said, his serious ten-year-old eyes saying more than his words. "Come. The others are at the river!"

The boys howled furiously and raced off.

"It's good you've come," Stone Wolf told his adopted brother as the boys sped past. "Your sons are too thin, and they ride like old women. Soon they'll become one with Horse and know the smell of freedom carried by the wind."

"Your sons, too, are learning," Freneau observed.

"They already know the important things," Stone Wolf argued.

"What's important today and what will be important tomorrow are not the same. Already Long Walker and other Oglalas trade with their relatives and bring beaver pelts to Fort William. In return the

Oglalas get good guns and bright cloth. They're not cheated, and the young men avoid the whiskey makers."

"Is that the future you see for my sons?" Stone Wolf asked angrily.

"I see them as traders, yes, but traders of a new kind," Freneau explained. "Already beaver's growing scarce. Next it will be buffalo and elk hides. Stories of this good country make their way eastward, and the people say, 'Let's go there. Here where the lakes are pure and the forests stretch skyward, we can make a new beginning.' They'll come as strangers, helpless as newborns, and someone will have to teach them how to live. Men will lead the way across Shining Mountains to the Oregon country. Our sons, maybe."

"No," Stone Wolf objected. "You speak of this country as if it belonged to you. Here we camp and hunt. Whites bring death, like the sickness that killed my daughter. They drive off the game with their guns and noise. Even those like you, Corn Hair, who try to understand, find it hard to walk the straight road, living in harmony with all around you."

"It's true, Stone Wolf, but if we, and our children, can't bring our peoples together, others will come who only wish to exterminate the tribes."

"Exterminate?" Stone Wolf asked. It was a rarely used word. A man might do it to sickness, but to a people?

"Brother, where are the *Mandans?* Have you heard the smallpox, the blister sickness, has killed half the Crows on Laramie River?"

"Half?" Stone Wolf cried.

"And that wasn't by design. Soldier chiefs talk of making war on all the tribes."

"Ah, we've met these blue coats and their guns," Stone Wolf said, laughing. "We sent them home naked!"

"Yes," Freneau said, grinning. "The Oglalas found them and shared the tale. But those were but a handful. If the soldiers chiefs wish, they could send a thousand riders onto the plains. Could you fight so many?"

"If we must."

"They won't come in summer, when the grass is good and your ponies are fat. No, they'll strike your winter camps, when the bands are scattered, and only the circling birds will tell of the dead."

"How can you know this?" Stone Wolf cried. "Why do you paint these terrible pictures?"

"I, too, dream," Freneau explained. "I've lived in both worlds, and I know this dark day will come. It's for us to slow change, to work for peace."

"Yes, but can such dark times be turned? I carry a medicine shield, and it may deflect iron-pointed arrows, even lead balls shot from good guns. But even its power can't cast the darkness from a man's heart."

"Nor can I," Freneau said somberly. "But maybe we can help the leaders come together and talk. Agreements can be reached. The old ways can be preserved."

"They must be," Stone Wolf insisted.

"We'll work hard," Freneau vowed. "And so will they," he added, motioning toward the children wrestling on a sandbar.

* * *

Summer was no time for imagining dark days, though. The buffalo hunt concluded, and the camp halted while meat was smoked and set aside for winter. The cherries were ripening, and girls walked the hills, collecting them in their reed baskets.

"*Ne' hyo,* I was too young to hunt Bull Buffalo," Crow Boy told his father, "but Arrow Dancer says there are deer in the thickets growing fat on meadow grass. It's time you made me a good bow. Then I can lead my brothers on a hunt."

Stone Wolf nodded. Not long before, Younger Wolf would have tended such matters. Now he was occupied with his own growing son and his new place among the chiefs.

"I'll craft the bow," Stone Wolf promised. "Maybe we'll hunt Deer together."

"That would be a remembered hunt," Crow Boy agreed. "Maybe you'll make three bows. John and Charles have only their knives. They're good iron knives, *Ne' hyo,* but no deer is so blind that he'd let a corn hair come so close that a knife could be used."

"Three bows," Stone Wolf said, nodding. "Tomorrow we'll cut young ashes. Go and ask Arrow Dancer to give you buffalo sinew for the bowstrings. It's good a bow is made by many hands."

Stone Wolf worked the ash trunks in the old way, taking time to mold them with his knife and burn the wood strong. Arrow Dancer and Whirlwind provided the bowstrings, and boys accepted the weapons with quiet smiles.

"Now we'll hunt," Stone Wolf told them. "Corn

258

Hair and I will show you the way. You must follow slowly, practicing patience."

"Yes, *Ne' hyo*," the three bowmen answered.

They set off early the following morning, Porcupine and Louis came to hold the horses, but the hunting was left to the older boys.

The thickets were overgrown with briars that summer, and thorns tore at bare thighs and legs. Never once did anyone cry out, though, and Stone Wolf nodded approvingly at the boys. Once they came across deer sign, he halted them.

"Now we must make prayers," Stone Wolf explained. "Long ago, when Boy first received the sacred bow, he was told always to walk the world in harmony with his fellow creatures. When hunger tormented him, he was to hunt. The spirits live in all things, my sons, and even the lowest crawling thing is part of the Great Mystery. When a man prepares to kill, he must pray the animal gives itself over to his needs. In such a way there can be a joining of both in the sacred way. To kill without remorse, or to strike out of anger, is to destroy the harmony of the world and bring misfortune."

"How is it done?" John whispered.

"We'll make a fire and smoke," Stone Wolf explained, taking a pipe from his hip. "We'll invite Deer to give himself to us. Then, when you see a buck or doe, you must silently ask his life."

"How will we know if the animal gives himself up?" Charles asked.

"You'll know, *'Naha'*," Stone Wolf said, touching the boy's bare shoulder. "No words will come, but a peace will settle over you. Notch the arrow only then,

259

for you'll have the true aim, and the kill will be assured."

"And if I miss?" Charles asked.

"Man Above will give the kill to your brother," Crow Boy said, grinning.

They kindled the fire then and smoked. John swallowed a bit too much smoke and was sick, but the others followed Crow Boy's example and did no more then touch the pipe to their lips. When Stone Wolf was satisfied, he prayed for good fortune and emptied the pipe bowl. Finally he buried the fire and led the way on deeper into the thicket.

Now sign was everywhere. The grass was heavily chewed, and no fruit remained on the chokecherry plants. Stone Wolf touched his fingers to the twin lines left by deer hoofs in the soft ground and smelled the air.

Soon, he thought as he continued.

They came to a clearing beside a small spring. Three deer drank from the overflow, and Stone Wolf moved aside so that the boys could string their bows. He watched with approval as each made the required prayer and prepared to shoot. Crow Boy gazed eagerly at the waiting animals, then motioned for John to take the first shot. The yellow-haired boy looked at his younger brother, who also yielded. It was right, after all, the eldest should make the kill.

John notched his arrow and pulled his bow taut. Then, repeating his prayer, he loosed the arrow. It crossed the clearing with a quiet whine and struck the deer in its shoulder. The deer turned in surprise, and Crow Boy shot. His arrow struck the animal flush in its chest, and blood bubbled from the buck's mouth as its forelegs collapsed.

"End the pain," Stone Wolf whispered as the other deer scattered. Charles reluctantly notched his arrow, then stared at the dying buck. The third arrow struck deep, tearing at its heart. The deer rolled onto one side and found its death.

Stone Wolf expected the boys to cry out to celebrate the kill, but instead they walked slowly forward, displaying respect for the dead buck. They withdrew their arrows, and Stone Wolf made the throat cut. Crow Boy and John hung the deer up so the blood would drain, and the younger boys finally arrived with the horses.

"You've done well," Porcupine declared. "It's a good buck, and we'll enjoy venison steaks."

"You put too many holes in the hide, though," Louis observed, stunning everyone by speaking so many *Tsis tsis tas* words.

"You've learned our language well," Stone Wolf declared.

"He doesn't talk much," Porcupine said, slapping Louis on the back, "but he listens."

"It's a good way to learn," Freneau said, examining the kill. "We'll eat well tonight. Dove Woman can make snake tasty, but venison she pounds into chewy steaks. You'll think yourself on a cloud!"

"Our mother cooked well," Charles said, sighing. "But she's gone."

"Our mother went away," Crow Boy explained, "but she wasn't a good woman. *Ne' hyo* asked Dove Woman to come to our lodge, and she's been a better mother."

"She has a cousin," Porcupine said, grinning.

261

"It's not allowed," John said, staring hard at his father. "Our mother isn't dead, and the church allows only one wife."

"Church?" Crow boy asked.

"Yes," John explained, producing a small silver cross from a pouch carried on his hip. "We're Catholic."

"Ah, I've heard of the cross people," Crow Boy said, nodding. "Their black robe priests have been among the Oglalas. Our cousins say they make signs and say prayers whenever the Lakotas come among them."

"There's reason," John explained. "The cross offers protection. And Oglalas are fierce people. They never smile."

"They smile," Crow Boy said, grinning. "When eating small white boys."

"They don't eat you," Freneau argued. "Just cut off a piece or two."

"It's not true," John complained. "We know many Oglalas. They make camp on North Platte River, and we trade with them. Long Walker once gave me a pony."

"He's our cousin," Crow Boy boasted. "He told me the black robes are all crazy."

"Not crazy," John insisted. "Different. When we first came here, I thought you odd, Crow Boy, riding ponies without a real saddle, going about nearly naked. Now I'm wearing a breechclout and swimming Shell River with women gathering water at the bank! If the priests come among you, listen to them. They carry truth and faith onto the plains."

"They stir up trouble," Freneau grumbled. "These

262

people have their own faith, John."

The two started to quarrel, but a wolf howled on the far hillside, and all turned to stare.

"No!" Stone Wolf shouted as Charles drew an arrow from his quiver. "Wolf is sacred. Never point a weapon at him."

"He's going to take the deer," Charles replied.

"No, he says to remember the old admonition. Walk the world in harmony. We have no cause to quarrel. We're all of us brothers now, and there's work to do. Come, let's skin the deer."

"And the wolf?" Louis asked.

"We'll give him a gift," Stone Wolf explained. "A leg to eat."

Later, when they returned to the camp, Stone Wolf saw John fingering his silver cross and staring eastward.

"This is strong medicine, you say," Stone Wolf said, nodding at the cross.

"For me, yes," John answered. "My mother's brother wears the black robe. I expect to follow his path."

"Not your father's?"

"He has other sons."

"And this uncle does not?" Stone Wolf asked.

"Priests never marry. They're devoted to the faith. That must seem strange to you, *Ne' hyo.*"

"My grandfather's uncle also kept the Arrows," Stone Wolf said, lifting the boy's chin. "He believed the Arrows were his life, and he never took a woman."

"You did, though."

"Yes, twice," he said, laughing. "A man must do as his path demands, and I felt need of family. My father

263

died young, and I knew too much emptiness in my lodge. I would miss my sons."

"Uncle Joseph finds his road hard," John confessed. "But I suppose they all are."

"It often seems so," Stone Wolf agreed. "Put the medicine cross around your neck. Don't hide it in a pouch. I can see it brings you peace and should be close to your heart."

"Papa will be angry."

"Share your feelings with him. A father often believes he knows best, but he also sees clearly what's in his son's eyes."

That night, as Stone Wolf walked alone under the stars, he saw Freneau sitting beside the river, surrounded by all their sons. It was surprising the boys had so quickly bonded themselves to each other. Stone Wolf was both proud and alarmed at his own boys' familiarity with white man's language and customs.

When Younger Wolf visited, he saw it, too.

"You hoped for this understanding, *Nah nih*,' Younger Wolf reminded his brother. "It's for them to be the bridge to the future, after all."

"Yes," Stone Wolf confessed. "But will it be a future with a place for them?" He hoped so, but he knew events beyond his control would determine that.

Twenty-three

In the two years that followed, great changes shook the plains. A new kind of white man came west, one determined to build, to reshape the land. Far to the east along Shell River soldier forts sprang up, and whites built villages of wood and stone. Closer, Fort William grew. Corn Hair Freneau wasn't the only trader to travel among the tribes. Bull Buffalo scattered northward, hurrying toward the wild canyon country farther west or the low hills above Powder River.

The *Tsis tsis tas* found themselves pushed west and south. When not assembled to make the New Life Lodge or perform the Arrow renewal, the bands would disperse across the plains. Many Suhtai camps now traveled north with the Oglalas and Sicangu Lakotas. To the south, bands fought the Pawnees, Kiowas, and Snakes for the good hunting ground below Fat River.

It was during this time that Younger Wolf acquired great fame by recovering two of the original medicine Arrows. One of the Buffalo Arrows and one of the

Man Arrows were gained by guile and persuasion.

"It's good we have the old Arrows back," the People agreed. "But what's to be done with them?"

To Stone Wolf the answer was obvious. The old shafts must be renewed. New points and fletchings could be provided, and they would reclaim their rightful place in the sacred bundle. The two new Arrows they would replace could then be taken to *Noahvose* and given as an offering to *Heammawihio*.

"We should celebrate the restoration of the old Arrows," Stone Wolf said. "How better than the giving away of this powerful medicine?"

It seemed to Stone Wolf that the People enjoyed new prosperity from that moment. Hunters never failed to find game, and the young men took ponies from the Crows and Pawnees in great numbers. Stone Wolf's medicine was renowned, and as he crafted new Buffalo Shields for the bravest young men, he dreamed of brave heart deeds and great victories.

Stone Wolf gazed upon his growing sons with pride. Arrow Dancer stood straight and tall in his fifteenth summer. He regularly rode with the young Foxes on raids, and he rarely failed to bring meat to the young men's lodge.

"Ah, when he makes his wild charges," Crow Boy exclaimed, "he never fails to kill Bull Buffalo!"

Stone Wolf mourned his eldest son's absence. Now Crow Boy, too, was often gone. Only twelve, he didn't yet ride into danger, but he often held the men's horses while they collected Crow ponies.

"They hurry themselves into men," Dove Woman grumbled.

"Ah, I'm thankful Man Above has given us so much of their lives," he told her. "It's boy's nature to be impatient. See how Porcupine gazes at the young men? Next summer he, too, will want to ride out and hunt Bull Buffalo."

"Our lodge is too quiet already," Dove Woman complained.

"Go to visit Younger Wolf and Hoop Woman," Stone Wolf suggested. "Their little ones will make you thankful ours are older."

"Little Dancer, their son, puts me in mind of Dreamer," she said, smiling fondly toward the river, where their youngest son swam with his age-mates. "And the girls . . . Your brother was wise to have two daughters. They won't ride off to the hunt and forget their mother."

Stone Wolf smiled and took her hand. In truth the boys were never far away. They might hunger for adventure, but they hadn't forgotten Dove Woman's talent for roasting meat.

The younger Freneaus often visited, too. Peter hunted meat for the fort people now, and John had gone east to learn the black robe medicine.

"Next year Charles and Louis may pass the summer with you," Corn Hair told Stone Wolf. "They tire of the trading and remember the good times enjoyed in your camp."

"You should come, too," Stone Wolf suggested. "Too much time among the whites has turned you soft."

"And old," Freneau noted. "It's the winters."

"No, it's the lack of a woman," Stone Wolf argued.

"Your wife has still not returned to you?"

"She won't," Freneau said, shaking his head. "She doesn't share my love of this wild country. She's well, though. John sees her. Her father's rich, and he sees she's provided for."

"He should send her back to her family!" Stone Wolf complained. "I've seen this trouble before. Men don't always know when to let go of the reins. Daughters must make their own path, even as sons do."

"Your daughter is dead, Brother," Freneau said, frowning. "It's easy to say it. Quite another thing to do it. I ache enough that my sons have gone. When it's Mary's time, it will be very hard."

"Hard, yes," Stone Wolf agreed. "But it's always the difficult things a man has to do. The easy ones are unimportant."

That summer, camped along Powder River north of Fort William, Stone Wolf's band came in conflict with the Crows. The two tribes had raided each others' horses since first acquiring mounts, and there had also been some hard fights. Stone Wolf had counted coup on them as a young man, and he often shared remembered tales of the Crow battles of his youth.

Arrow Dancer remembered those stories, and when the Crows struck Red Bird's ponies, it was only natural the Dancer spoke of recovering them.

"*Ne' hyo,* I have accepted the pipe," the young man told Stone Wolf. "I go to smoke with Red Bird and the other Foxes. When we finish, perhaps you'll paint my face for war."

."Have the men considered this well?" Stone Wolf asked. "There will be a council surely."

"Tonight," Arrow Dancer explained. "The crier is making his rounds even now. Red Bird will go, though, and many young men are certain to follow. You'll paint my face and make medicine?"

"After we talk," Stone Wolf promised. "If there's to be war."

That night when the men gathered in council, Red Bird spoke hard words.

"We've suffered enough at the hands of these thieves," Red Bird declared. "My nephew was killed by them last year, and now they take my ponies. I would kill them all."

"Is it Crow ponies you seek or battle?" Stone Wolf asked. "You talk of men, not horses."

"If we kill the Crows, we'll easily retake the horses," Red Bird said.

"And once blood is shed?" Stone Wolf asked. "The Crows take ponies, and we take theirs. It's an old game. But if you strike down a man, his son's blood warms, and he comes to kill us. We then must avenge our dead, and it continues."

"Not if we kill them all," Red Bird said. "Crows are nothing. We've killed them often."

"Some of us have," Wood Snake agreed. "Red Bird, you've ridden to war, but how many of these young men have counted coup? We've shot up our lead hunting, and now our guns are empty."

"We have arrows," Red Bird argued.

"What drives you to demand blood?" Stone Wolf cried.

"They insulted him," Thunder Coat said, stepping to the side of the older man. "He stood guard, and they disarmed him."

"Enough!" Red Bird shouted.

"They quieted him and cut his belt," Thunder Coat added. "This is how they treat a blooded warrior. You've all seen Red Bird's battle scars!"

"Come with me," Red Bird told the others. "I've had a dream. We'll drive the enemy."

"There's more to this dream," Stone Wolf said, noting the Bird's tormented eyes.

"Yes," Red Bird admitted. "When we meet these Crows, I must show them my courage. I'll make a suicide charge."

"*Ayyyy!*" the young men shouted. "He has a brave heart."

"Come with me," Red Bird pleaded. "Help me find a brave death."

"Our concern isn't death," Thunder Coat said solemnly. "It's life."

"It will be a hard fight," Talking Stick said, standing and eyeing the young Foxes. "I, too, have dreams. Black crows fill the heavens in my vision. They peck at the flesh of our many dead."

"We should smoke and consider it well," Wood Snake suggested.

"Come or stay," Red Bird replied. "I'll do this thing alone if I have to. My sons are all dead now, and my nephews ride with the Suhtai. My days are long, but I won't end them in disgrace. These Crows will regret striking me!"

Stone Wolf sat quietly while the chiefs argued over

270

raiding the Crows. Only Red Bird among the head men was in favor of the ride, but the young men boiled over with eagerness.

"A brave man should not ride alone against the enemy," Whirlwind declared. "We'll pray and paint ourselves. I will lead the fight with my Buffalo Shield."

"It's for all of us to go," Stone Wolf finally said. "But consider well before striking a mortal blow. For each Crow who dies, some Crow will attack our camp."

"We'll kill them all!" Yellow Hand Pony boasted.

"They are too many," Stone Wolf argued. "And we are too few."

For two days the young Foxes sang and danced, warming their blood for battle. Stone Wolf prepared charms, and the Buffalo Shields were made ready. Finally the men painted their faces and chests.

"I give you what protection I know," Stone Wolf explained as he painted Arrow Dancer with the red bittersweet herb paint. The Wolf presented his son with two good ponies, each marked with the wolf paw medicine of his father's family.

"Hold your head high as you ride, *Naha'*," Stone Wolf said, "for only strong men have worn these brave heart symbols."

Young Charles Freneau offered the Dancer a silver bracelet, and Younger Wolf provided a necklace of bear claws. Finally Stone Wolf tied owl and eagle feathers behind the young man's ears.

"Stay vigilant, *Naha'*, and look with eagle's far-seeing eyes," the Arrow-keeper urged.

"Who will fight at your side?" Crow Boy asked as

he led his brother's horses to where the war party was assembling.

"Ferret Boy," Arrow Dancer answered. "Next summer, perhaps we brothers will ride together."

"If you're not careless," Crow Boy said, gazing seriously into his brother's eyes. *"Nah nih,* I know you. You'll ride in harm's way, as always. Watch out for Crow tricks, and remember the medicine prayers *Ne' hyo* has taught us."

"I remember them always," Arrow Dancer said, taking the horses and moving away.

It was, as Red Bird had foretold, a remembered fight. There was no surprise, for Crow scouts spied the raiders long before the *Tsis tsis tas* found the enemy. By then the Crows had formed a long line in the hills above Powder River. Three young men rode out as decoys, but Wood Snake held back the young Foxes.

"They've too often used this old trick," the Snake shouted. "Let's show them what we think of their Crow trap!"

The *Tsis tsis tas* howled like low dogs and waved their lances at the decoys. Then Red Bird rode out and faced the three.

"See this old man, Crows!" Red Bird screamed. "I'm the one you insulted! See the scars left on my chest by your fathers? I won them bravely, honorably. You who quirted me, who scorned my strong arms and brave heart, come and test them now. I'm here, waiting!"

The young Foxes cheered, and Red Bird dismounted. There he stood, stripped to the waist, painted black like death and waiting. The Crow decoys halted. Then one turned and charged. Calmly, with great patience Red Bird drew an arrow, notched it on his bowstring and pulled it taut. The Crow was only four horse lengths away when Red Bird loosed the arrow. It struck the young Crow in the throat and threw him back from his horse.

"Ayyyy!" the Foxes shouted as Red Bird walked over and cut away the dead enemy's forelock. Waving the bloody scalp at the remaining decoys, Red Bird invited their charge. The young Crows shouted back, turned, and flew at the old man.

Red Bird sang his death chant as he notched a second arrow. Again he waited until they were close before shooting. This arrow tore through the lead Crow's shield and pierced his belly. Red Bird then danced away from the other rider's shot, notched another arrow, and shot the last of the decoys through the back.

"Ayyyy!" the *Tsis tsis tas* cried as Red Bird scalped the two Crows. When the Crows on the far hill remained, Red Bird dragged one of the bodies out and tore away its war shirt. As he prepared to bare the corpse, a great angry howl rose from the hills. The Crows charged like a wall of fire on the prairie, enveloping Red Bird in a cloud of dust and gunsmoke. No one saw how Red Bird died, but a Tall Crow rode out, waving his hair.

"Brave up!" Wood Snake cried. "It's time we ran the enemy!"

273

Now came the *Tsis tsis tas* charge, and it was a terrible thing to see. Those with guns fired them, and the others lashed out with lances or shot arrows. Great confusion gripped the hillside, and for a time it was difficult to tell Crow from *Tsis tsis tas*. Some of the Crows, reeling from the ferocity of the enemy's charge, fled westward toward their camp. Others, angered at the death of the decoys, stood and fought. Many died.

Arrow Dancer carried a brightly decorated lance. The stone point was one carried by his grandfather, and perhaps others before that. It wasn't sharp like the iron points carried by others, but it was heavy and made a dangerous club. Twice the Dancer drove back older men with the lance, and another retreated when he recognized the wolf medicine on Arrow Dancer's pony.

"Here's a man to fight!" Ferret Boy screamed, turning to chase a young Crow toward the river. Arrow Dancer followed his friend, for there were two other Crows rushing to rescue the fleeing boy. Ferret Boy swung away from the onrushing enemies, but his horse fell, throwing him across the ground.

"Brave up!" Arrow Dancer called as he raced at the Crows.

The Crows were caught by surprise as Arrow Dancer darted between them, clubbing one across the forehead and throwing his horse into the second. The first rider fell, dazed by the blow, and the second was crushed under his falling horse.

"Join me, Ferret Boy!" Arrow Dancer called as he turned his shaken horse around. Before him the first

Crow rose to his knees and stared at the stone point of the lance.

"Strike him!" Ferret Boy urged as he limped over.

"See how I strike the enemy!" Arrow Dancer shouted. He then nudged his pony toward the defenseless Crow and touched him lightly on the shoulder. The Crow stiffened, and Arrow Dancer jumped down from his horse. With the flat of his hand, he struck the Crow again. All around them men paused in their individual battles to watch the two young men stare eye to eye at each other.

"Here's a brave man!" Arrow Dancer shouted, grinning. Then he turned, remounted his horse, and rode over to rescue Ferret Boy.

"Ayyyy!" the warriors, Crow and *Tsis tsis tas* alike, cried. And the lines pulled away. Each band recovered its dead, and the *Tsis tsis tas* turned back toward their camp.

Stone Wolf was kept busy two days mending wounds and offering medicine to the bruised and battered survivors. Many families began their three days of mourning by tearing their clothes and loosening their hair. Old Red Bird's lodge was torn down, and his belongings were given away. Soon only the memory of his last fight remained.

Crow scalps now decorated the shields of Thunder Coat and his brother, Talking Stick. Some good horses were taken from the slain Crows as well. But mostly the talk in the council was of Red Bird, the Crow decoys, and Arrow Dancer's coup.

"Ayyyy!" the Foxes all agreed. "It was a brave rescue. He rode through the enemy to his friend, ignor-

275

ing their bullets and arrows. His medicine was strong that day!"

"Yes," Whirlwind said, rising. "He saved my brother from the Crows. I give two horses away to celebrate this deed."

"I'm honored by my friend's brother," Arrow Dancer answered, avoiding the eyes of his elders. "I did only what we are pledged to do, one for the other."

"Ah, they are brother-friends," the men murmured. "It's a good thing to revive this old tradition."

"To count a coup should not go unrewarded," Wood Snake announced as he approached Arrow Dancer. "To strike the enemy is a brave thing. To put your hand on him is rarer still. Here, brave heart, accept these feathers."

Wood Snake tied two eagle tail feathers atop Arrow Dancer's hair so that they fell downward along his neck. All the council cheered and sang to mark the occasion.

Now Stone Wolf rose. Crow Boy led two horses out as presents, and the Arrow-keeper helped his son toward the fire.

"This is my son," Stone Wolf began. "Long has he carried a boy's name. Arrow Dancer he has been, but now he's proven his brave heart and can wear the old name no longer. I give it away."

"*Ayyyy!*" the others howled.

"Our father wore a brave name," Younger Wolf said, joining his brother beside the fire. "Iron Wolf, he was called. In the old, remembered fights, he carried the stone-tipped lance and touched the enemy in the old fashion, even as this young one did in the Crow fight at Powder River. It's a good name, Iron Wolf, and the People have been too long without it. Today my brother and I give it to our heart, this son of the People."

Both men gripped the young man's shoulders, and Iron Wolf trembled as he embraced them. Crow Boy made the giveaway, and the men rushed to greet the newest of the wolves.

"Ne' hyo, I feel tall," the young man told Stone Wolf.

"You *are* tall," Stone Wolf replied. "It's I who feel tall."

Twenty-four

Red Bird's fight, as it would always be remembered, did not end the People's trouble with their old foe, the Crows. Parties of boys were forever raiding horses, and occasionally hunting parties fought along Powder River. As the hard face moons of winter approached, Stone Wolf suggested moving south of Shell River into the country once roamed by the Pawnees.

"It's also the land of our cousins, the Arapaho," Wood Snake said, grinning. The Snake had a fondness for Arapaho women.

"The Kiowas also like that country," Thunder Coat argued.

"When didn't we send Kiowas running!" Yellow Hand Pony exclaimed.

"They camp with the Snakes on Fat River," Stone Wolf told the others. "We'll go east of there."

"It's good country, with wood and water where the two rivers meet," Wood Snake said, frowning. "But the Arapahos are on the plain."

"It's no place to winter," Stone Wolf declared.

"Winds blow the snows in white clouds across the land, choking and freezing any who camp there."

"He's right," Beaver Foot, an old man chief, agreed. "Once, when I was a boy, I saw a lodge buried in snow on Fat River, where the land is broken east of the Shining Mountains. Later, when the thaw came, a whole village was there, buried."

"We'll go south and east then," Wood Snake said, turning to the other chiefs. When no one objected, it was considered to be decided.

It was while in the winter camp, with his family gathered around him, that Stone Wolf sought the future in a dream. Many times he and Younger Wolf had climbed a hill and built a fire. Now Stone Wolf left his brother to watch the camp. Crow Boy came instead.

"Ne' hyo, it's winter," the boy had objected when Stone Wolf announced the plan. "Look at the skies. The clouds are dark with snow. It's no time to leave camp."

"It's a good time," Stone Wolf argued. "The nights are not yet cold, but our enemies are keeping to their camps. There's high ground nearby where we can build a camp and invite the dream."

"Is it so important?" the boy asked. "Often in winter dreams come to you unbidden."

"This time I have questions."

"What questions?"

"Ah, you look familiar, but I don't think we call you *Heammawihio."*

Crow Boy matched his father's grin, and they rode to the hill together.

It proved to be a remembered time for both. Stone

Wolf had often gone off with young Iron Wolf, bu'
Crow Boy had rarely been with his father when one
brother or the other hadn't been along. As the two sa'
beside the fire reading the heavens or smoking the
pipe, Stone Wolf came to see deeply into his son's
thoughts.

"Soon I'll go to the young man's lodge," Crow Bo'
had declared. "I've hunted Bull Buffalo, and I've held
horses for the men on horse raids. Soon I, too, wil
win a brave name."

"Your brother carries my father's name," Stone
Wolf noted.

"And I'm not tall enough to be called Touches the
Sky. The next Cloud Dancer should keep *Mahuts*."

"Yes," Stone Wolf agreed. "That's a task to fall into
the hands of my son, though."

"Iron Wolf and I have talked of it," Crow Boy ad
mitted. "We carry our mother's Crow blood. Perhap:
Dreamer will walk the medicine trail."

"He's young, and I grow weary."

"You have many summers yet to see, *Ne' hyo,*'
Crow Boy argued. "Surely a grandson will relieve you'
burden."

The notion of bearing the burden so long tor
mented him, but Stone Wolf didn't share his feelings
His sons had to make their own way, and if necessar'
others would keep the Arrows.

That first day they smoked and prayed, but al
though Stone Wolf slept, no dream came. He ac
cepted no food and only scant water, but denia
afforded him nothing. On the third day Stone Wol'
cut himself so that the bleeding kindled a fever. H'
grew weak with hunger, and weary with fatigue, bu'

he forced his eyes open, singing brave heart songs or dancing. When he finally collapsed, Crow Boy wrapped him in elk hides and stoked the fire.

Stone Wolf had prayed for four visions. He wished to see each of his sons standing tall in the years to come, and his great hope was that one would keep *Mahuts*. But no man writes his dreams, and so when the future revealed itself, it was not all Stone Wolf had hoped.

First Iron Wolf appeared. He rode a tall horse at the head of the young Foxes, waving the decorated stone-tipped lance and holding a shield.

He's taken warrior's trail, Stone Wolf silently realized.

Crow Boy, also, carried a shield, but instead of the wolf's head markings on his brother's, Crow Boy's shield resembled his father's, with a white skull dominating the center. In place of the sacred Arrow symbols, Crow Boy's shield was marked with eagles and hawks.

They ride the soldier road together, Stone Wolf noted. Ah, that was a good thing.

Next the dream filled with a shadow, and Stone Wolf had difficulty interpreting it. A riderless horse grazed on a lonely hill. Then it raced down the slope to a camp. Thereafter Stone Wolf saw himself in a great council, celebrating brave deeds and planning horse raids.

Clouds darkened the dream, and terrific flashes of lightning lit the heavens. Stone Wolf saw Shell River crowded with long, hoop-topped lodges. The river was full of swimming boys, most pale as fawn skin. Bull Buffalo lamented the arrival of these strangers.

281

"They come to our sacred places and carve their words in stone!" Bull Buffalo cried. "Many die of sickness or drown, but always more come. There's no end to them!"

Last Stone Wolf saw little Dreamer standing tall, preparing to hunt Bull Buffalo. His brothers brought him a good horse, and he climbed up atop it and followed them down a winding trail.

"Did the dream come?" Crow Boy asked when Stone Wolf awoke the following morning. "You cried out loudly twice, and once you whispered my name. I thought you were calling me."

"No, just gazing upon our future," Stone Wolf explained. "I saw little clearly."

"Did you see me a great horse stealer?" Crow Boy asked. "A warrior counting coup?"

"You'll do all these things," Stone Wolf assured the boy. "I was searching for something else."

"An Arrow-keeper?"

"Yes," Stone Wolf admitted. "I saw no one, but there are other boys about and some young men willing to guard the welfare of the People."

"Surely one will take your place. My son perhaps."

"I didn't know you had one."

"I don't," Crow Boy said, grinning. "Not yet."

Stone Wolf then accepted a cup of spring water from his son. As they visited, he put the dreaming behind him and spoke instead of hunting and scouting.

When he returned to the camp, no one asked him what he'd seen. Dove Woman did inquire about the boys, but he offered no explanation for a time. It was later, when the hard snows began to fall, when Stone Wolf described the dreams to Dove Woman."

"You've seen much, but it tells you so little," she said, sighing.

"Enough to know our sons will be good men," he argued.

"I knew that already," she grumbled. "You saw lodges on Shell River. That's not a welcome notion. Game will grow scarce there."

"Yes, and when the need is greatest of all, there will be few men to make medicine and find understanding."

Stone Wolf mostly found comfort in his sons' strength, though. As winter passed into memory, and the band moved north to renew the Arrows, he nodded approvingly when Iron Wolf and Crow Boy raced across the hills, closely pursued by Porcupine and Dreamer.

"They've grown tall, *Nah nih,*" Younger Wolf declared as he rode alongside.

"Brother, you've taught them well," Stone Wolf replied.

"It's their father's greatness," Younger Wolf insisted.

The Arrow renewal brought the scattered bands together once more, and Stone Wolf's heart quickened at the sight of so many lodges. It seemed the People were finally recovering from the sickness and death that had so often stalked them.

"*Ayyyy!*" Younger Wolf shouted. "It's good to be alive to see so many young men preparing for the hunt!"

"Yes," Stone Wolf agreed. But as he prepared elk

tooth charms for relatives and friends, he kept a watchful eye on Shell River. The image of the strange lodges troubled him now more than before, for as he prepared Porcupine for the boy's first hunt, Stone Wolf's sleep was troubled by disturbing dreams. Not since Firebird had lit the sky did the world have such a strange feel to it.

"Ne' hyo, don't worry," Iron Wolf said when Stone Wolf passed a new ash bow into Porcupine's hands. "He has brothers to ride with."

"Yes," Crow Boy agreed. "We are three now!"

"Soon four," Porcupine said, glancing back to where young Dreamer stood watching enviously.

Yes, Stone Wolf told himself. The little one had seen his seventh summer. He wouldn't be long kept from man's road, either.

Once the prayers and preparations were completed, the hunters moved north. Bull Buffalo seemed to have forsaken Shell River, and most of the young men were sent off to scout.

"It seems only yesterday we led the way," Wood Snake remarked to Stone Wolf as they sat beside the fire, warming their hands as the scouts departed.

"It was," Stone Wolf answered. "Hawk Wing hunts this summer, and I remember well when his father, Charging Hawk, was slain."

"Soon it will be our grandsons." Wood Snake said, laughing. Whirlwind already had two sons, and Painted Snake, as Ferret Boy was now called, walked the river path with one maiden or another when not hunting.

"It's appropriate, I suppose," Stone Wolf declared. "We've had our seasons."

"You talk like old men!" Younger Wolf grumbled as he shook off a rare summer chill. "I'm tired of waiting for children to find Bull Buffalo. *Nah nih,* are you young enough to ride with your brother this morning?"

"Ah, I'll do it," Stone Wolf replied sharply. "I'm tired of eating river fish. I hunger for a buffalo steak!"

"*Ayyyy!*" Wood Snake shouted. "I'll come, too. We old ones will strike Bull Buffalo's trail!"

They were but three, though, and the young men were many. Stone Wolf led them westward, toward Laramie River, and soon they came upon buffalo sign.

"We're not the first, though," Younger Wolf noted, pointing to a small party of riders on the next ridge.

"Crows?" Wood Snake asked, readying his rifle.

"Worse," Stone Wolf said, laughing. "Our sons."

The men swiftly took cover in a stand of cottonwoods and watched as Painted Snake and Iron Wolf led the way along the ridge. Suddenly Crow Boy pointed to his left. Instantly the scouts turned and made their way down the slope.

"Bull Buffalo's here," Younger Wolf said, sniffing the air.

The horses also caught the scent, and they stirred with anticipation. Stone Wolf kicked his pony into a gallop, and his companions followed. They broke out into the open in time to glimpse the herd moving slowly south. The scouts raced each other to be the first to strike Bull Buffalo.

"They should send word to the others," Wood Snake muttered.

"Yes," Younger Wolf agreed.

"Ah, did you ever turn away when seeing your first herd?" Stone Wolf asked. "Even my old man's heart urges them on."

As they watched, Crow Boy raced out ahead of the others. The spotted stallion he sat wasn't the fastest of Stone Wolf's many horses, but mount and rider were as one that day. The others used their quirts, but they fell farther behind. The herd started to run, but Crow Boy cut inside the watching bull and slapped a cow with his bow.

"Ayyyy!" Crow Boy screamed across the plain. "I am first!"

The scouts then swung wide of the herd, and the buffalos thundered on past a bit before slowing. Soon after, they resumed their peaceful grazing.

Crow Boy wasn't content with being the first to sight the herd or the first to count coup, either. Once the hunters were gathered, and the ceremonies conducted, Crow Boy raced ahead of his brothers and made the first kill.

"Ne' hyo, I thought he would find a cow to shoot or a small bull," Porcupine said excitedly. "Instead he charged the lead bull itself. *Ayyyy!* He killed it with his second arrow."

"Porcupine also did well," Iron Wolf explained. "He killed a calf."

"And only required a quiver of arrows to do it," Painted Snake added.

"I had the greater challenge," Porcupine insisted. "Anyone can hit a big bull. My quarry was small. Don't grieve over the lost arrows, *Nah nih.* I'm a good arrow-maker."

286

"But a poor shot," Iron Wolf said, laughing. "It's good to be one or the other, though."

It was later that summer when Crow Boy won his name and was invited to join the Fox Warriors. Though the boy was but thirteen, Iron Wolf and Painted Snake had agreed he should accompany them on a raid against the Crow pony herd.

"His eyes are keen, and he never tires," Iron Wolf declared.

"He's gone before," Painted Snake added.

"Only to hold the horses," Whirlwind had complained.

"As all of us once did," Iron Wolf argued. "He's my brother. I'll watch him."

As it happened, though, it was Crow Boy who did the watching. Twice the others started into ravines when Crow Boy warned them back.

"See there," he said, pointing to a scrap of cloth hanging on a cottonwood branch. "Cloth. Only our enemies wear such clothes."

The second time Crow Boy noticed a trail cut through a brier thicket.

"No buffalo or wild pony did this," he explained.

Finally, when they located the pony herd, it was Crow Boy who spotted the guard camp.

"Quiet," Iron Wolf urged. "We'll dismount and lead the horses away."

"Better to stay mounted," Crow Boy argued. "There are only three watching, and they are just boys."

"You're old yourself," Painted Snake said, grinning.

But again the older boys followed Crow Boy's lead. He approached the guard camp silently, found the watcher's asleep, and stole their guns. Then, one by one, he clubbed them, tied their hands and feet, and moved on to the next.

"Now we can run the horses," Crow Boy noted, and the raiders did just that. They reached the *Tsis tsis tas* camp with over a hundred ponies, and the People shouted their approval.

"It was a remembered thing," Iron Wolf declared as he recounted the tale to the council. "We might have made those Crows captive, but they were old enough to bring us trouble."

"The horses are more use," Painted Snake agreed.

"It's good you brought off so many horses," Wood Snake told the raiders. "Better yet that no one was hurt. You've done well."

"It was all my brother's doing," Iron Wolf said. "He was first to strike the buffalo, and now he has been first to touch the enemy. *Ayyyy!* It's good another son of Stone Wolf walks man's road."

"Yes," the men murmured their agreement.

"Stand, boy!" an old man demanded, and Crow Boy rose slowly.

"You're not tall," the old one said as he stepped over and lifted Crow Boy's chin with a withered hand. "As you see, I was never a giant myself."

The others laughed, but the old man remained serious.

"Long ago, when I was in my fourteenth year, I also led the way. So I've done ever since. I've counted coup on Crows, Kiowas, Pawnees, Snakes, even on the hairy faces. Now I'm bent over with old age, and my sons have climbed Hanging Road. There is no one left to give my name."

The council stirred in anticipation, and the old man gazed solemnly into Crow Boy's eyes.

"What am I called?" the old man asked.

"All know you," Crow Boy said, stepping back a pace. "Goes Ahead! Crier of the Foxes."

"I'm so called no longer," the old one said. "I take my boy name, Big Ears." The others laughed, but Big Ears hushed them. "You, now, are Goes Ahead."

"*Ayyyy!*" the young men howled. "It's a brave heart name!"

Iron Wolf walked to where some of the captured horses grazed and brought Big Ears two of the best.

"You need horses, Uncle," Iron Wolf said. "I give you these two in honor of my brother, Goes Ahead."

Again shouts erupted, and men rushed to congratulate the young man who had won a name.

Twenty-five

With three sons hunting and raiding, Stone Wolf gave over to them the responsibility for providing meat and devoted himself to the obligations of an Arrow-keeper. The renewed prosperity of the People brought many young men from the ten bands to the Arrow Lodge in search of medicine. Others came to ask *Mahuts* questions. And when no one came, there were always the children of the camp to entertain.

Many boys had come to help with the healing cures since White Horn had become Talking Stick, but now Dreamer was old enough to gather roots and kindle the fire. The boy missed his brothers and was happy to share his father's work.

"Ne' hyo, soon I'll ride with them," Dreamer said. "Who will make the fire then?"

"Someone whose heart calls him to walk the medicine trail," Stone Wolf answered.

In truth, Dreamer himself studied the ceremonies and curing with great interest.

"Ne' hyo, why does the starving bring a fever?" he would ask. "Why do you let your blood flow?"

Stone Wolf answered with patience, hoping to kindle in the eager boy's mind an understanding for the harmonious world Man Above designed.

"All we hope to do is restore the balance, *Naha'*," Stone Wolf told his son. "All manner of sickness can torment the body and the spirit. Poisons must be drawn out. Often the Sweat Lodge can revive the harmony. Also a singing will drive off the afflicting demons."

Sometimes Stone Wolf would awake to find Dreamer thrashing about in his sleep.

"Ne'hyo, he also dreams," Porcupine would say as he watched his small brother.

Yes, we named him well, Stone Wolf thought. And as the boy told of the future he saw, his father found reason to smile. Perhaps, after so many helpers, a new Arrow-keeper was at last walking at Stone Wolf's side.

That summer Stone Wolf's own dreams were troubling. Rarely did a night pass without some glimpse of the strange long lodges with the hooped covers. Equally troubling were the parties of white horsemen who skirted the hunting camps.

"Who are these men?" Stone Wolf asked his brother.

"I don't know," Younger Wolf confessed. "They don't trap, and they don't trade. They have hungry eyes, though, and they make pictures of rivers and hills. They say they only come to look, but I don't trust their words."

No, Stone Wolf thought. A hungry-eyed white man was cause to fear.

By summer's end one great mystery was finally solved. Iron Wolf appeared at the Arrow Lodge with news he'd seen the hoop-covered lodges.

"Where?" Stone Wolf asked.

"On Shell River, not far from the traders' fort," Iron Wolf explained.

"That's no place to build a camp," Stone Wolf observed.

"Ah, but these hooped lodges are on wheels, *Ne' hyo*. They are pulled by horses!"

"Wagons?" Stone Wolf cried.

"A long line of them," Iron Wolf explained. "Beside them walk many pale people."

"Men?"

"Yes, and women. Little ones. A whole camp, with many cows and horses."

"Now I see it," Stone Wolf said, frowning. "White man means to make a road of Shell River."

"Is that a bad thing?" Iron Wolf asked.

"You haven't seen a white man's road," Stone Wolf said, sighing. "Corn Hair has told me how the wheels cut deep into Mother Earth, scarring the land. Soon the grass will be chewed to nothing, and the game will vanish. Shell River is Bull Buffalo's road. If he comes no more, how will the People live? What meat will keep us fed in the hard face winds? What will we wear?"

"They can't make a road through our country," Iron Wolf argued. "Peter and John have told me of the white people's laws. They need a paper. Our chiefs will never agree to one."

"I remember such a paper signed near Muddy River," Stone Wolf said, frowning. "Ah, the soldier chiefs said, it's a greeting from our chiefs to you. Here are fine presents you can have if you touch the pen.' Soon the whites came, swallowing that good country. Yes, they were the hungry-eyed ones, and we were tricked. No great chiefs signed their paper, *Naha'*. It doesn't matter to them. A name only is needed, and they are satisfied. It's a bad thing they come."

"We should stop them," Iron Wolf suggested.

"Perhaps, but whites have long traveled Shell River. I must smoke on this, *Naha'*. Then perhaps we'll ride out, you and I, to see these strange lodges."

"Yes, *Ne' hyo*," Iron Wolf readily agreed. "I'll ready our horses."

Stone Wolf solemnly entered the Arrow Lodge and filled a pipe. Dreamer entered quietly and sat beside his father.

"You'll ask *Mahuts* about the wagon people," the boy whispered.

"Yes," Stone Wolf answered. "But I fear there's no good choice for us to make."

"I saw these people in my dreams," Dreamer whispered. "There was blood and fire. Great suffering."

"What else?" Stone Wolf asked, studying his sons' tormented eyes.

"Later, I heard mourning cries in our camp," Dreamer said, shuddering so that Stone Wolf drew the boy close.

"In our camp?" the Arrow-keeper asked.

"Yes," Dreamer replied. "I didn't understand. People were crying, and Iron Wolf said, 'Our brother is dead'!"

Stone Wolf calmed his son, then built up the fire. As he lit the pipe and invoked sky, earth, and the cardinal directions, he sensed something terribly wrong with the world. He tied two eagle feathers to the medicine bundle and asked the Arrows, *"Mahuts,* what must we do?"

The answer came slowly, as if whispered on the wind.

"Save the innocents," it seemed to say.

"Did *Mahuts* answer?" Dreamer asked as Stone Wolf stepped from the fire and began assembling his medicine pouches.

"You didn't hear?" Stone Wolf asked.

"No, *Ne' hyo*. It's for the Arrow-keeper to hear, you've told me."

"Yes, that's so," Stone Wolf agreed. *"Mahuts* said to save the innocents. I'll ride out with your brother and see what can be done."

"What does it mean, 'save the innocents'?" Dreamer cried.

"I'll know when we arrive, *Naha',"* Stone Wolf assured the boy.

"How?"

"My heart will tell me,"

When Stone Wolf stepped from the Arrow Lodge, he found Iron Wolf had summoned the Foxes.

"It's best we ride in strength," Iron Fox explained.

"Yes," Wood Snake agreed. "Should we carry our shields, old friend?"

"I won't lead you into a fight," Stone Wolf promised. "None of us has made proper preparations."

"I read your eyes, *Ne' hyo,"* Goes Ahead objected. "It's important, this thing we go to do. Tell us."

"I can't," Stone Wolf replied. "My thoughts are muddied like a river crossing. I can make no sense of them."

"Ah, the ride will clear the confusion," Wood Snake said confidently. "Come, Foxes, we ride to look at these wagon lodges. Maybe we'll trade with them. Maybe we'll take their horses."

"We could leave them naked like the blue coats," Whirlwind suggested.

"No, this is no war band to be tricked," Stone Wolf told them. This ride would be no game.

They were half the day reaching Shell River, and a bit longer locating the white wagon people. They had their wagon lodges formed in a square, with their horses inside. At first Stone Wolf was baffled by this odd camp. Then he saw the Lakotas.

"Ne' hyo," Iron Wolf called, pointing to a mixed band of Oglalas and Sicangus watching from a slight rise just ahead.

"How many?" Stone Wolf whispered.

"Thirty perhaps," Iron Wolf answered. "Maybe more. They're clever at hiding, the Lakotas."

"Yes," Stone Wolf admitted.

He and Wood Snake rode out from the rest and hailed the Lakotas. A tall Sicangu chief, Spotted Eagle, greeted them. The two tribes had traveled together often, and they had no trouble understanding each other's language.

"Hau!" Spotted Eagle called. "Brothers, have you come to join our fight?"

Wood Snake turned to Stone Wolf, who said, "Perhaps. My dreams have been troubled. They call me here."

"You're Stone Wolf, who keeps the sacred Arrows," Spotted Eagle said, nodding. "It's a good thing you add your strong medicine to our struggle."

"What's happened here?" Wood Snake asked.

"Much," the Eagle answered. "Come. I'll show you."

Stone Wolf and Wood Snake dismounted and followed the Lakota chief a short distance. There, resting

on a blanket, was a young Sicangu boy of perhaps fourteen summers. A lead ball had smashed his left leg below the knee, and he fought back pain as two young
men fought to halt the bleeding.

"This is a thing I should do," Stone Wolf said, slip-
ping a buckskin bag from his shoulder and searching it.
At last he found a manroot and shaved a bit off.

"Boil this to make a tea," Stone Wolf told one of the
young Lakotas. Then, after invoking the aid of the spirits, he drew out a sharp flint knife and examined the leg.
It wasn't hard to locate the misshapen ball and work it
out of the swollen flesh. It hurt considerably, and Stone
Wolf was grateful Man Above brought on a faint. The
young man slept fitfully as Stone Wolf removed two
slivers of bone. Then he added yellow healing powders
and bound the wound. He added splints to protect the
injured bone and help it heal. Finally, when the boy
awoke, Stone Wolf insisted he drink the root tea.

"Your medicine is strong," Spotted Eagle said, gripping Stone Wolf's hands. "He's my son."

"It's good to have strong sons," Stone Wolf noted.
"The leg will heal."

"Now we'll punish the whites!" Spotted Eagle
shouted, and the other Lakotas howled their approval.

"Wait," Stone Wolf called, urging restraint.

"We must punish them," Spotted Eagle argued. "My
son rode to trade with them, and they shot him. Here,
in our country, they shoot boys who ride the river as
they've always done."

"Who did it?" Stone Wolf asked.

"A wagon boy," one of the young Sicangus said. "No
older than Eagle Claw himself."

"It's a misunderstanding," Stone Wolf suggested.

"No man who knows the country would shoot a La-kota! A fearful boy shot your son."

"If he's old enough to carry a gun, he should under-stand a peaceful greeting," Spotted Eagle complained. "My son carried no bow, no lance. He left his weapons behind, on the hill. His face wasn't painted, and his horse's tail was not tied as for war."

"Let me go and talk with these people," Stone Wolf pleaded. "My heart warns it's not right they should all die."

"Is this the man we once heard speak strong against letting white traders come among his people?" Spotted Eagle asked in dismay. "Have you grown soft in old age?"

"What do your eyes tell you?" Stone Wolf asked, turning toward the angry Lakotas. "Would you strike me blindly, as the wagon boy shot your son?"

Spotted Eagle softened. Turning back, he saw his son gazing up with alert eyes.

"He's right, *Ate*," Eagle Claw said. "The one who shot me was afraid. There's one among the wagon people we know."

"Yes," Spotted Eagle agreed. "Young Corn Hair's boy."

"Freneau?" Stone Wolf asked, growing cold. "Ah, now I understand."

"Yes?" Spotted Eagle asked.

"Freneau is his brother," Wood Snake explained. "Corn Hair's sons have ridden to the hunt with us many times."

"Go and speak with your son then," Spotted Eagle said, nodding. "As you saved my son, I'll save yours."

Stone Wolf walked to his horse, remounted, and

started down the slope toward the wagon people. He rode slowly, holding his hands out to show he wasn't armed. The terrified wagon people gazed at him over their long-barreled muskets, many of them cocked and ready to fire.

"Ne' hyo!" Peter Freneau called, stepping out from the wagon wall and greeting his adopted father. "I'm glad to see you!"

"Ah, it's good I came," Stone Wolf said, frowning. "You are in a hard place, *Naha'.*"

"You've spoken with the Lakotas?" Peter asked. "How's the boy?"

"Alive, but lame," Stone Wolf answered. "Your people picked a bad one to shoot. His father leads the Sicangu."

"Spotted Eagle. Yes, I recognized him. How many ride with him?"

"Enough," Stone Wolf said, dismounting. He led young Freneau aside and told of the bad hearts among the Lakotas.

"I warned them against loading their rifles," Peter said, sighing. "Already a small girl was accidentally shot by her brother and killed. Now this! They think they can defend themselves, but at dusk, when the Lakotas come, we'll all of us die."

"Not the smaller ones," Stone Wolf argued. "They'll be accepted into the tribe."

"I had my dream, *Ne' hyo,* but it's brought me to an early death."

"No, you can come away with me," Stone Wolf suggested. "I mended the boy's leg. Spotted Eagle will allow you to go."

"And the others?"

298

"Wrong's been done," Stone Wolf pointed out. "The Lakotas expect payment."

"Surely not fifty lives for a wounded boy."

"You don't understand," Stone Wolf complained. "These people scar the earth, disturbing the harmony of our country. It's for that we would punish them."

"And will you kill the others, those who follow?" Peter asked. "They'll come, and soldiers with them. The traders at Fort William will hear gunshots, and when they ride out to investigate and find murdered women, they'll insist blue coats be sent. That will be the end of your harmony, *Ne' hyo,* not our coming."

"And if we run the Lakotas?"

"You'll be preserving peace."

Stone Wolf paused, considering his choices.

"You'll come away with me?" the Arrow-keeper asked.

"Ne' hyo, do you think I've changed so much? Could you ignore your obligations?"

"If you stay, you may die."

"Should I fear the long sleep? No, *Ne' hyo,* you and my father taught me better. I won't abandon the helpless ones."

"Then it's for us to save you," Stone Wolf said, gripping the young man's hands.

"If you can't, set me up high," Peter said, swallowing hard. "At least I left my hair long. It will make the Lakotas a good trophy."

Stone Wolf hesitated to let the young man return to the wagon people, but Peter pried his hands free and retreated. Stone Wolf remounted his pony and hurried to speak with Spotted Eagle and the Lakotas.

The Arrow-keeper shared all Peter Freneau had said,

first with the Lakotas and then with his own people.

"I owe you a life, true," Spotted Eagle admitted, "but not all of them. Someone must pay for the wrong done my son."

"Then someone will," Iron Wolf said, turning toward the wagon camp. He set his lance aside and approached the whites with hands extended to his sides. Freneau stepped out to speak with his old friend. They talked several minutes. Then Iron Wolf accompanied a young white boy back toward the hill.

"This is the one who shot Eagle Claw," Iron Wolf explained.

"Yes?" Stone Wolf asked. "It was you?"

Iron Wolf translated his father's question, and the boy nodded fearfully. Tears formed in the corners of his eyes, and he shuddered as Spotted Eagle drew a knife and cut open his shirt.

"He's afraid, but he doesn't run," the Lakota observed.

"Yes, he's afraid," the young Lakotas said, laughing. "He's made water."

Spotted Eagle hushed them.

"It's right a wrong should be punished," the Sicangu chief asserted. "Yes?"

Again Iron Wolf translated, and the boy paled. Then, with trembling hands, he grasped Spotted Eagle's hand and drew the knife up against his shivering chest.

"I got a ma and pa down there," he said, shivering. "Brothers. A sister. I didn't mean to hurt anybody, but I did. No reason everybody ought to suffer for it. Just make it quick, won't you, mister? I heard about the slow death, and I wouldn't favor that."

300

Iron Wolf interpreted the words, and Spotted Eagle lowered the knife.

"Their ways are strange," the Eagle observed, "but a man who would suffer for his people can walk the straight road."

"Yes," Stone Wolf agreed. "What should we do, old friend?"

"Restore the balance," Spotted Eagle said, turning to his son.

"Yes, *Ate,* match the wounds," Eagle Claw agreed.

Spotted Eagle sheathed his knife and raised a lance instead. With a single blow he shattered the white boy's leg. The boy screamed out and fell, clutching the broken limb.

"Heal him," Spotted Eagle said, resting a hand on Stone Wolf's shoulder.

"Why?" the whites asked when Stone Wolf brought the boy down the hill.

"Wrong was done," Stone Wolf told Freneau. "He'll long remember this."

"We all will," a big man said when Peter Freneau translated. "They'll pay for this."

"They might have taken his life," Peter argued. "Mr. Harrison, anybody but Spotted Eagle likely would have. He's let the rest of us go, and I wouldn't have bet a nickel on that happening. It's Stone Wolf's doing."

"And who will set the boy's leg?" Harrison cried. "He'll be lame, and for what? Shooting an Indian!"

"He won't be lame," Peter said, tearing the boy's trouser open from heel to the knee. "My father will set it. He's a medicine chief."

"He isn't really your father," a woman cried. "We met Mr. Freneau at Fort William."

301

"Not my father?" Peter cried. "Who else could have saved us?"

The wagon people returned to Fort William, for Stone Wolf insisted the Harrison boy have rest to allow the mending of the leg to begin. Peter Freneau welcomed the decision, for it afforded him the chance to offer presents to the *Tsis tsis tas* for their help. Two fine ponies were presented to the Arrow-keeper, and Iron Wolf was given a fine new rifle.

"You did well," Marcel Freneau told Stone Wolf as they sat beside Laramie River, watching the young whites swim with the fort Oglalas and the *Tsis tsis tas* visitors. "Our peoples are different, yes, but alike as well."

"I wish these newcomers sought to understand us better," Stone Wolf lamented.

"Yes," the trader agreed. "If you hadn't come, there would have been a terrible slaughter. Peace on the North Platte would have come to an end."

"We've done no great thing, my sons and I," Stone Wolf argued. "In the days to come, when more pale people arrive, we may all wish these people had paid with their lives so that others wouldn't follow."

"They'll come anyway," Freneau insisted. "As we've both always known they would. But maybe our sons can forge a peace."

Stone Wolf looked hopefully at the river, where Dreamer and little Tom Freneau splashed alongside each other. He wished he could believe such a peace possible. But how could it be when there were so many angry hearts? It took so few to start war.

Twenty-six

Stone Wolf moved his band south that autumn to the Swift Fox River. There, many of the other bands had been struggling against the Kiowas and their fierce Snake and Apache allies. It was good buffalo range, and the Arapahos, old friends of the People, had come down as well. So many hunters in this land where the Pawnee, too, roamed, was certain to cause conflict.

The young Foxes welcomed the chance to fight these old enemies. The Snakes were famous horse stealers in the south, where they took good Mexican and American horses from the settlers. They always had too many animals to guard well, and small bands of Arapaho and *Tsis tsis tas* raiders were always sneaking in and running some north.

"Who will ride with me to take horses?" Thunder Coat asked one night as the first cool wind whipped across the flat country north of Swift Fox River.

"I will go!" Talking Stick shouted.

"I, too!" others cried.

And so Thunder Coat led the Fox Warriors across

the river into enemy country. They were gone but a short time when they came upon great herds of horses. A party of Snakes gave battle, but no one was badly hurt. When the Foxes returned, bringing along many horses, they were greeted with shouts and brave heart songs.

It was a hard time for Stone Wolf. His sons followed Younger Wolf on raids or hunted in the northern hills with Whirlwind and Thunder Coat. As the hard face winds arrived, old wounds made themselves felt, and when not making the healing cures or making medicine prayers, Stone Wolf sat close to the fire and warmed himself.

"Ne' hyo, the criers are out," Dreamer explained one morning as snow flittered down in a light wind.

"Ah, send one to speak with me," Stone Wolf urged, and the boy stepped outside the Arrow Lodge. Soon he returned with Yellow Hand Pony, lately made a crier by the other young Foxes.

"I come to summon a council," the Pony explained. "Kiowa raiders have been seen, and Thunder Coat is carrying a pipe. We'll smoke and make a war party."

"In winter?" Stone Wolf asked. "With snow already painting the land?"

"Yes, others, too, speak against it," Yellow Hand Pony admitted. "But we'll smoke and talk of it tonight. Perhaps you'll ask *Mahuts.*"

"It's for the pipe carrier to do," Stone Wolf grumbled. "Has everyone forgotten?"

Indeed, many had, for already young men were readying their war ponies. The chiefs quickly condemned these premature moves and drove the younger

304

Foxes to the council. As the fire blazed in a circle cleared of snow, Wood Snake reminded the young men of their obligations.

"Winter is a hard time for the People," the Snake said. "Many must keep to their lodges, and game is scarce. Above all a Fox must guard the defenseless ones and the buffalo meat which will feed them until the grass greens once more. It's good to take Kiowa ponies, yes, but we should watch these raiders and see they don't strike our camp. It's no time for the young men to ride off hunting honor."

"Old man's talk," Thunder Coat muttered. "Have our chiefs forgotten battle makes the blood strong? Brave up! Join this struggle."

"It's easy to talk," Younger Wolf said, rising. "I know a young man's heart hurries him at his enemies, but it's necessary to make medicine, sing and dance and pray. *Mahuts* is with us, and the Arrows should be consulted. A war party who rides with power meets with success."

"When all these things are done," Thunder Coat argued, "the Kiowas will have escaped. We should ride now, before my sons have grown tall and my hair has gone white with age."

"I remember another who talked this way," Younger Wolf said with a frown. "He was called Bear Claw, and he urged us fight the Pawnees."

The other men stirred uneasily, for all recalled the time when *Mahuts* was lost to the People. As Younger Wolf shared the story, he gazed somberly at each of the young men's faces.

"Bear Claw ignored the power of *Mahuts,* and he

305

neglected to make the required prayers before taking the war road," Younger Wolf added. "Two summers past, when we were renewing the Arrows, Bear Claw and the Bowstrings broke away to raid the Snakes. Do you remember this, brothers? Some were in the north country, not yet arrived, but Bear Claw wouldn't listen. He insulted the Arrows and hurried from camp.

"Long ago Bear Claw was warned he would come to a bad end for mistreating the Arrow-keeper and ignoring the rituals. This time he rode with many brave men into enemy country. A large band of Kiowas with their Snake and Apache allies fell upon Bear Claw's band, killing and scalping every one of them. Later, when relatives reached the place where they were killed, only bones remained.

"Remember this story when you speak of hurrying into a fight," Younger Wolf urged. "Don't get the brave hearts killed. Make the proper prayers, and I will join you. *Ayyyy!* We'll make a remembered raid. Cool your blood now and make medicine. Later we'll dance and sing, kindling the fire in our veins once more."

Thunder Coat was unconvinced, but the others howled their agreement. For once a chief's voice had carried the day.

The strike against the Kiowas was well-planned. Scouts kept a watchful eye on the raiders while Stone Wolf made the medicine prayers. *Mahuts* blessed the attack, and the young men painted themselves and prepared their ponies.

"Your heart remains troubled, *Nah nih*," Younger Wolf observed. "You don't fear these Kiowas?"

"No," Stone Wolf replied. "They only come for horses. We're old enemies, and we've always met each other with respect, making the good fight and giving each other honorable death."

"What worries you then?"

"It often appears to me that while we fight our neighbors, the whites creep in behind us and steal the earth."

"It was you who saved the wagon people."

"Yes," Stone Wolf said, sighing. "My dream told me to save the innocents. To kill the children would have darkened our hearts. Even so, perhaps we can find peace with these others."

Thunder Coat's war party rode out that afternoon, but the Kiowa horse stealers were clever. They evaded Thunder Coat and struck the People's pony herd instead. War cries swept the camp that night, and those men remaining in camp hurried to dress themselves and grab their bows.

"Protect the camp!" Wood Snake shouted. "Brave up. We're Foxes! It's for us to do the hard things!"

One group of Kiowas was driving horses southward toward the river while the rest rushed into camp, knocking down lodges and terrifying the little ones.

Stone Wolf had thought his fighting days over, but he had not yet passed his fortieth summer. He pulled the cover from his shield, dabbed paint on his face, and balanced an old stone-tipped lance lightly in his powerful right arm.

"Come and test my shield!" he screamed as he stepped out into the night. "Nothing lives long. Only the earth and the mountains!"

Some of the younger men saw the Arrow-keeper and calmed themselves. They collected bows, lances, even war clubs and formed a line. Three Kiowa riders charged, but they were cut down in a hail of arrows. A fourth rushed toward Stone Wolf on foot, but the Arrow-keeper deflected the Kiowa's lance with the Buffalo shield and clouted the young man across the forehead, knocking him senseless.

"I am first!" Stone Wolf shouted as a boy might to count his coup.

"I'm second," young Hawk Wing cried.

"I'm third!" two others yelled as they fought each other to touch the enemy.

Then a party of women fell upon the Kiowa boy with their knives. They tore off his shirt and cut him up. He managed to get away, though, and he stood for a time with his back to the Arrow Lodge, facing them bravely.

"Wait!" Stone Wolf shouted as Yellow Hand Pony prepared to shoot the boy with an arrow. The Kiowa staggered, for one hamstring was severed, and blood flowed down his chest from the many cuts. One of the women had gashed an ear, and another had cut away most of his hair. His face had been battered by the lance, and his eyes were swollen shut. He was blind.

"He fought well," Wood Snake declared, joining Stone Wolf. "Even now, naked and defenseless, he doesn't run. *Ayyyy!* A lance carrier could do no better."

The Kiowa followed the voices with his good ear, but he made no plea for his life.

"Let him go," Yellow Hand Pony suggested as he

lowered his bow. I'll find him a Kiowa pony. Perhaps it will take him home."

"Yes," others agreed. "Give him his life."

But even as Yellow Hand Pony found a horse and brought it toward the Arrow Lodge, the bleeding Kiowa stumbled and fell. Once on the ground, he touched a knife, gripped it, and crawled forward, stabbing at the ground.

"No," Yellow Hand Pony cried when Hawk Wing notched an arrow.

But now there was nothing else to do. The boy screamed loudly and sang his death chant. Then he charged at his tormentors, and Wood Snake struck him down with a lance.

Six Kiowas were killed in the attack, and another was taken captive. Stone Wolf would have let the Kiowa go, for he was too old to be taken into the band. A woman whose daughter was trampled by a Kiowa rider cut the captive's throat, though.

The surviving raiders were driven off by Younger Wolf, who had broken away from Thunder Coat's band when he suspected the Kiowas had backtracked. All the horses were recovered, and Iron Wolf counted two coups with his stone-tipped lance.

Next day the camp was put back in order, and the wounded were tended. The Kiowa bodies were taken across Swift Fox River and left to the wolves and birds. Only the brave boy was put on a scaffold, for his courage had touched Yellow Hand Pony, and the young man insisted honor be awarded this enemy.

As for Thunder Coat, he returned in time to watch the scalp dance. He complained bitterly the delay had cost him his chance, but Yellow Hand Pony and Wood Snake, who had stayed to guard the camp, insisted he was deaf to advice.

"Younger Wolf found the enemy," Wood Snake noted. "Watch the experienced ones. Theirs is a good path to follow."

Praise was also heaped on Stone Wolf, who rallied the young men.

"Our Arrow-keeper protected the women and children," Hawk Wing observed. "We left-behinds fought well in his shadow."

Stone Wolf recorded the fight on his winter count, painting the faceless Kiowa on the elk hide. The People spoke afterward of it as the night the blind boy fought, and stories of it were recounted often that winter.

As the snows deepened, the men drove their ponies to cover and prepared for the long freezing time. Stone Wolf sat close beside the fire, with Dreamer on one side and Dove Woman on the other, sharing often-recounted stories and teaching Dreamer the medicine prayers. That winter was also a time of much dreaming, and the Arrow-keeper often grew gloomy at dusk.

"My brother says you've seen things," Iron Wolf told his father when he, Goes Ahead, and Porcupine came to share a meal. "What have you seen, *Ne' hyo?*"

"Much," Stone Wolf told them. "Hard days to come. Great honor for my sons."

"Tell us," Goes Ahead urged.

"Yes, tell us," Porcupine added.

"I've seen the skies full of falling stars. I've seen the camps of the People burning under a summer sun. I've seen snows painted red with the blood of the helpless ones."

"Ne' hyo, no," Iron Wolf gasped.

"These things lie far in the future," Stone Wolf told them. "When the Arrows have passed to another, and their power has been broken. We must all work hard to see it doesn't happen."

"Yes," the young men agreed.

"One thing will come sooner," Stone Wolf continued. "A great flood will sweep Shell River."

"A flood?" Goes Ahead asked. "Should we warn Corn Hair?"

"It's not a flood of water," Stone Wolf said, sighing. "No, this flood is white men. They'll come like locusts to chew all the grass, and they will sweep Fort William away into memory. In its place they'll put up stone lodges and bring blue coat soldiers to protect their river road."

"We will fight them!" Iron Wolf vowed.

"Yes, we'll fight them," Stone Wolf agreed, "but the flood will sweep us away, too."

"How can it be possible?" Goes Ahead asked. "A world without the People?"

"Can it be stopped, *Ne' Hyo?*" Porcupine cried.

"Maybe," Stone Wolf said. "I've had another dream."

"Tell us," Porcupine pleaded.

"In this I've seen a great band of people split apart

311

by a thunderbolt. In their place rests a painted lance marked with the symbols of *Tsis tsis tas* and Suhtai, Lakota and Crow, Kiowa, Apache, Snake, and Pawnee. This lance is also struck, and its splinters are scattered by the winds. But always the pieces know of a greater belonging.

"In the horse-fattening moon pipe carriers will ride the country, bringing word of a council of many nations. Here stand the separated bands with their broken lance. Singers join voices, and the drum beats a song. Men dance, and women take husbands. Those who had been enemies are relatives now, and the lance is made whole again."

"It's not possible to bring so many bands together, to put aside the old hatreds," Iron Wolf argued. "Some among us have lost brothers and fathers to the Kiowas and Crows. There can be no forgetting such bad heart memories."

"Perhaps not," Stone Wolf said. "It was only a dream."

"Your dreams hold great power, *Ne' hyo*," Goes Ahead argued. "Maybe we should smoke on this idea."

"You could send a pipe among the many bands of our own People," Porcupine suggested.

"Yes," Goes Ahead agreed. "I would carry such a pipe. Others, too, would do it."

"Yes," Stone Wolf told them. "But the People will gather to make New Life Lodge, and it's then we'll talk of remaking the old lance."

"Yes," they agreed. "That's a good time."

312

The young men shared their father's dream with others, though, and soon the chiefs sent for Stone Wolf.

"What talk is this of making peace?" Wood Snake asked. "How can there be peace with our blood enemies?"

"You remember the blind Kiowa," Stone Wolf said. "Was it such a hard thing to honor him?"

"He was a brave heart," Wood Snake declared. "Brave men are all brothers."

"It's how many see the Kiowas and Apaches already," Stone Wolf argued. "We are more alike than different. Even the Snakes used to trade peacefully with our fathers. We must make peace with these southern brothers."

"It will be a hard thing to manage," Younger Wolf said, shaking his head.

"Ah, Brother, but we are Foxes. Ours has always been the difficult thing to do. We'll try."

"Yes," Younger Wolf agreed. "We'll try."

Twenty-seven

That following spring, even before Stone Wolf could send pipe carriers out to the scattered bands, a young man called Little Chin, who had been among the Arapahos, arrived with a message from the southern tribes.

"The Snakes and Kiowas wish to make peace," the young *Tsis tsis tas* explained. "We heard these good words in the Arapaho camp of Little Raven, whose Apache relatives also wish to smoke with us and put aside our quarrels."

"This would be a good thing," Stone Wolf declared. "We've spoken of such a peace here, in our winter camps. It's for all the chiefs to meet and decide, though, and there will be men whose blood is up for revenge."

"Yes," Little Chin agreed. "The others understand. They have collected the scalps taken from Bear Claw's party and wish to return them. Also the Snakes promise good presents. They'll give the men, and the women and children, too, good horses to ride. And we will all promise friendship."

The Foxes spoke of it among themselves and thought it a good notion. Even the bad hearts considered the generous offer and deemed it fair.

"We could steal some horses, but never so many," Painted Snake declared. "If we have peace with these people, we can return to Shell River and fight the Crows."

Younger Wolf and Wood Snake rode out to meet with the other chiefs, for they were the head men of the band. Some days later they returned with news the chiefs had decided to make the peace.

"*Ayyyy!*" the young men howled. "It's good."

Younger Wolf then forbade any man from riding out to raid the Kiowas, Snakes, or Apaches.

"These people will be our friends soon," the Wolf declared. "Nothing must be done to break the agreement!"

The chiefs had decided to assemble all the People and their Arapaho allies on the south bank of Swift Fox River, where Two Butte Creek feeds the main stream. That was a day and a half's hard ride from where the white man Bent had his trading post. A great mass of dead wood lay alongside the creek, and the open country provided space enough for a great encampment. No hills blocked one people's view of the other's campground, either. It was necessary, after all, that nothing be hidden. Too many retained suspicions of the old enemy.

When Stone Wolf arrived with his band, the Arapahoes were there already. Some Apaches had arrived, and they sent pipe carriers out to speed the

Kiowas and Snakes to the meeting. Most of the People, meanwhile, hurried to Bent's Fort, as the place was called, for the generous gift of many horses had to be returned. Good blankets, shiny beads, looking glasses, and bright cloth were assembled to offer the gift givers.

Two days passed. Then four Kiowa men and a boy, together with two Snakes and an Apache arrived. These visitors joined the chiefs, smoked, and the peace was agreed. A Kiowa offered to hand over the scalps, but Eagle Feather, who spoke for the *Tsis tsis tas,* refused them.

"If we take these things," the Feather said, avoiding the Kiowa's bag, "relatives may see them, and bad feelings will follow. We're at peace now. Take them away and bury them."

"Yes," the other chiefs agreed. "It's better such things shouldn't come between us."

Eagle Feather then announced to the People that peace was made.

"These who were once our enemies are now our friends," High Backed Wolf added. *"Ayyyy!* It's good. Those who have brought presents should come now and give them over."

The Kiowa chief Little Mountain rose, saying the Kiowas, Snakes, and Apaches were already rich in horses.

"Our people build a road here to bring you horses we would present to you," the Mountain explained. "But if you have other presents to offer, we'll accept them gladly."

316

Soon the gift giving and feasting began. After the main body of Kiowas and Snakes, with their Apache friends, joined the encampment, the great camp circle spread out like a sea of lodges. The Snakes brought the promised good horses, and all the *Tsis tsis tas* and Arapaho people even to the smallest child took a good horse away. Some men received five or six, and the chiefs got even more. Never had Stone Wolf seen as many ponies as the Snakes brought to give away!

Young men visited the other camps, and many walked with maidens along Two Butte Creek, whispering as they wrapped a blanket around each other. Great numbers took wives, and the mixing of the children of all the peoples was great.

"This will make a lasting peace," Stone Wolf observed. "Truly the old broken lance is mended. We are all one heart again."

The dancing and good fellowship continued for days. When finally the bands separated, the People made their way north and prepared to make the New Life Lodge. It was good the world be remade, even as the old peace had been restored.

"It's a good day to be alive, *Nah nih*," Younger Wolf said as the brothers walked the low hills outside the great camp of the People. "Soon we hunt Bull Buffalo again, even as we've done so often."

"Life is a sacred hoop," Stone Wolf said, nodding. "We turn our life in circles, one flowing into the next. Soon it will be our day to climb *Noahvose* and

be one with the Great Mystery. Ah, it's good w
have sons to carry on."

"Good sons," Younger Wolf agreed. "But we hav
summers yet to hunt, and coups to count."

"Dreaming to do, and men to lead."

"New things to see," Younger Wolf declared
"And old ways to preserve."

"How many wondrous things have we seen in ou
lives?" Stone Wolf asked. "The Buffalo Shield. M
son's first kill. The time we hung by the pole in Ne
Life Lodge."

"The day we ran the Crows," Younger Wolf said
smiling. "Our grandfather's stories. This coming o
the peace, *Nah nih,* brings me the most pleasur
yet."

"More than Hoop Woman?" Stone Wolf asked
grinning.

"No, but it was as long in coming. Soon Dreamer
too, will take his first steps on man's road. The
Little Dancer. It's good they're still small, for boy
stretch themselves tall too soon, I think."

"There have been all these good things," Ston
Wolf said, gazing at the boys splashing together i
the river, at the cook smoke curling skyward, an
the little ones kicking a rawhide ball past the cam
dogs.

"All these things," Younger Wolf echoed. "An
more lies ahead, *Nah nih.*"

"More, yes," Stone Wolf whispered as he gazed a
the setting sun. "Better? Perhaps. Only tomorro
knows that."

RED-HOT ADULT ACTION WITH E.J. HUNTER'S
HEAD HUNTER

#1: ARIZONA HELLCAT   (2095, $3.95)

#4: SIN CITY   (2360, $2.95)

#6: ARIZONA BUSTOUT   (2630, $2.95)

#7: TOMBSTONE TEMPTRESS   (2847, $2.95)

#8: NEVADA CLAIM STRIPPER   (3049, $2.95)

#9: TOOLS OF THE TRADE   (3241, $3.50)